*D*rawn

Dear,
Candy Lynn
Happy Reading!
Lilliana Andersen xxx.

By Lilliana Anderson

2013

2

Thank you
for reading!
Love always,
Lilliana

xoxox
♡

Books by *Lilliana Anderson*

Coming in 2014

Drawn Trilogy

Drawn

Beautiful Series

A Beautiful Rock

The Confidante Trilogy

Confidante: The Madame

Entwined Series

Our Lives Entwined

For information on upcoming releases visit

www./lillianaanderson.com

ISBN-13: 978-1494372347 (CreateSpace-Assigned)

ISBN-10: 1494372347

Design by Ember Designs

Printed by CreateSpace Publishing USA

Contents

Dedication

For all the women, who see it like it is.

'Love is as much of an object as an obsession, everybody wants it, everybody seeks it, but few ever achieve it, those who do will cherish it, be lost in it, and among all, never... never forget it.'

~ Curtis Judalet quotes

Foreward

Where do I start? Drawn has been my secret obsession for a year. It's been my baby. It's been my joy. And it's been my fear.

I don't think I have ever been dragged into a book so emotionally, before this one. The others, while I felt a part of them, just didn't possess me quite as much as this one did. I think that's why I'm so nervous to let this one go, and why I've held on to it all year.

Honestly, in the beginning, I was going to just write it on my own, show it to no one and then release it with my eyes shut tight.

But now, here we are. I pray that you like it, and can understand my reasons for writing this nod to the alpha male.

Yes. It's an alpha male book, but it's not like all the others you have read lately, and if you stick with me. I promise you that come May – I'm going to take you on a very wild ride with the final two instalments.

Happy Reading

Lilliana xoxox

Acknowledgements

First and foremost I must thank my beta and proof readers for working so hard for me on this novel. Marion of Making Manuscripts (www.makingmanuscripts.com), Tammie, Mary, Doraine, Kassi, Lindsey, Anna, Betchy, Billie, Candice, Celsey, Megan, Kristina and Kristine. I know it has been such a busy time for all of us, but for those of you who could get back to me in time - your input was AMAZING! It's made this book so much better than if I had have done it all alone. Thank you!

Thank you to my editor, Maria Johnson, for trawling through my manuscript for errors and always working me into her schedule. A big thank you to my husband for his unending support, his plot help, and his encouragement.

Thank you to my street team and to everyone who has agreed to review for me – my heart fills up every time I see your enthusiasm for my work!

I'd also like to thank the wonderful team at Apple and Smashwords, who set up all of my preorders and trust me to upload my books on time – I truly appreciate your support!

A big thank you also goes out to everyone who has been watching me on my social networks and talking to me/ putting up with my randomness while I write. The small interactions we have, really helps to break up my day and stave away the loneliness that can creep in while immersed in your writing all the time.

I also want to thank my kids for cuddling up next to me while I type and waiting patiently until I've finished my thought – you're all beautiful!

And of course – thank you to all of my readers. Without you, I would be writing to the crickets.

Mwah! Xoxox

1

"Are you sure that moving out of home is what you want for your eighteenth birthday?" my father asks a week before the actual day. "Has it really been that terrible living here?"

"Oh no, dad! Don't think like that. It's just that all of my friends are either living in uni housing or they're in flats of their own. I just don't want to feel left out anymore," I attempt to explain.

My father just growls in response, he's not happy about this change at all. And I understand that. Ever since my brother died, he's kept a very close eye on me. I mean, I've had a 6pm curfew since I started high school which continued on into university.

He has always claimed that it was because I was so intelligent – he wanted me to focus on my studies. Although, I'm pretty sure he was just making sure I had no time for a social life.

Not that that stopped me – where there's a will, there's a way. And I've managed to have my fair share of teenage experiences, despite my restrictions.

My mother butts in as she wanders into the kitchen and pours herself a cup of coffee. "Oh, leave her alone Barry. It's perfectly normal. She wants to stand on her own two feet. I don't blame her. You're so damn strict with her all the time."

"There's nothing wrong with wanting your family close," he grumbles.

"Of course there isn't, dear," my mother coos, sliding an arm over his protruding belly as she kisses his cheek. "But she's going to be an adult. We can't keep her locked up forever."

My parents have one of those silent exchanges that always ends with them kissing, so I take that as my cue to leave.

"I'll see you both tonight. I have a train to catch," I say, as I stand up from the stool I was occupying and pick up my navy blue Crumpler laptop bag.

"Have fun, honey," my mother calls. "I hope you find something."

Walking toward the train station, I squint against the warm Australian sun and dig inside my bag for a pair of sunglasses. As I slide the dark shades over my eyes, I can't help but smile to myself as I check my watch.

Today is my first whiff of freedom. My friend Aaron is taking me apartment hunting, and I can't wait. Pretty soon, I'll be eighteen, and I'll be able to legally go out and have fun without having a curfew to get back in time for.

Swiping my travel pass, I enter the station and after a short wait, board the sterile steel carriage of the train, disembarking a stop later at Kingswood station. I make my way over the pedestrian bridge and walk toward the older styled apartment block where Aaron lives.

He moved in with a new flatmate only a couple of weeks ago and since I haven't visited him here yet, I double check the message on my phone containing his address to make sure I have the right place.

Once confirmed, I enter the foyer through the brown painted aluminium and glass door. To my right, is a bank of letterboxes and just in front is a narrow set of stairs that wind up the couple of flights to his floor.

Each floor seems to have five apartments on it. I'm looking for number nine and find it on the second floor, right near the landing on my right.

I knock loudly on the faux wood, chipboard door in an attempt to be heard over the music booming from the inside. Then stand back, and wait patiently as I hear the music shut off and footsteps coming toward the door.

When it opens, I'm immediately taken aback by a set of unusually light brown eyes, set in a lean, stubbled face, topped off with dark hair, messily spiked. Their owner practically fills out the doorway, and I thank Christ I'm so tall and can almost look him in the eye, because in my periphery I can see that he's *gulp* shirtless. *I will not look down, I will not look down*, I assure myself, trying to ignore the round pecs and defined abs that are calling to me. My heart beats solidly against my chest as I stare directly into his questioning eyes, hoping I appear calm.

"Hi, I'm Etta, Aaron's friend. He said to meet him here," I say to who I'm assuming is Aaron's roommate Jeremy, while trying to sound confidant and unperturbed by his thoroughly ruffled and very sexy appearance.

Taking a deep breath as I await his response, I inhale his smell, my stomach growls audibly, he smells like… bacon?

The corner of his full mouth turns up in an amused grin as my cheeks flame from my stomach's rudeness.

"I'm making bacon sangas. You want one?" he asks me, stepping aside to let me through.

"Ah sure," I reply, stepping inside and setting my things on the vacant chair at the two seater dining table to the right of the front door. Jeremy picks up a shirt and slides it over his head, and I'll admit that I eye licked him a little while his face was hidden under the material.

My eyes scan the apartment, noting how meticulously clean it is for an apartment that houses a couple of male university students. To my left, there are two doors that are closed, presumably leading toward bedrooms and a bathroom door between them which lies open.

The living area is open planned. It's basically one big rectangle that houses the lounge, dining, and kitchen. A two-seater black leather couch sits in front of a rather large flat screen TV that is attached to the wall above an antique looking, Jacobean style sideboard, that houses the DVD player and stereo system.

There is some very modern looking art adorning the walls. They feature lots of shapes, lines and duotone colours. I particularly like the one that's hanging above the dark-stained pine, dining table. It kind of looks like a glass of red wine, hitting a black surface and exploding.

To the right is a small kitchen where Jeremy is still cooking strips of bacon and buttering slices of bread. The scent of the pan and the sight of the man standing over it, causes my mouth to water and my stomach to nag at me with both hunger and a nervous attraction. I continue to look around the room, trying to keep myself from staring at him as he works the pan.

Right next to the door on the wall, I notice a pin board covered in small pieces of paper. Stepping closer, I lean in, scrutinising the collage, releasing my breath in awe as I notice that they're all sketches.

Reaching out, I touch a yellow post-it note with my finger. On it is a perfect sketch of a girl, leaning up against a tree. It's so small and so detailed, that I feel myself leaning even closer to have a look.

The sound of plates being placed on the table brings my attention away from the board, and I'm once again entranced in those light coloured eyes. His gaze flicks from me to the plate, and I snap out of it, moving to the table to sit down and eat.

"Thank you," I say as I pick up my sandwich and take a bite, closing my eyes as the greasy-bacony-goodness flows over my taste buds. "That's delicious," I practically moan.

Smiling, he sets a can of coke in front of me before moving over to the pin board and flipping it over. I frown slightly as I'm now faced with a board pinned with a calendar, bills and a few photos.

He makes his way over to the table and sits across from me, raking his hand through his messy jet black hair and popping his own can of coke before taking a thirsty gulp.

"Sorry, I didn't realise I wasn't supposed to be looking at that," I say, indicating the now flipped pin board.

"It's fine," he says, focusing on his sandwich. "I normally flip it when I'm expecting someone. Um, what time are you supposed to be meeting Aaron?"

"One, although I'm a little early," I reply glancing at my watch. It's twelve fifty two, and I've already been here for five minutes.

"Ah ok," he says, before filling his mouth with almost half of his sandwich. He must be hungry.

"I didn't just steal half your lunch, did I?"

He grins around his food, covering his mouth slightly as he shakes his head in the negative. Swallowing he says, "Don't sweat it, I'm happy to share. So how do you know Aaron?"

"We're studying for the same degree."

"Ah, of course," he says, his eyes twinkling at me as he finishes devouring his sandwich and starts to wash it down with his can of coke. "Here," he says, reaching out and popping the top of my can, twisting it around so the mouth is facing me.

"Thanks," I say again. "You make a really good bacon

sandwich."

"Thank you," he nods, as he sits and watches me eat, his eyes still twinkling in what looks like amusement over the top of his can while he takes another swig. "So how long have you and Aaron been dating?"

"Oh. No. We're friends. We have been since the first day of uni. I mean, we dated for a while, but the age difference became a bit of an issue. So that was the end of that."

"Why was your age a problem?" he asks, taking another sip.

"Because when my dad found out I was dating an older guy, he cracked it and forbade me to go out with him – although, I think it was really just the whole 'dating' thing that was an issue."

"Do you always do what your dad says?"

"Why wouldn't I?" I shrug. "I mean, it's not like he's super unreasonable. He's just strict. Especially after my brother died, he just wants me close. I can understand that."

"Sorry to hear that."

"Why? It's not like you killed him. He got drunk and fell in the river." I shrug, feeling there wasn't much more of an explanation needed.

He studies me for a moment, his eyes on me seem to bring the surface of my skin to life as if I can actually feel everywhere he sees. Taken aback, I reach for my can of drink and lift it to my lips, hoping my cheeks aren't flaming too brightly.

"You keep mentioning an age difference. If you're doing the same degree as Aaron, you'd have to be at least 20. You're third year right?"

"Yeah, third year, but I skipped a couple of grades in high school, so I'm only eighteen – well, almost. My birthday's next week."

"A couple of grades? Geez, what are you? A genius or something?"

"Not quite. There just isn't a lot to do but study when you're not allowed out."

I can see this information rolling around in his head as he regards me for a moment.

His brow creases as he leans back in his chair. "So, let me get this straight - you're an eighteen year old girl, and you've come here on your own, to the apartment of a man you've never met, and eaten lunch with him like it's no big deal. What if I was dangerous?"

Suddenly I bristle a little. "Excuse me? How is visiting the home of a friend suddenly dangerous?"

"You obviously have zero life experience. I don't blame your dad for being so strict with you."

"What? Of course I have life experience. Probably more than most girls my age."

"Really? How many high school parties did you attend?"

Shifting uncomfortably in my seat, I'm not sure if I want to answer – I never got invited to parties in high school. No one wanted to invite the girl who was younger and smarter than everyone else. I missed out on everything social about high school. All I did was study.

But once university started, even though I was younger than everyone, I was finally able to socialise. The Bar Café on campus holds social events that start at lunch time. On top of that, my lectures and tutorials, don't take up the whole day. So I'd leave home before nine and get home before dinner at six. As far as my father knew, I was in class or studying at the library – I could fit a lot of fun in around those hours. And I did my damnedest to join in with everything I could.

"You didn't go to any parties did you?" he asks, narrowing his eyes as he assesses me.

"No ok, no one wanted me around. I totally missed the party scene in high school – are you happy?" I snap, more out of embarrassment than anger. "What's it to you anyway? It's not like I'm totally sheltered. So what if I didn't have a social life in high school? I've had one since I started uni – I've even managed to have boyfriends. I'm not totally clueless."

"It matters because a girl like you shouldn't be entering the apartment of guys you don't know."

"I can assure you that I'm quite capable of looking after myself," I tell him.

Shaking his head he sets his can down. "It doesn't matter, a girl

– no matter how strong she is, is no match for a guy when she's cornered."

"My father teaches Aikido. I trained with him every day until I was twelve. I assure you – I'm fine. Plus, in case you haven't noticed, I'm a bit of an amazon."

"Oh, I noticed – you look like an Amazon princess or something." His eyes move over me appraisingly before moving back up to my face. "It's part of the reason I think you're making a big mistake. It's great that you know how to defend yourself but it's not going to help you if you're trapped is it?"

Annoyance flashes, hot in my chest as I push back from the table. "Listen, this is obviously a bad idea. Just tell Aaron to call me when he gets in. I'll wait for him in the park across the street. I'll practice my self-defence skills while I'm there in case I get mugged by one of the little grannies coming out of the post office." Shaking my head, I roll my eyes. "Thanks for the food," I add as an afterthought, as I stand up and gather my things to leave.

He rises as well, watching me as I sling my bag over my shoulder and turn towards the door. With a speed that seems unnatural for a man with his bulk, he suddenly slams his body up against mine, effectively pinning me against the door.

"What are you doing?!" I shriek, my heart beating wildly in my chest as I struggle against his body. He leans his face close to mine and I go still, his warm breath on my face sending shivers over my body. I should probably be scared right now but instead, all I can focus on is the firmness of his chest against

30

the softness of my own, and the beautiful colour of his eyes staring into mine with what looks like concern.

"Do you see what I'm talking about?" he whispers close to my ear, his voice threading its way through my senses, making me dizzy and short of breath. "Sometimes a man will be faster and more trained than you are. It's not safe for you."

My eyes flutter and the only sound that escapes my mouth is a whimper-like 'huh'. I can't believe how affected I am by him, I just met him.

As our eyes lock, and I feel sure he's about to kiss me and hold my breath, waiting for him to do something. My phone chooses that moment to start playing Young Girls by Bruno Mars. I gasp as he releases me and steps back, moving immediately to the table to clear away our plates and empty cans.

With a shaking hand, I reach in my bag and pull out my still ringing phone. Frowning, I slide my finger across the screen to answer the call.

"Uh, hello?"

"Etta? Where are you? I've been waiting for you for ages. I thought you were coming over today?"

"Uh… no, I mean yes – yes I'm coming. Um, what number apartment are you in again?" I ask, eyeing the man who I had thought was Jeremy in front of me as he leans against the sink with his muscular arms folded over his broad chest, watching me with darkening eyes.

31

"Nine."

"Nine," I repeat as I open the door and look at the number, now noticing the scrape marks from where it has obviously spun countless times. Reaching up with my finger, I slide the number up to its original position and press it in place so that it's now a number six.

"Um… hello?"

"I'm here. I'll be at your place in a couple of minutes. See you soon," I say before disconnecting and turning my attention back to my deceptive host, pointing to the number on his door. "You might want to use something a little stronger than Blutach to keep that in place in future. It will save you getting unwanted visitors."

"You were definitely wanted," he says watching me intently.

Shaking my head, I ignore the clenching of my insides as my body responds to him. Instead, I call him a jerk and step out into the hall way. Closing the door quietly, I take a moment to calm myself down before looking at the doors around me, quickly locating number nine on the other side, almost diagonal from this door.

As I step away, I jump slightly when the music starts up again in the room behind me. I can't believe that guy just took me into his apartment when he knew I wasn't here to see him. To what? Teach me a lesson about self-defence? I don't care how sculpted-from-marble-by-the-hands-of-the-gods you may look – who the fuck does that?

I walk towards the correct door, pray that my face isn't too red and knock. I'm immediately greeted by another Adonis and almost gasp at the sight of him as well. What the hell is this? The secret hiding place for all of the god's love children? I'm wondering if I knock on every door I'll find a model like creature living inside.

"Jeremy is it?" I ask, double checking this time.

He grins, his blue eyes almost getting lost in his perfect smile. "That's right, come on in. Aaron's just hunting for his keys," he grins, stepping aside to let me in.

I can't help but notice the stark contrast in the state of the two apartments. This one is basically a mirror image of the one across the hall, but as you'd expect for the home of two single men – it's not the tidiest place in the world.

"I'll be right out," I hear Aaron call from the bedroom.

Jeremy moves some papers, books and clothing from one of the couches and gestures for me to sit down.

"Geez, you're a tall one," he comments, looking me up and down.

"So I'm told," I respond, smiling politely.

"You know, I used to think I was a pretty decent height. I mean, I'm almost six foot, but then I moved up here. Is there something in the water supply or something?"

"Who knows," I shrug before attempting to steer the

conversation away from my six foot, one height. "Where were you living before?"

"I'm from Victoria. Grew up on Phillip Island," he nods.

"So you're a bit of a surfer then?"

"Not really," he laughs.

"Found them!" Aaron declares from the doorway to his room, holding his keys up triumphantly. "Hey Etta, thanks for waiting," he smiles moving over to the couch and planting a kiss on the side of my cheek. His stubble grazes my skin as he brushes past.

"No problem. Are your ready to go though? We'll have a few places to look at."

"Absolutely. I just need my wallet…"

***

Twenty minutes later, Aaron has located his wallet and we're saying goodbye to the real Jeremy. As we walk down the hallway, I try my hardest to keep my eyes from straying to the door at number six – what is that guy's game anyway? Why not just tell me I had the wrong room?

"What's going on?" Aaron asks me, looking over his shoulder. "You seem a bit skittish."

"Oh it's nothing. I just had a bit of an altercation with your neighbour over there."

"Who, Damien?"

"I don't know his name. I just knocked on the wrong door at first because his number was upside down."

He rolls his eyes and shakes his head slightly. "Doesn't surprise me. That guy's a grade A fuckwit in my books. He's some kind of artist and has girls streaming in and out of there all the time. He's the kind of guy that gives the rest of us a bad name." Shaking his head, he runs his hand through his sun streaked blond hair then abruptly pauses, tapping on his pockets before exclaiming, "Oh shit. I left my phone on the charger. Meet me downstairs in the car?" he says, as he passes me his keys.

Rolling my eyes at his absent mindedness, I can't help but smile as I take the keys from him. Knowing Aaron, he'll be another twenty minutes trying to find his phone too.

The moment I step in front of number six, the door bursts open, and my arm is caught by a very strong hand. I spin my arm around effectively evading his grip, and step away.

"What the hell is your deal!?" I hiss out, not wanting to cause a scene in the hallway.

"I'm sorry, ok – at first, I was just having a joke. But when I realised how young you are, I realised how dangerous it could be for you if this happened somewhere else."

"I can look after myself," I told him through gritted teeth, extending out my arm and pushing him in the chest. He doesn't even move.

35

"Obviously," he says, a slight grin turning up the corner of his mouth as he holds my eyes.

"Is everything ok?" Aaron asks as he emerges from his apartment. He moves to stand beside me, his arms crossed over his firm chest as he looks between myself and Damien.

"Aaron," Damien says with a nod.

"Damien," he responds.

"So, you dated a minor huh?" Damien starts.

"Fuck you. She was seventeen when we dated. The legal age is sixteen dickwad."

"I was referring to the fact that legally, you aren't an adult 'til eighteen. But if you want to tell me about your sex life, that's fine too."

"Um...guys. I'm standing right here," I say, although my words fall on deaf ears.

"Well, we can't all go around using the fact that we're an 'artist' to trick girls into sleeping with us," Aaron bites back, using his fingers to quote the word.

Damien presses his lips together as he regards Aaron, then turns his attention to the stairwell. "Speaking of art, here's my next model now." We all turn to see who he's talking about, as the most gorgeous looking brunette I've ever seen walks, no, she slinks, up the last few stairs. "Sucks to be me huh?" he says, directing the comment at Aaron.

"Damien." She oozes his name in greeting. "Are we having some kind of party?"

"No Bec, these two were just stopping by." He steps to the side a little as she glides past us all and into his apartment. "It was nice to meet you Etta. I'm sure I'll be seeing you soon."

"I don't think so," I retort, feeling all agitated by that girl's entrance, hating that in my mind, I'm comparing myself to her, as well as hating the pang of disappointment I feel over seeing her with him.

"We'll see," he grins, closing the door and leaving us both standing there.

"Don't let him get to you. He's just a jerk," Aaron says, placing his hand on my back and guiding me toward the stairs.

"He doesn't bother me," I lie, pretending to shake off the interaction. "Although, what the hell is with this building? Are you only allowed to live in it if you're ridiculously good looking? I feel like I'm on an episode of Next Top Model!"

"Do you think I'm ridiculously good looking?" he grins, nudging me lightly with his shoulder.

"You and Jeremy could be brothers, you look very much alike."

"That's not answering the question," he laughs.

Rolling my eyes, I return his laugh. "You know I think you're hot Aaron. You're the man I got myself into a hell of a lot of trouble over," I remind him, referring to the reason we were forced to break up. "Although, it's lucky I refused to name you. I just called you 'my boyfriend', otherwise dad might have hunted you down and then pulled me out of school altogether."

"The whole thing was a bit of an overreaction I thought, but hey – you're almost eighteen. Freedom is on the horizon," he affirms, opening the car door before I hop inside.

"He was just scared that I was going to end up like Craig," I comment, defending my father. The loss of my brother is something my family felt intensely and as much as I've wished for my freedom, I've always understood my father's motives.

When Craig was fifteen, he started rebelling against my dad. Being raised by an Aikido sensei meant that discipline and respect were a huge focus in our household, and as Craig got older, he felt that my father's rules were too restrictive.

He started sneaking out with his friends. I don't know exactly what they did – I was only twelve at the time – but I do know that he changed a lot in that last year. He was belligerent, and at times incredibly hateful toward my parents, and was always preaching to me about how the other kids are allowed to have fun and we should be able to as well.

I guess I admired him for standing up to my parents, which is why I never told them that he was climbing out of his window every night. Each night, when I went to bed, I would pull up my blinds and sit there, waiting until I saw him go. He always knew I was there, and would turn around grinning at me, pressing his index finger to his lips to remind me to keep quiet.

I would wave him off, and go to bed, trying to imagine all the fun he'd be having out there with his friends. In my mind, it was all parties and fun times – and I guess, based on how he died, it probably was.

Occasionally, he'd bring something back for me – a shiny stone, a hair clip – just silly things that he obviously came across while he was out having fun. He'd slide them to me surreptitiously at breakfast with a wink when no one else was looking, and I treasured each one like he'd given me a star from the sky.

Then spring came, and with it, the storms that swell the Nepean River to bursting point, increasing the speed of its current as the water rushes, carrying debris and other obstacles in its haste to return to the ocean.

A storm had raged for days, making it so that my brother was forced to stay home for a couple of nights. When the rains had finally cleared, I could tell from his demeanour that he was eager to leave and be with his friends.

I waved goodbye to my brother for the final time that night, and I'll never forget that last grin as he ran toward his freedom, he didn't even place his finger to his lips to remind me, he just smiled and ran into the night.

When I woke the next morning, it wasn't to my brother, sitting at the breakfast table and the hope of a treasure. It was to my parents sitting on the couch, holding each other and crying as a police officer explained to them what had happened.

I stood by and listened as the officer spoke, saying that my brother and his friends had gone down to the river, drinking and messing about as teenagers are wont to do. At some point, my brother separated from the group and fell into the rushing water, and due to his inebriated state, he didn't make it out alive.

Eventually, I felt so guilty that I broke down and told them that I knew he was leaving. As a result, it was deemed that I couldn't be trusted and my life became school, home and study. Of course, as I got older, I started to rebel too. I guess I followed in my brothers footsteps a little too closely, because when my father caught me sneaking out my bedroom window, he immediately nailed it shut and after interrogating me about why I was sneaking out and who I was going to see, he forbade me to date and kept even closer tabs on my whereabouts.

And so, the countdown began. I decided that the moment I turned eighteen, I was moving out and having a life of my own – I can't live with all that fear anymore. I miss Craig too. I just can't mourn him forever. I need to live, and I know that's what he would have wanted – he'd want me to be free.

"Let's go and get your life back by finding you some place to live," Aaron announces as he starts the car, breaking into my thoughts.

"Good idea," I say smiling, knowing that wherever my brother is right now, he'd be smiling too.

2

Aaron's and my version of looking at share houses, involved going to the uni and taking numbers off the various flyers posted on notice boards, then making phone calls while we sat at the café, drinking and eating our weight in coffee and blueberry muffins.

By the end of it I was bloated and shaking like I was going through withdrawals, but at least we had two places we could go and see that afternoon.

The first place was a townhouse that was around a fifteen minute walk away from the uni itself. When I called, I spoke to a girl named Jessica who said that their other roommate had to leave unexpectedly, and since they couldn't afford the rent on their own, they needed someone quickly.

"This looks alright," Aaron comments as we pull up out the front of the townhouses. The place we're looking at is the very first one, so its caramel coloured, side wall faces the street. "Although, if those are the bedrooms, you might want heavy curtains," he says, indicating the side windows and the street light above us with his cobalt blue eyes.

Jessica greets us at the door, she's a tiny girl with light brown hair and dimples when she smiles. "Come in," she says, holding her hand out to shake mine and then Aaron's.

A small grin pulls at the corner of my mouth as I notice her do a double take when she's confronted with Aaron. It's probably exactly how I responded when I first met him. He's wonderfully tall, a good inch above me, has blond sun streaked hair and big blue eyes that seem to glow like jewels from within his tan face. He's one of those lean athletic looking guys, so he's not overly muscled, but he's beautiful to look at. I tend to joke that that's the only reason I keep him around. But that's not true - he's a good friend, and he's never made me feel like a child. Other guys would have just moved on after my dad banned me from dating him, but not Aaron, he's a loyal friend.

"So what degree are you doing Etta?" she asks as she shows me through the townhouse. Downstairs is all white walls and beige carpets in the small living and dining area. The furniture is all second hand but comfortable looking, and there are a few nick-knacks around as evidence that this is a girl's home.

"Communications," I reply, following her around as I take in the amenities. There is also a small kitchen, laundry and second toilet downstairs, as well as a postage stamp courtyard out back.

"Ok, one of my friends does that. She's first year as well. Do you know a girl called Tanya? She's really little with curly blonde hair."

"No, sorry. I'm actually third year."

"Really? Sorry, I thought you were my age."

"I am," I reply. "Well, I'll be eighteen in a few days."

She gives me a questioning look, and I briefly explain the whole skipping grades thing to her as she leads us upstairs to see the bedroom and main bathroom area.

"She left her furniture behind, so you're welcome to it. I know she took a trip with her dad to Ikea and got it all there at the beginning of the year. You'll have to provide all of your own linens and pillows and whatnot."

The bedroom is fairly simple, it has a built in cupboard for my clothes, a tall boy with a mirror on top of it, along with a small computer desk, swivel chair and a single bed in the middle.

"What's the rent?" Aaron asks, as he moves over the window and tests the thickness of the curtains.

"One-fifty," she replies.

"A week?" I ask.

"Yeah, then we divide all of the bills between us. You shop for your own food though."

"Great," I say, following her back down the stairs and into the living area.

"So when do you think you can move in?" she asks, surprising me, as I thought she'd at least want to talk to her other housemate before giving me the room.

"Oh… um," I start.

"If you need time to think, that's cool. I just thought, if you like it

– you can have it. We need help with the rent and you seem nice, so…" she tilts her head to the side a little and bounces a shoulder.

"You know what? Yeah. I'll take it. I'll have to move in next weekend. My Dad will flip it if I move in this week," I tell her.

"Sounds great," she says.

We work out a few of the particulars of the move, such as a deposit to hold the room and my portion of the bond money, and by the time we have finished, the front door opens.

"Kensi," Jessica exclaims. "Come and meet our new flat mate, Etta."

"Oh you got one. Great," she says, dropping her knapsack on the floor and walking over to me, her short severe black bob barely moves as she walks.

I stand from my seat to shake her hand. "Nice to meet you," I say.

"Holy shit. Look at the size of you."

Smiling politely, I return to my seat. Although my sitting height is almost the same as Kensi's standing height, she has birdlike limbs and very pale features, made even starker by her dark crimson lipstick.

"So 'Etta' huh?" Kensi confirms, sitting on the chair next to Jessica. "Is that your whole name or is it short for something?"

"It's short, for Henrietta actually. Although I won't answer you if you call me that," I grin. "It's a horrible name."

"Better than 'Kensi'," she laughs. "You should try spelling that all your life. I've been called 'Kendi' 'Kenny' 'Kenthi' – the list goes on."

"Listen, since your moving in and all, maybe we should all go out beforehand?" Jessica suggests, looking behind her at Aaron who's been sitting on the couch playing with his phone while he waits for me to finish up. "Are you guys going to the Scarlet Party at the World Bar next Thursday? It's free for all UWS students. "

"I remember getting the email for it, but I hadn't really thought about it," Aaron replies.

"Oh, hello there," Kensi says, spinning in her chair. "I didn't see you when I came in."

"I'm Aaron," he says, standing to shake her hand in greeting.

"Well, I can see why Etta likes you Aaron. You're obscenely tall too," she grins, raking her eyes obviously over his body as she touches her tongue to her front teeth.

"Everyone is tall compared to you Kensi. You're a waif," inserts Jessica, before turning back to me. "Anyway, it would be great if you could come. We'll meet at the Uni Bar and watch the pool competition, have something to eat and then get the train in with everyone else."

"That sounds perfect," I say, grinning like a Cheshire cat. This will be the first outing I'll have as an eighteen year old. What better way to celebrate than going to my first University party?

***

"Are you serious?!" I whine. "What do you mean I can't go? I'll be eighteen. It's not like I'll be the only eighteen year old in the entire student body! It's a university party!"

My father doesn't like the idea of me going out next Thursday and continues to lay down the law. "No daughter of mine is going to some drunken uni student party. You have no idea what goes on in those places," he points out.

"That's only because I've never had a chance. If I had have been a 'normal' person growing up, then I would have gone out with my friends in high school like everybody else did," I argue, using my fingers as quotation marks. "Mum! Help me out here," I beg, looking at her beseechingly. As strict as my father is, my mother is a soft touch. After Craig died, I became her primary focus. It's made us very close, more like friends than mother and daughter, and as a result, she is my biggest advocate in the fight against my father's rules. She hasn't been able to get him to lift the rule on my curfew, but she has gotten him to understand that his rule ends on my eighteenth birthday.

"Barry, she's right. In a few days' time, she'll be an adult. You can't keep her here forever," she reminds him, and I know the moment she says something, he will relax a little. There is something special about my parent's relationship. When my father looks at my mother, his tough exterior melts away, and he turns to mush. It's amazing to watch.

"But she's still so young at heart," he argues with her. "And what if something happens? I just…"

"Dad, I'll be fine. I'm not Craig. I'm not going to get so drunk I can't look after myself. You've been training me since I could stand up. I know how to fight, no one's going to do anything to me. Just please. This is the first time I've actually been able to say yes to something like this. Plus they're my new flatmates. I'd like to go out and have some fun with them," I insist.

He exchanges glances with my mum, and they do that silent conversation thing again. I don't know what's going on beyond a few head tilts and raised eyebrows.

"I'll tell you what. You come and train at the studio this Thursday. Show me you can still take care of yourself - then I'll have no issue with you going," he concedes. I look at my mother again, who shrugs her shoulders in a manner that tells me to take what I'm given.

"Fine," I exasperate, wishing he wasn't so damn over protective. I'll bet no other girl going to this party will have to literally fight her way out of the door…

***

On Thursday afternoon, I rock up to my dad's martial arts gym to prove to him that I can take care of myself. I'm still so angry at him for making me do this. I know I could just say no and go out anyway. But I can't escape my upbringing – it's his house, his rules – which is half the reason why I'm leaving. I know that even though I'm legally about to become an adult, it's not going to matter to him. He will still find a way to place restrictions upon me no matter how much I fight.

I want to live freely. I want to make the rules. So, I'll have to find my own way in this world. With or without my father's blessing.

But today, I'm still living under his roof. I'm still seventeen – so he gets his way.

I bump my hands against the glass entry door to push it open and make my way past the gym in front to the dojo out back. I haven't been to my dad's gym for years. Not since I was a kid really. But it all looks exactly the way it always has. Blue mats cover the floor of the training area in the dojo. Around the walls are sparring weapons and pads. There's a long row of staffs and wooden swords hung horizontally in a custom made rack on the wall in the far corner. There's also a bit of Aikido inspired paraphernalia – posters, photos of dojo members participating in tournaments, as well as a really cool display of my dad in his prime. I always loved looking at these as a kid, especially the one where he's jumping through the air and his ponytail is flying behind him. It looks like something out of a movie.

My dad doesn't have a ponytail any more. Now his brown hair has turned grey and thinned out around his temples. He keeps it cut close to his scalp and seems to feel that he can balance the hair loss on top of his head by adding a bushy beard. For some reason, his beard has turned an auburn colour, so for once in our lives the whole family matches.

I have long and incredibly thick auburn hair which I get from my mother's side of the family – she has the exact same hair, so she's always been great at showing me how to tame it. We also all have blue eyes, although where my mum's are a clear blue, my fathers and mine are more segmented and flecked with bits of green and hazel.

Pulling the elastic band from my wrist, I lift my hair high up on my head and fasten it away from my face as I walk toward my father. He's standing in the centre of the room, talking to a few of his students. He's well into his forties now, but he is still a formidable form, his broad strong frame and over six feet of height has him dwarfing most of the students. All except one.

"Shit," I hiss under my breath as I approach. It's Damien. Immediately, my face begins to burn with the memory of the day before. I'm not sure if it's embarrassment, nerves or just plain anger. But I do know that seeing him, makes me a little scared. I'm not sure I can think to react properly with him here.

I ball my fists at my side and give myself an internal pep talk as I approach – you can do this. He just caught you off guard yesterday.

"Ah, you're here!" my father calls in my direction as I move toward the group. I do my best to keep my gaze trained on my father's face and smile.

"Wouldn't miss it," I say as I come to a stop beside him.

"Ok, this is my more advanced group. I've told them a lot about you before, so they're pretty keen to see what my daughter can do," he beams amusedly. He knows full well that I haven't trained properly for over five years. Besides the times he's convinced me to train with him in our backyard – I've been avoiding Aikido like the plague. Once upon a time, I was a good fighter and he was proud of that, but after Craig died, I didn't want to train anymore. It was too sad training without him, so I've stayed away.

The students all greet me kindly. I simply nod in their direction, unwilling to make eye contact with Damien. But I can feel his eyes on me. It takes all of my will power to keep my eyes trained on my father – all of it.

"I've selected Damien to spar with you. He's the most advanced of the group, so if you can keep up with him then we have a deal," he smiles, his eyes twinkling with excitement. I can tell he's loving that he got me here, and knowing him, he's chosen someone he doesn't think I can beat. Well, I'll show him…I hope.

I risk a glance at Damien, whose mouth is turned up on one side as his light eyes bore into mine. My heart starts thudding loudly in my ears and suddenly I'm feeling a little warm. Why does it have to be him?

"Nage Waza" my father announces.

"Throwing?" I question, my brows raised as I glare at my father. He's doing this on purpose. I shouldn't have come.

Mumbling under my breath, I curse myself for being so damn agreeable. If I had have been your typical teenage girl, I would have just threatened to move out earlier instead of agreeing to a fucking training session to prove my worth.

I follow as everyone pairs off around the mats, and stand across from Damien waiting for the call to start.

"You knew who my father was yesterday didn't you?"

He shrugs and smiles in response, shaking his limbs out and rolling his neck, preparing himself to train.

"Whatever," I sigh, doing exactly the same thing he is. Damien has the club gi on, but I'm simply in a pair of black leggings and a fitted aqua gym shirt. It's highly inappropriate clothing for Aikido, but I don't own a gi. I told my parents that I lost it years ago, although honestly, I burnt it. I didn't want to wear it ever again.

"Give me a push," Damien tells me, as we move around each other. We didn't establish who would attack and who would defend – we're just sizing each other up, daring the other one to start first.

"Fine," I say, readying myself for a swift reminder of the way these katas work.

Lunging forward, I push at his chest, knowing that with his level of training, there was no way I was actually going to connect. Although he surprises me, stands there and takes it.

"You can do better than that," he says with a grin.

"Why? So you can flip me over and be the guy who beat up on

a girl? I don't think so," I retort.

"Push me," he insists.

Glancing sideways, I see my father watching, so I push again, still not with my full force. Once again he doesn't budge. "Push me," he demands, with a growl.

Something about the way he is speaking to me really pisses me off, so I push again, really putting my weight behind the shove, fully expecting that he's going to throw me on the mat. Still he doesn't budge, he doesn't apply any moves – he just stands there, looking at me like I'm wasting his time.

"Maybe you should go back to a beginner's class. It's been a long time since you've trained."

He says it with such disdain that it infuriates me, I forget myself. I forget where I am, and who I'm dealing with, and I just charge him. Big mistake.

Twisting his body, he sidesteps me, causing me to rush past him. Which is embarrassing enough, if not for the fact that he then grabs my wrist and spins me back toward him. He's so fast that I don't even know how to respond. His other arm slips under my armpit and before I know it, my feet are off the floor and I'm dangling over his shoulder.

"There's the fire," he comments, as he sets me down. "Now. Your turn."

"You want me to lift you up on my back?" I query, dubious of my ability to lift such a large man.

"Henrietta, you seem to be forgetting one of the primary principles of Aikido – you won't be using your strength – you'll be using my momentum. We'll go through it slowly and then we'll do it fast. Ok?" he says, his voice soft and gentle all of a sudden. I find myself nodding, trusting that I can do this.

Slowly, he talks me through the steps of the kata. We repeat it, step by step, three times. We're not really exerting ourselves, but I find myself breathing a little heavier as my body buzzes around him. There's something about this man – he's…intoxicating.

As we perform the last move, he doesn't break away. Instead, he leans close to my ear and whispers, "Are you ready for me?"

My heart thuds like the beat of a bass drum in a marching band. Swallowing hard, I try to slow my breathing before answering. "Yes," I whisper. "I can do it."

"Good," he nods, a pleased grin pulling at the corner of his mouth.

As he comes toward me with a fast push, I react correctly, with the moves he's just shown me. This is all stuff I've learned in pieces before, but with my lack of practice, I'm very rusty and have to think to react. Whereas for Damien, he's so well trained that he's instantly reactive.

The first time, I'm a little slow, and I don't hoist him onto my back. But when we do it again, I perform the move seamlessly.

When his feet lift off the floor, I can't help but laugh out with pride. I did it.

"Excellent. Now for the rest of it."

"There's a flip isn't there?" I laugh.

"Yes, there's a flip," he grins.

"Alright. Let's get this bad boy done," I say, giving it my all straight away this time.

As I rush him with my push, he spins, pulls and hoists me onto his back, tilting his body so that I roll straight off and onto the mat.

"You ok?" he asks, holding his hand out to help me up when I spend a moment longer on the floor than I really should.

Taking his hand, I nod. "Just a little winded. I'm not used to this anymore."

"You need to go through it, or do you think you can flip me?"

"I think I can flip you," I say, feeling confidant after managing to lift him.

"Good girl."

Rushing me, I perform the move in return, hoisting him off the ground and rolling him off my back. A great sense of pride floods my body as I successfully perform the move. But he's quick, he grips my wrist and pulls me with him, causing me to

54

suck the air back in surprise as I go flying to the floor along with him, slamming hard into the mat by his side.

Fighting for breath, I lay there – defeated and embarrassed. Cursing my own hubris as I try to get my lungs working again. Damien stands easily, holding his hand out to me again to help me up, a self-satisfied grin upon his face as those light eyes of his watch me gasping amusedly.

"Leave me alone," I pant, slapping his hand away.

"Are you upset that I caught you off guard again?" he asks grinning.

I roll my eyes at him, just as my father comes over beaming, slapping Damien on the back like they're buddies. Well, I'm glad he's got someone to be proud of.

Fuck this. I get up and start to leave. My pride is hurt and I'm angry that I'm probably not going out next Thursday. My father wanted proof that I could handle myself, not proof that I could hit the ground gracefully. Although, I didn't even manage to do that.

As I head toward the door, I shake my head. Finally I was going to go out and behave like a normal uni student, and Damien fucking… - I don't even know his last name; is messing with my life.

I hear my father call after me, but I just keep going. I want out of here.

"Hey Henrietta, wait up!" I hear from behind me as I start to walk home.

"Just go away Damien, you've embarrassed me enough lately. I don't need you to rub it in," I call back.

"Come on. You can't get the shits with me for dropping you. It was just training," he points out, as he catches up to me.

"No. It wasn't just training for me. I had to prove I could handle myself so he'd let me out next Thursday night. This is the first time that I've been invited out and have actually been old enough to go! Now, because of you, I get to be Nigel No Friends at home alone AGAIN! I'm sick of it. I just want to go and be normal. Doesn't anyone get that?"

His brow furrows as he watches me rave on. "Hang on. Back up a bit. You were supposed to prove you could hold your own in an advanced class so you could go out with your friends?" he clarifies.

"Yes. He doesn't think I can take care of myself. He's over protective," I explain.

"Yeah, but most guys aren't going to be fourth dan, like I am. You'd beat a regular guy hands down."

"Try telling him that."

"Come with me," he says, grabbing a hold of my hand and leading me back into the gym.

Admittedly, I notice the hand hold - a lot. I want to pull my hand away, the heat of his body is like an electrical charge racing up my arm. But I don't want to make this any stranger than it already is, so I keep holding on, and when he releases my hand as we enter the dojo, my hand feels horribly empty.

"Wait here," he instructs, and I nod, interested in what he's planning.

I stand by the door and watch as he jogs toward my father and has a quiet conversation with him. All I can see are a few glances in my direction as my father listens to Damien, his hands folded over his chest.

The conversation ends with a nod from my father who then looks at me and beckons me with a tilt of his head.

As I approach, I look at Damien, hoping to see some sort of explanation on his face, but his features are completely impassive. So I'm left wondering what was said.

"You can go next Thursday," my father informs me.

"Really?" I squeal, feeling like a little girl, who is finally allowed to go on a sleepover.

"On one condition. You continue to train. Damien will be your Sensei. He's obviously more capable of teaching you than I am."

"What?!" I spit out. "No! That's not ok Dad!"

"Take it or leave Henrietta. It's all I have to offer." With that he turns and strides off, but pauses, turning back to me and saying,

"Oh, and Henrietta. I want you training indefinitely. If you want your mother and me to help support you until you finish uni, I suggest you fulfil this one wish for me."

"But…" I start, but he's moved off, leaving me with my mouth open and Damien looking impressed with himself.

"Don't look so happy with yourself." I tell him.

"What?" he asks looking innocent.

"I'm really not sure…" I say, shaking my head as I wonder exactly what his role is in all this.

"Hey, at least you get to go out next week. In the meantime, I'll be picking you up tomorrow morning at six. Be ready."

"I'll just meet you here," I respond, trying to think of jobs I can apply for so I can support myself and get out of this.

"I'll pick you up," he insists, ensuring he has the last word by abruptly turning and walking off.

Mumbling under my breath, I pick up my bag and head outside to walk home. Even though it's almost six o'clock, the sun is still shining brightly, the weather still warm.

Removing my water bottle from my bag, I take a cooling drink as I trudge along in the gravel along the side of the road. There's no actual footpath here as it's mainly an industrial area, but once I make it to the end of the road, it will all become residential again.

Kicking up a cloud of dirt, a brand new, dark grey metallic, Subaru XV stops in front of me.

"Why are you walking on the side of a busy road?" Damien asks through the passenger window as I approach.

"Going home," I state obviously.

"Don't you drive?"

"Well no, but I live two blocks away. It's not far."

"Get in." I'd like to say he offered me a lift, but it was more of a command than anything which instantly gets my hackles up.

"I'll be fine," I state, continuing to walk ahead. He drives at a crawl alongside me.

"What does it hurt to get in? It's hot, you just worked out, and now you're breathing in car fumes while you walk through gravel that's full of broken glass and probably a few used syringes."

"Why would I get in your car? I hardly even know you."

"You know me just fine. You even visited my house. We had lunch together – remember?" he grins, creeping the car forward just enough so that when he flings the door open, it's blocking my path. "Come on, get in," he says gently, his eyes pleading.

"This is pointless," I huff as I get into the car, doing my best to seem unaffected by him, and whatever it is about him that makes me want to do anything he says, but at the same time, run like hell.

"Seatbelt," he points out, indicating the silver buckle, still sitting against the side of the car.

Reaching for it, I stretch it across my body but slip as I try to click it in. I'm obviously more nervous around him than I thought.

"Here," he almost murmurs, taking the buckle from my hands and deftly clicking it into place. All the while, my heart is hammering again, and I'm doing my best to make my breathing sound normal as my blood temperature starts to rise.

Reminding myself of his ability to embarrass me, I focus on that as he pulls into the stream of traffic.

"Why did you do it?" I ask.

"Do what?"

"Let me into your apartment yesterday."

"I wish I knew." He pauses at the red light and looks over at me. Our eyes lock for a moment and that feeling I've been fighting starts to win over again, invading my mind like a gaseous cloud, making me dizzy.

We drive the rest of the way to my parent's house in silence. I don't question how he knows where it is. I just assume he's been here before for something to do with my dad – any other possibility seems a little farfetched and stalker-ish.

"I'll see you in the morning," he confirms as he pulls up outside.

Nodding, I get out of the car and walk up to my front door, not looking back until I'm safely inside and can spy on him through the peephole for long enough to see him drive away.

"Who was that?" my mother asks from behind me.

"One of dad's students," I reply, leaning into the window next to the door as I watch his car disappear down the road.

"How was training? Did your dad agree to release you?" she jokes.

Turning away from the window, I lean against the door jamb to face her. "Yes, but with conditions," I sigh.

"Oh no. What's he going to do? Make you wear a GPS tracker?"

"No. Worse. He's making me train again. He said that if I don't, you guys won't help me when I move out."

"That man," my mother grumbles. "Don't worry, I'll talk to him. You don't have to train if you don't want to. I know it's hard for you without Craig around."

"It wasn't horrible going there today. But it just reminds me that he's gone. I'd prefer not to go there."

"I know," she coos, giving me a hug. "I know. I'll sort him out."

"Thanks mum," I say, before heading into the bathroom for a shower, glad that my mum is going to talk to my dad.

I'll admit, that once I got going today, I didn't mind training. But the thought of constantly doing it, is a little hard to handle. All of my memories of training revolve around my brother. I quit for a reason, and I'm not keen on returning – regardless of who my teacher is.

3

Where are you?

It's six-fifteen the next morning. I was trying to sleep. Instead, I'm staring at my phone, wondering exactly how Damien got my number. Deducing that he must have gotten it off my father at some point.

Why? I type out in reply.

When I don't get an answer after a few minutes, I return my phone to my bedside table and roll over, trying to return to my sleep.

Five minutes later, just as I start to drift off, my phone starts vibrating and dancing atop its wooden perch, startling me awake again.

"What?" I say, knowing it's Damien. "How the hell did you get my number?"

"Come outside," he instructs.

"I'm trying to sleep."

"I don't think your father would be happy if I start beating on his door. Come outside," he insists, hanging up.

For a moment, I stare at the phone, debating whether or not to do what he's asking. Not really wanting him to wake my parents, I swing my legs out of the bed and go to the window, pulling aside the curtains to see him standing against his car waiting for me.

Holding my hand up, I signal that I need five minutes. He nods, tapping his watch to let me know he's timing me.

Rolling my eyes, I step away from the window and open my wardrobe, pulling out a pair of tracksuit pants and an old band t-shirt. Pulling my thick hair into a high pony tail and pinning my fringe back, I move to the bathroom where I put on some deodorant and quickly brush my teeth before splashing some water on my face.

As I make my way toward the front door, I quickly scrawl a note to let my parents know I've gone out, grab my bag and shoes, and attempt to quietly exit the house.

Leaning against the entry way of our avocado green, weatherboard house, I slide my feet into my runners, then trot down the concrete steps, pausing in the centre of the path to adjust the heel of my shoe where it's digging painfully into my ankle.

"Glad you could make it," Damien smiles as he opens the passenger door for me.

"Why are you even here? My mother spoke to my dad, and I don't have to train anymore," I respond.

"Is that a fact?" he asks, looking highly amused.

"Yes it is. But since you obviously weren't informed, I'll train with you – once."

He grins and nods his head. "Just hop in," he tells me.

I get into the car, grabbing a hold of the seatbelt and clicking it in place before he can do it for me again.

Closing my door, he walks around to his side and starts the engine, u-turning in front of my house to drive us toward the gym and dojo that my father owns.

While my father is primarily an Aikido Sensei, he has branched his business out to be an actual gym that opens from midday to midnight, offering fitness classes and personal training. It was an ingenious decision really, as the dojo wasn't making a huge amount of money on its own. But adding a gym that was more affordable than the big chain gyms, has been what's kept him afloat and able to keep the dojo going.

"Why don't you have a Gi?" he asks.

"I got rid of it," I explain. "I haven't had one since I was about twelve. Plus I hate those black skirty things."

"Hakama," he corrects.

"I know what they're called. I'm not an idiot," I state.

"Then call them what they are. Don't dumb it down. You're a smart woman Henrietta."

"Would you please stop calling me 'Henrietta'? I prefer 'Etta'."

He just looks at me briefly, not giving me an answer as he pulls into the car park at my dad's gym.

"So you're trusted enough to be given keys huh?" I ask as he unlocks the front door.

"Looks like it," he responds, keying in the alarm's code.

Standing back, I look him over, head to toe. He's dressed in a pair of black gym pants with a double white stripe going down the side, a tight black ribbed singlet that shows off his well-defined arms and broad shoulders. On his feet are a pair of black runners.

"Where's your gi?" I ask.

"In my bag," he replies, raising his gym bag a little as he walks ahead of me, flicking lights on. When he pulls the sliding door open leading into the dojo, he stops and sweeps his arm in front of him to indicate that I should enter.

"Why were you willing to do this?" I ask as I walk in and watch him slide the door shut. "You know – train me. What's in it for you? Is my dad paying you?"

"I enjoy teaching and you obviously need more practise. Your technique is sloppy and your reaction time is poor. If something really did happen to you, I can't see you overcoming your opponent."

"What are you talking about? You said yourself that I would be fine against a regular person."

"And you probably would be. But what happens if your attacker is someone like me? What if they know more than you do? What if you react around them the way you do around me?" he practically whispers, moving closer to me, so our bodies are almost touching.

I tilt my head back slightly, holding his gaze and fighting my urge to rock on my toes to connect our lips.

"And how is it that I react around you?" I ask, my voice unintentionally quiet and breathy.

"Exactly like this," he breathes, reaching up to move the stray hair that has escaped from my clip. I hold my breath, unwilling to even blink while he refastens it, as I refuse to even let my mind acknowledge how much my body is crying out for him. "Now let's get started. I want you to strike me."

He takes two steps away from me, and I literally have to shake my head slightly to remove the fog that seems to have settled on my mind. "Aren't you going to get changed?"

"Just strike me."

See, this is what I hate about Aikido – the part where you're the attacker. You always end up on the floor, and you very rarely get to connect any of your hits. When you're training with someone who knows what they're doing, it feels like you're fighting against air because they are never where your strike lands. The whole point of it is to anticipate your opponent and use their own movement against them. Essentially, they make you feel like a marionette puppet as they take control of your limbs.

"Come on," he insists, his brows raised as he beckons me forward.

"Do you think you can just walk me through it, instead of making me attack you so you can throw me on the ground?" I ask, hands on hips as my nerves set in. I'm not equipped for this kind of training anymore. It's been too long and I really dislike falling.

"You can either attack me and train, or I can just throw you on the ground anyway. Your choice."

"Fine," I grumble, reaching up and tightening my hair as I ready myself to get this over with.

Rushing forward, I attempt to punch him in the face. I choose the face because at this point in time, I wouldn't mind it if my fist actually connects and leaves some sort of a mark on that smug face of his. But of course, it doesn't. Instead, he deflects the blow by pushing my arm to the side, and pulling me past him so I'm off balance, before landing a blow on my chest that causes me to fall on my arse.

As he did yesterday, he holds his hand out to help me up, but I'm annoyed. I didn't really want to be here, and now I'm going to have a bruised tailbone – I really need to remember to roll with the fall instead of fighting it. It's something I'd do, had I continued with my own training, but now, my natural response is to always fight to remain standing.

"I can get up on my own," I remind him, although he doesn't listen and reaches further to grip me by my upper arms and haul me to standing.

"Roll next time," he says, a seriousness in his expression before he instructs me to work through the move on him.

We continue on with the training session, taking turns as to who attacks and who defends. I'm still not landing properly, so I'm really feeling it by the time I get flipped on my back for the tenth time.

"Enough! Enough!" I say, placing my hands on my face in frustration. He's just too good, and I'm too tired. I've only pulled off two successful moves. The rest of the time he's out manoeuvred me. I've simply had enough.

He holds his hand out to me, pulling my arm to help me up.

"We'll do this again tomorrow," he informs me, breathing steadily, despite our vigorous workout.

"What if I don't want to do this again tomorrow?"

"Then I'll stand outside your house, honking my horn until you come out."

"You wouldn't do that. My dad would kill you."

"Honestly, I think he'd thank me."

"For what?"

"Getting you training again."

"Is that what you're doing this for? My father's approval?"

"Not at all. I'm doing this because you're young," he says tapping his head, indicating that it's my mind he feels is young. "You're inexperienced in the world. You can fight, but you're too trusting."

"I am not," I argue.

"Henrietta. Think about how we met… you're too trusting."

"Maybe I'm just good at knowing who to trust. Have you thought about it that way?" I argue, hands on my hips. "Unless of course it's you I shouldn't be trusting. In which case, why would I want you to train me? This makes no sense. I don't want to train. I want to make it one last week at home. Move out and have a life of my own. This is my last year at uni. I just want to have some fun and feel like a regular eighteen year old. I know how to defend myself Damien. I know how to fight. Most girls don't know anywhere near as much as I do and they go through life just fine."

"I don't think you're like most girls."

"What does that even mean?" I ask, feeling confused and frustrated by his inability to answer a specific question.

"It means that I will pick you up at six tomorrow, and every day after that."

"Until when?"

"Until you can beat me."

"What if that never happens?"

"Then you're stuck with me. Come on," he says, picking up his bag and heading toward the door. "I'll take you home."

"Jesus Damien. I can walk you know."

He just looks at me with his eyebrows raised, holding his bag by his side until I concede and follow him.

Once again, he opens the door for me, only this time he is faster than I am, and does my seatbelt again for me.

"Stop it!" I yell, slapping at his arm as he reaches it around me. "I'm not a baby."

He pauses as the seatbelt clicks in place, keeping his arm around me as he turns to look in my eyes. He's so close that I can feel his breath and smell the workout mixed with his soap and deodorant on his skin.

Snapping my eyes away, I look down as I speak. "I'm not going to keep training with you," I tell him defiantly. "Beep your horn all you want. I'm not doing it."

He breathes in, as if his patience with me is wearing thin and withdraws his arm from around me, walking around the car and entering on his side.

"What's so bad about training with me?" he asks as he starts the car.

"Why does it matter? Can't I just say 'no, I'm not training' and be done with it?"

"Not if you want me to leave you alone," he states calmly.

"I quit training because it reminds me of my brother. It's something we always did together. We would train with dad in the dojo outside our regular classes. Then we'd train together at home. We drove my mum insane with the amount of broken vases we amassed, but we loved it. When all the other siblings hated each other – we still got along; even though he was three years older than me. I don't want to train with you because I don't want to be reminded that he's gone," I explain as we pull up outside my house.

I put my hand on the door handle, wanting to get out of the car and away from this guy I know nothing about, but who seems to think he has a say in my life. But he presses the button on the console and locks me in.

"Let me out," I say sternly, flicking the lock upwards by hand. Instantly it drops down again. "Let me out!" I repeat.

"Just wait. We're not finished."

"Well I am finished. You made me train when I didn't want to and it won't be happening again. I'm done. Training didn't keep my brother alive. There's no fucking point. Sometimes shit just happens and there's nothing you can do about it. Knowing how to disarm a guy and toss him on his back isn't going to change anything. Just let me out."

"I'm sorry Henrietta," he says. "All I want is for you to be safe."

"Stop calling me Henrietta. I don't need you to keep me safe. I don't need another father."

Sighing, he presses the button again and grants me my release.

"I'll see you around then, Henrietta," he says as I go to close the door.

"Fuck you," I grunt. Stepping away from the car and heading up the path to my front door and the safety of my own home.

When I get inside, my mother and father are already at the dining table eating their breakfast. "Have you eaten?" my mother asks the moment she hears the door close.

"No. I'll just have some fruit and yogurt," I say, trying to seem unruffled by Damien as I head straight for the fridge.

"How was training?" my father asks, between sips of his tea.

"Annoying," I answer with a bounce of my shoulders as I take the yogurt over to the bench top and grab a bowl.

"Who were you training with?"

"Damien, of course," I state, as I slice a banana into my bowl.

"I thought you didn't want to train. Are you finally interested again?"

"I'm not interested. He made me go."

"How did he make you?" my mother laughs, knowing me to be incredibly stubborn and unwilling to bend for most people. "You were dead against it yesterday afternoon."

"He threatened to unleash a cacophony of epic proportions upon our household. You should thank me – I rescued your sleep," I inform them.

"So he was going to toot his horn until you came out?" my father translates, to which I nod, licking the excess yogurt off my spoon as I carry my bowl to the table. "I knew there was a reason I liked him," he smiles.

"Oh you like him now?" my mother laughs.

"Our daughter is training again. How could I not like him?" he beams.

"Because he could be trying to make moves on our daughter," my mother counters, looking at him pointedly.

"No. He wouldn't be that stupid," my dad states confidently, to which my mother shakes her head and continues eating her breakfast.

"Dad, your priorities are so messed up. Don't you mind that he used my love for my family against me? That could mean that he isn't really that great a guy."

"You're training. I'm happy," he smiles, standing from the table to take his plate and cup to the dishwasher.

"Don't get too excited. I told him it was our first and last session.

I only went because you conveniently forgot to tell him not to train me."

"I did tell him not to train you. I spoke to him last night," he informs me.

"Then what the… You know what? It doesn't matter, I'm not going again anyway," I state, trying to ignore the questioning voice in my head that is demanding to know what Damien's deal is.

"Listen, I know going to this was a big thing for you. But you must know that your brother would have wanted you to keep going. Maybe instead of training with Damien you can start doing the weekly classes again? Craig wouldn't want you to give up something you loved because of him," my mother puts in, reaching across the table to squeeze my arm.

"I loved Aikido because of him. It's just not the same." Getting up, I deposit my dishes in the dishwasher as well, then head straight for the shower to get ready for uni.

Sometimes I feel like I'm forever being told to live my life as if my brother was still around. But how can I? Everything and everyone is different with him gone. It's as if his ghost resides in our house, watching and judging everything we do. Although, it's not his actual ghost, it's my parent's perfect representation of the son that died. The one that didn't sneak out every night, the one who didn't rebel.

Every time someone says 'It's what Craig would have wanted', I just want to scream, 'You didn't even know him!'

In truth, he would have wanted me to run for the hills, to go out and have fun. If I wanted to quit Aikido, he would have been ok with that – as long as it was what *I* wanted. He would never have expected me to do something that makes me unhappy.

These are the times when I'm angry at him for leaving me. If he had have just accepted the house rules for what they were, he never would have died, and I wouldn't be so miserable with a set of parents who have spent the last six years too petrified to let me out of their sight.

Everyone just needs to accept that he's dead. His wants don't matter anymore. We all just need to deal with that and move on.

***

"What's up your arse today?" Aaron asks, regarding me as I take the seat next to him in the lecture hall and twist the desk over my lap so I can set up to take notes.

"Nothing, I'm just tired. I didn't get much sleep."

"Well, maybe this will cheer you up," he says, placing a small rectangular box on my desk.

"What's this? It's not my birthday 'til Tuesday." I glance at him, smiling as I pick up the box and untie the purple ribbon that surrounds it.

"It's a big birthday. I wanted to be the first one to give you something," he smiles, watching me as I remove the lid.

Inside the box is an oval shaped, brushed metal keychain.

Holding it up, I turn it over in my hands, reading the inscriptions on both sides. One says 'Home Sweet Home' and the other side says 'Etta'.

"Oh wow. This is really thoughtful Aaron. Thank you," I say, leaning in to him and hugging him tight as I kiss him on the cheek.

Grinning, he turns a little pink. "No worries. I just thought with the move and all…"

"It's perfect. Really it is," I beam, taking his hand and giving it a squeeze as our lecturer calls us all to attention. "Thank you," I say again in a whisper, as I turn to the front of the room to listen, all the while keeping a hold of the smooth metal in my hand. This is really the most thoughtful gift I've ever received.

4

"Happy birthday!" my mother singsongs, as I trudge out of my room on Tuesday morning at 8am. "What would you like for your birthday breakfast?"

"Anything with caffeine," I groan, covering my face with my hands. You'd think I hadn't even slept by the way I was feeling when my alarm went off this morning. It's not like I've been training lately either. Surprisingly, Damien actually respected my wishes and didn't show up, honking his horn until I came out. Although, I'm not sure if I'm happy or a little disappointed in that.

When I'm around him, I feel things. That's a very ineloquent way to put it, but I don't feel normal around him. I'm not sure what it is. I'm not sure if I'm attracted to him or if I'm scared of him, and I find myself constantly on guard, but at the same time, hoping to run into him.

It's driving me a little mad, as I keep thinking I see him everywhere. He's in my dreams, he's on the street. I even thought I saw him when I was at the movies with my mother on the weekend.

I just can't name what that feeling is. It's not that hope you feel when you like someone – it's different to that. I guess I just feel…aware. It's strange. It's disconcerting and more than a little confusing.

My mother sets a mug of coffee in front of me. Thanking her, I take a sip. "Where's dad?" I ask, carefully placing the mug back down on the table in front of me.

"He's outside, working off a bit of steam. He's not taking your birthday well," she confides.

"I know. But I need to have my own life mum. I just want one year on my own. Uni will be over and before I know it, I'll have all this work and responsibility. I just want one year with no rules, no restrictions."

She cups my chin in her hand and looks at me, her lips pressed together, and her eyes glassy. "I do understand, honey. It's just hard for us to see our little girl grown up so fast. You'll have to give your dad time."

It's at that moment, he chooses to burst in through the back door, his face flushed and his breathing rapid from his early work out.

"Happy birthday, sweetheart," he says as soon as he sees me.

"Thank you dad," I smile, noting the hint of sadness on his face.

He walks toward me and places a small bag on the table in front of me. "I know your present is the move and all, but I wanted to give you something on the day."

"Oh dad," I breathe, touched that he's being so thoughtful even though this birthday spells the end of his authority over me. It's not like he's been horrible to me at all. I certainly don't see him as some sort of evil tyrant, I just feel shackled and I'm ready to be free.

"Open it," he urges, nodding toward the black bag with brightly coloured 'happy birthday's all over it in different fonts.

Looking inside, I move the white tissue paper to the side and locate a burgundy velvet pouch at the bottom.

"You got me jewellery?" I ask smiling. My father has never bought me anything girly before. As I open it, I glance over at my mother who is leaning against the bench top and watching our exchange with an absent smile on her face.

Slipping my fingers into the opening to loosen the string, I reach inside and slide out a black tube bracelet, held together by a silver ellipse.

"It's a Ki bracelet," he explains, taking it from my fingers and offering to clasp it to my wrist. "It's to keep you centred."

Turning my wrist from side to side, I admire the sleek design. "Thank you Dad. This is beautiful. I'll wear it always."

He nods, leaning his bulk down to kiss me on my head. "Happy birthday," he says again, before announcing that he's going to take a shower.

"Did you know about this?" I ask my mother once he's out of ear shot.

"No, he did it all by himself," she smiles. "You ready for

something to eat? I can toast some banana bread if you like?"

"Yeah mum, that would be great."

I spend the rest of the day with my parents. My mother has taken the day off work, and my father has left the running of the gym to his employees for the day. We torture my father by shopping for items I'll need to move out with, as well as a dress for the Scarlet Party on Thursday night.

It's a simple dress - red of course, and sleeveless, with an asymmetric mid-length skirt. It's one of those halter neck designs with black binding on the neck and a black and gold trim on the waist that acts like a belt.

While I'm not that into dresses, it's actually kind of cool – and it's not super girly, plus, it doesn't have any sequins on it, which I hate. It's just …nice.

By the time we're done, you can tell my dad is itching to go home. He's not big on shopping, so I really appreciate him spending the day being dragged around without complaining.

Feeling exhausted, I head to my bedroom to deposit some of our purchases on the floor while my mother and father store a few of the other things in the living room. As I walk down the hall, I brush my fingertips over the door leading to my brother's room, wishing he was still here. It's basically a shrine in there, not one thing has changed since he died. It's as if it's sitting there, waiting for him to return.

Once again reminded of my family's loss, I lay on my bed and take out my phone as a distraction, quickly responding to the happy birthday messages from my friends. They all know that we're celebrating my birthday together at the Scarlet Party on Thursday.

I know that spending the day with your parents isn't the normal thing for an eighteen year old to do. I'm supposed to be celebrating my legal freedom by having a big party or spending the night getting drunk at some club or bar with my friends. But today is a family day. It's one of my last ones.

In a few days, I'll be out of here, out on my own. As much as I love my parents, and as much as I know it hurts them that I'm leaving, I need to think about myself. I can't live with my brother's ghost forever. It's already been six years since he died, and while I miss him every day, I just can't live with the sadness his absence brings to this house anymore. I need to live. I can't mourn anymore.

5

Is it wrong that I'm so excited about going to the Scarlet Party that I actually woke up early this morning? Like 5am early? It's only 8am now and I already have my dress ironed and ready… I know – who even irons these days? But I'm all fidgety with nothing else to do today but wait until it's time to meet everyone at the uni bar.

I think I'm driving my mum crazy with my constant pacing. She works from home as a Virtual Assistant to various small companies that can't afford to hire someone to work for them full time. So I guess me walking around the house aimlessly is ruining her concentration.

"Would you just go for a run or something?" she says eventually, her eyes closed as she forces her voice to stay calm.

"Oh, it's fine. I'm happy hanging around here," I reply, clapping my hands together as I continue to pace.

"Honey, I insist. Please, get out of this house and work off some of that excess energy."

"But I have uni in an hour," I retort.

"Then you can get ready and walk to the uni instead of catching a train. Please Etta, I can't concentrate with you huffing and puffing out there."

I hesitate in the doorway of her office, it's already fairly warm outside, and I don't want to have to wear a giant hat to protect my fair skin from the bright February sun.

"Go!" she commands, shooing me away with her hand.

"Um… ok," I call, grabbing my bag as I head out the door.

It takes me a good forty-five minutes to make it on campus, and the first thing I do is head to the café to grab a cold bottle of water. As I stand outside, I lean against the wall in the shade to cool down before I go to class.

"Hey, I thought that was you," says Aaron as he approaches me. "How does it feel to officially be an adult now?"

"The same so far. I haven't done any 18-year-old things yet," I reply taking a mouthful of water.

He raises his eyebrows at me as a grin spreads across his lips. He knows full well that I've done plenty of 18-year-old things. I just haven't done them legally yet.

"I mean I haven't been able to officially use my ID yet."

"Well, we will fix that for you tonight. Are you going to crash at your new place or do you want to crash at mine?" he asks, taking the bottle from my hands and taking a mouthful for himself.

"I hadn't thought about it. I was actually just planning on going home. I only have tonight and tomorrow before I move out. So I thought I might be responsible and not drink too much tonight to freak the parental unit out."

He hands the bottle back. "Thanks," he says. "Yeah, that might be a good idea. We can go out again next week if you want to have a big one."

"We can go out any time. I'm about to be granted my freedom. The rules will soon be mine to make," I smile.

"You know, it's strange thinking of you as eighteen. You seem so much older all the time," he muses as we begin to make our way to the lecture hall.

"I don't know if that's a compliment or if you're telling me I look haggard," I laugh.

"No Etta – it's a compliment. You're so far from ever being called 'haggard' and you know it. I guess it's just that we started uni at the same time, and I've always thought of you as the same as me. You've never seemed as though you were five years younger than me."

Besides the mature age students, Aaron is actually one of the older students in third year. Most students started straight out of high school. But Aaron didn't start until he was twenty – he took a year off to work and travel before focusing on his studies.

"You're just saying that to be nice," I say.

"No. It's true - you're amazing."

He stands aside to let me into the row of seats ahead of him, and I'm glad to be able to turn away from him, and glad that the lecture hall has dim lighting. His compliment has caused a deep flush to heat my cheeks. I've always thought he was pretty amazing too.

***

"Show me, show me, show me!" my mother sings as she makes her way up the hallway to the bathroom where I'm getting ready for my night out. I've used the flat iron to straighten my thick auburn locks and applied a deep pink lip stain. For my eyes, I've kept it simple, by brushing brown eye shadow over my lower lid and smudging it at the corner, topping it off with some black mascara.

"Oh honey," she breathes, looking me up and down. "You look gorgeous. Wait there, I want to take a photo to show your father."

"No mum please," I beg.

"Just one," she says, dashing off to grab her phone.

When she returns, I turn around and let her take her photo, feeling like an idiot as she clicks away.

"Just one more. Can you smile in this one - please? You look so pretty."

I give my mum the smile she's after, as a horn honks outside, letting me know that Aaron is there to pick me up.

"Isn't he going to come in to get you?" she asks, glancing out the window at his parked car.

"It's not a date mum," I remind her, as I pick up my bag.

"Doesn't mean he has to beep at you," she comments.

Smiling, I ignore her quip. "Thank you for the dress mum," I say to her as I start to leave.

"I expected you to choose pants," she smiles, touching my arm lightly. "Have a great time tonight. Stay out as long as you like. Be good – and drink if you wish. I promise to deal with your father."

"Thanks mum," I whisper, giving her a quick hug.

On my way out, I can't stop smiling as she leans against the door jam and keeps calling out for me to have a good time. I'm now wondering who's more excited about this. Me or her?

"Holy shit Etta. You look smoking hot tonight," Aaron remarks as I get in the car.

"Thank you," I smile. "You don't look so bad yourself. I like this look on you."

He's wearing a pair of red jeans with a fitted black t-shirt. You can actually see the hours this man puts in at the uni gym through his clothes, and I wonder why he still doesn't have a girlfriend. I don't really think he's dated much at all since we broke up.

As we approach the campus Bar Café, I'm feeling a little overdressed. Most of the people milling about the campus are wearing casual jeans and t-shirt type outfits as they move from class to class. My phone goes off in my bag, signalling that I have a message.

Still coming? It says.

I smile as I reply to Kensi, *Yes, we're outside.*

When the bar comes into view, my smile grows wider as I see Kensi and Jessica, both in red dresses, leaning against one of the outside tables, talking to a few other people dressed in a similar fashion.

"Yay! You made it," Kensi squeals, dancing about excitedly as she holds a bottle of beer above her head.

"Wouldn't miss it," I return, grinning like crazy. I've been to the uni bar before, but I've never been able to go out with everyone afterward. I've always had to keep to my curfew. Now suddenly, I don't have one, and I can't stop smiling.

"I love that dress," Kensi says. "I wish I was tall enough to wear something like that. Long dresses make me look like a baby," she laughs.

"There has to be a benefit to being a giant woman," I laugh in return.

"We haven't been to one of these pool competitions before. Are they any good?" Jessica asks, directing her question toward Aaron.

"Um, yeah. They're not too bad. I normally buddy up with a few friends. That's them over there," he says, nodding toward a group of people we know from our classes.

"Can you play pool Etta?" asks Kensi, as she lifts her bottle of beer to her lips.

"A little, I know the rules. But I'm rarely here long enough to play," I reply, hoping they don't really expect me to play in the tournament.

Our other friends wave us over to their table. "Let me introduce you to our friends," Aaron offers, guiding us all over to our usual group of Jenny, Kylie, Daniel, Carl and Adam, who are already seated and drinking at an inside table.

Kylie jumps up and hugs me. "Happy birthday! We thought we'd sit inside today since your legal now," she bounces.

"It was your birthday?" Kensi asks.

"Yeah Tuesday," I smile, turning to introduce them before everyone gets caught up discussing my age again. "Everyone, this is Kensi and Jessica. They're going to be my housemates as of this weekend," I tell them all proudly.

"Oh my god! You found something already? That's fantastic," squeals Jenny.

"And I hear you're coming out with us tonight," Carl adds.

"I sure am," I grin.

"Does that mean she can sub in for me with this pool thing?" Adam asks. He seems to be all arms and legs and from what I hear, is solely responsible for the constant losses this group is amassing in the pool competition.

"Don't try and rope her in," Jenny puts in. "Adam you'll be fine. The men play the pool and the women sit around and drink and giggle. It's the rules, and it has been for years."

"What's going on?" I ask Aaron.

"Adam doesn't want to play," Carl explains.

"But we need a forth," Aaron responds.

"Etta can do it," Adam insists.

"Alright, well if you want me to – I'll play. I can sink the balls, I just can't do any fancy tricks," I offer, realising that I'd actually prefer to play pool more than I'd prefer to watch for a change.

"Sounds perfect. Of course you'll partner with me," Aaron smiles.

"Of course," I grin back.

Aaron and Karl rise from their seats and make their way over to the sign up area. It's at that moment I get a prickling sensation dancing over my skin. When I look around for the reason, I notice Damien, sitting at the bar, beer in hand, watching me.

The moment I catch his eye, he tilts his glass toward me and smiles, giving me a wink. The corner of my mouth twitches as I try to fight my smile, although the blush comes anyway and I'm sure he notices because he laughs a little as he takes a sip of his drink.

"We're all set," Aaron says as he makes his way back over. "Can I get you a drink?" he offers, pointing toward the bar.

"Yeah, actually. That'd be nice," I smile, glancing toward the bar where I just saw Damien. He's still there, but he's joined by two other guys now as well as that Bec girl who was at his room on Monday. She catches me watching and smiles, like she's some sort of a feline, playing with her prey as she slides her arm over the back of Damien's shoulders before whispering something in his ear.

"What'll it be?" Aaron asks, stealing my attention away.

"Surprise me," I smile, unable to force my attention away from Damien and Bec long enough to decide for myself.

He laughs. "I'll try and get you something nice."

"Thanks."

Quite a crowd has gathered now that the tournament is about to start, and as I watch Aaron push through it, I find my eyes straying to find Damien. Although he's not there anymore. Actually, I can't see him anywhere.

"Here you go. I don't think you've tried this one before," Aaron says as he hands me a watermelon vodka mixer.

"Thank you," I smile, accepting the bottle, and taking a cautious sip. It's actually quite nice.

"Are you looking for someone?" he enquires.

"No. Just looking around," I lie.

A short and very pale skinned guy stands up on a makeshift stage and taps the microphone. He's wearing round Harry Potter style glasses and has shoulder length, lifeless brown hair.

"Attention everyone. The tournament is just about to start. I'd like you all to note where your names are on the whiteboard. We'll be running three games at a time, so listen up and pay attention for when you're called."

He announces the names for the first three games, and we all either return to what we were doing or move to watch the other games as the players rack up the balls.

"We're not playing for a while. You want some food while we wait? My shout," Aaron asks.

"Yeah actually, I'm starving. What are you thinking of?" I ask, looking over at the wall menu.

"Maybe a bowl of chips?"

"Perfect." I take a seat at the table with the others as Aaron goes to order.

"So are you and Aaron dating?" Kensi asks. Her silky dark hair and severe bob frame her heart shaped face. It works on her and makes her look porcelain doll-like.

"We used to. But not anymore," I reply, taking a sip of my drink.

"They were hot and heavy for a while," Jenny adds in. "But Etta's younger than the rest of us and things didn't work out for them."

"So what's World Bar like? I haven't been before," I ask everyone, wanting to steer the conversation away from my dating history.

"It's a club," says Daniel. "Music, dancing, drunk people. Everyone goes pretty mental at the Uni parties. It should be a great night."

"Yeah, I have no idea why they would want us to wear red. It's going to look like a pulsating artery in there tonight," Jenny says, looking down at her dress and smoothing her hand over the skirt.

"I think it will look awesome," Kensi adds.

"Here you go," Aaron says, as he slides into the bench seat next to me and places a basket of hot chips in between us. The others pinch a few too, and we all chat for a while until it's time for us to play.

"Aaron Stevens and Etta Davis."

"We're up," he says, nudging me in the arm.

"Don't expect any miracles," I warn him. "I'm really not that great."

We get handed our cues by someone who I'm assuming is a helper of the event.

"Head or Tails?" he asks, holding a coin on the edge of his thumb. "Winner gets to break."

"Ladies choice," says one of the guys from the other double.

"Heads," I call, with a bounce of my shoulder.

The helper flicks his thumb up and sends the coin flying in the air as we all watch until it lands on the green felt with a light thud.

"Heads it is!" he calls.

Grinning triumphantly I high-five Aaron, before heading to the top of the table to start. Leaning forward, I slide my cue over my fingers as I aim at the white ball. With a short burst, I thrust the wooden pole forward, hitting the ball so it breaks apart the neatly arranged solid and striped balls.

"Great work!" Aaron whoops as a cheer breaks out around us. Somehow I managed to sink six balls and can choose whether we are playing for the striped balls or the solid coloured balls.

"Stripes," I call, taking aim at the blue ten that is clearly able to be hit into the pocket.

After sinking another four balls, I finally miss one. The crowd groans, and claps, shifting their attention to the other team as their first player takes aim.

"You're good," Aaron murmurs behind my ear. "All these years, I've missed out on having you as a partner."

"Thank you," I smile, leaning on the cue as I wonder if there is a double meaning behind his comment.

"Although I have to admit, I'm kind of disappointed. I was hoping I'd have to show you how to play."

A grin creeps across my face as his hands slip around my waist. "I'll just have to settle with being forward then," he adds.

A delicious warmth creeps over my body, beginning where his arms are and spreading until I feel my cheeks heat. I lean back against him slightly, as he rests his chin on my shoulder and observe the game taking place in front of us.

I let out a disappointed sigh when our opponent's next shot misses. Now it's Aaron's turn, which means he'll need to let go.

Taking the cue from my hands, he picks up the blue cube of chalk and rubs it over the tip, blowing lightly on it to remove the excess. He does a bit of a walk around the table as he decides which ball to go for. As he leans forward to take his shot, I can't help but observe the way his jeans tighten over his arse and bite my lip, feeling a little like a lioness in heat.

"I'm pretty sure your father won't be too impressed with those thoughts you're having," Damien says from behind me. I can't even say that he startled me, as just before he spoke, that pickling sensation crept over my skin again. It's as if I expected him, and now, here he is…

"What are you doing here?" I ask over my shoulder, without turning my head.

"Watching you," he whispers close to my ear, causing me to stiffen slightly, unsure as to whether he's teasing me or not.

"Are you watching me for fun? Or did my father send you here to spy on me?" I ask, trying not to let myself turn around and look at him.

"Your dad just wants you safe Henrietta. You can't blame him for worrying," he says so softly, I'm the only one who could possibly hear him.

"Don't you have a job or something to go to?" I deflect, finally turning my head to look at him, but missing him entirely as he switches sides.

A low chuckle rumbles in my ear, sending chills skittering, deliciously through my body. "It's possible this is a pure coincidence. I'm a student here Henrietta. Perhaps my being here, isn't about you after all…"

I roll my eyes slightly and huff out my breath before turning my head to tell him to back off. But when I turn, he's gone, and I'm left wondering if I imagined the whole exchange.

6

"Who knew that Etta here, would be the reason we finally win that bloody pool comp?" Karl laughs. "We've been getting guys to team up with us, when all we needed was a good lookin' sheila." He stretches his leg out between the train seats as we ride a Tangara to Parramatta station so we can attend the Scarlet Party at the World Bar. The carriage is full of students from our university, all dressed in Red and all slightly buzzy from some pre-party drinks. Even I'm feeling a little buzzed after drinking three vodka mixes over the last couple of hours.

"Karl! You're not in Orange anymore - don't call girls 'sheilas'. Especially ones who are obviously a lot classier than the girls you're used to being around," Jenny points out.

"Don't bag out Orange chicks, it's not like Penrith is a huge step up in this world," he responds haughtily.

"What's the issue with Orange chicks?" Jeremy asks from next to Kensi. He's joined us to go to the party, and she seems to have taken an immediate liking to him, making sure that she slid in the seat at just the right time so she could flirt with him more easily.

I smile and listen as the debate rages on about the virtues – or lack thereof – of Western Sydney versus Country girls, rolling my eyes occasionally when the points get too silly. I'm sitting next to Aaron, his arm resting on the top of the seat behind me, just close enough to brush against my skin as the train jostles us about. It seems as though a grin has been placed firmly upon my face. Silently, I thank my mother for getting my dad to let me out tonight.

Oh, and I guess I should thank Damien a little too. After all, he did convince my father I could take care of myself. Damien is in the same carriage, but he's not sitting with us, nor is he wearing red. He's head to toe black again, as he sits next to the stair well with a couple of his friends and that girl, Bec. I don't know why, but I really dislike her. I think it's the way she looks at me – like I'm beneath her or something.

We all walk in a massive group up Church Street until we arrive at the bar. For a while we need to wait in line. I find it amusing as passers-by turn their heads at the wall of red clad party goers that weaves up the street, waiting to get inside.

The moment we step through the doors, we're enveloped in the thumping beat of the room. It's not only the music, but the energy in here too. Everyone is excited and ready for a good time.

"Drinks?" Karl yells over the music, tilting his hand toward his face in the 'drinkie drinkie' motion.

Aaron takes my hand and guides me toward a table as Karl and Daniel go and get everyone some of the discounted drinks. For the next hour, we all sit around the table, initially sharing chairs until we loosen up a bit and girls start to make their way onto boys' laps as the alcohol continues to flow. Before I know it, I've lost count. Everyone wants to shout me a drink to celebrate my eighteenth, and I'm really feeling it.

When I watch Kensi drag Jeremy onto the dance floor, I decide that's exactly what I want to do too.

"Dance with me," I yell over the music, tugging on Aaron's hand. Smiling, he follows me onto the dance floor as I bounce around, swaying to the music.

He pulls me toward him, swaying along with me. "Are you having a good time?" he asks next to my ear.

"Yeah. The best," I grin, sliding my arms up around his shoulders, my head fuzzy and my vision slightly blurred. "You're very tall," I comment, the thought coming to me suddenly. "I like that you're tall."

"And you're a little drunk," he laughs.

"Me? No, I'm just really happy. You're the one who's drunk," I say, trying not to trip over my words as my lips lose their feeling.

"It's true. I'm pretty fucking smashed actually."

"I'm not smashed. I'm just really happy," I say again, as if it's the first time I've come out with it.

He laughs at me. "I'm happy too. Although, do you know what would make me really happy?"

I look at him and bounce my shoulders, wanting to know the answer.

99

"This," he says, as he stops dancing and takes my face into his hands. He tilts his head down toward me and I feel small. I feel gloriously small.

As our lips collide, my insides melt. I've never lost my attraction toward Aaron, and to have him kissing me again, feels wonderful, like I'm re-visiting a favourite holiday destination. I can't tell you how long Aaron and I dance and make out for, but eventually we come up for air.

"Do you want another drink?" he asks.

"Definitely," I agree. "I'll meet you at the bar. I need to visit the ladies room first."

"Sure thing," he smiles, kissing me briefly before heading back toward the bar.

As I push my way through the crowd toward the bathrooms, my head starts spinning. I touch my hand to my forehead, suddenly not feeling so good.

Slamming my hand against the door, I step through before realising that I've exited into a back alley. There's not a huge amount of lighting out here and my drunken mind is struggling to focus.

But I'm sure I see people. People fighting.

"What the hell?" I question, as I step a little closer. There's a lot of yelling going on as a group of about twenty people stand around cheering and shouting at whoever is in the centre of their makeshift circle.

My curiosity draws me closer, and I peer over the shoulder of a young guy with dark curly hair, gasping when I see Damien in the middle, his shirt off, muscles glistening in the heat of the night, as he stands there, poised and alert. Four other guys are charging him, fierce expressions on their faces as they attack.

I push forward, my intoxicated mind thinking that he needs help and that somehow, I am capable of giving it. The group seems to have coordinated their attack and split into two, grabbing at his arms on both sides.

"Oh no!" I gasp, forcing my way to the front of the crowd. Damien pushes toward two of his assailants, dropping down so that he can spin under his arms, crossing them over so that all four men are now standing together. He pushes as they pull, and drops them in a pile on the asphalt ground.

I freeze where I am, watching as they come at him over and over again. As one strikes out, Damien takes his arm and twists his body, flinging him into another attacker as he turns to deal with the two on his other side. It's like a flurry of motion that leaves the four men groaning and clutching their limbs painfully.

"Who's next?" he yells, looking around the circle as one of the guys I saw him with earlier walks around collecting money. As his eyes land on me, his expression changes. "What are you doing out here?" he demands.

"I…" I start, but I don't get to finish as my dizziness twists in my stomach and erupts out of my mouth, spewing all the food and drink I've had onto the ground in front of me.

"Shit." I hear hissed around me, mingled with a few groans, as those close by jump clear of the spray.

Leaning forward, it's as if a faucet has been turned on, and I can't stop until my stomach is painfully empty.

"Finished now?" a soft voice asks. I look up, suddenly realising that Damien is holding me up and keeping my hair out of my face.

"I think so," I groan, trying to stand.

He holds me against him to steady me as I struggle upright.

"Can you walk?" he asks calmly.

"I think so," I attempt to say again, but it doesn't sound like that. My mouth is struggling to speak, and my body doesn't even want to move. I sag against him, my head dropping onto his shoulder. As I feel material instead of skin against my face, I wonder when he managed to put his shirt back on, and then I pass out.

7

"Oh god," I moan, as I attempt to sit up. My head feels like it's attempting to leave my brain behind on the pillow. Clutching at my forehead, I force myself upright, swinging my feet over the side of the bed, my soles coming into contact with…carpet? I wriggle my toes – my floor doesn't have carpet.

Slowly, I open my eyes and look around. It takes a moment for my vision to clear, but in front of me is a tall chest of drawers, finished in a high gloss black lacquer, their handles hidden underneath a curved exterior, edged in white laminate.

The bedside tables are exactly the same, and besides a bedside lamp, no surface holds anything on top, it's all perfectly clear. And except for where I've been laying, the king-sized bed is perfectly made too, with a white bedspread and a charcoal throw blanket at its base.

Above the bed is a large canvas painting, it's all grey, with white circular shapes and flecks of black paint, you can actually see the texture of the paint on there.

"How are you feeling?" a deep voice, softly asks.

I turn around, wincing when my head punishes me for my movement, squinting through the pain as my eyes land on Damien, who is sitting on a chair in the corner of the room. It's as if he's been watching me sleep.

He lifts the glass of water he has sitting on a small round table beside him and rises to walk over to me.

"What am I doing here?" I croak, taking the glass of water as he holds it out to me.

"You don't remember?"

"I remember dancing. I remember drinking. Then I wanted to visit the bathroom but I ended up outside… and you… you were fighting?"

He smiles, only one side of his lip turning upward as he reaches out and removes the now empty glass from my hands.

"You had a bit too much to drink, passed out, and I brought you here to sleep it off."

"How did you get me here?"

"With great difficulty," he laughs through his nose. "But I couldn't really take you home. Your father would have my head."

"Oh no! What time is it? I should be home. He'll refuse to let me move out."

"Relax, your mum texted to see if you were still out and having fun. So I replied for you – told her you were still at the party and still having a great time. She said to keep going, and let her deal with your dad. I think you're pretty safe, but… you smell like spew."

"Oh shit," I moan, looking down at my new dress and seeing

splatters of sick on it from the vodka mixes I was drinking. "I'm dead."

"No you're not. Here, put these on," he says, throwing a pair of boxer shorts and a t-shirt at me. "We can get that cleaned in the laundry downstairs."

"Are you going to stand there and watch me?" I ask, as I pick up the clothes.

Grinning, he shakes his head. "I thought you might want to take a shower first. There's a clean towel in the bathroom," he says, nodding toward the door.

"Oh, of course," I stammer, pushing through my legs to stand. Although I'm still feeling dizzy and stumble forward a little.

Damien rises instantly and steadies me, his arms sliding around my waist and holding my elbow. "You made a right mess of yourself, didn't you?" he points out, his voice so gentle, it causes emotion to prick behind my eye.

I simply nod, my own self-pity winning over as a tear manages to escape and slide down my cheek.

"Come on," he says softly, as he leads me out of the room and into the bathroom. Due to the sick feeling in my stomach, I drop down on top of the closed lid of the toilet and lean against his vanity while he prepares the shower for me.

"You're very tidy," I comment, looking around and noticing how clean the tiles and basin are in his bathroom.

"Not every guy is a pig," he says, running his forearm under the water to test the temperature. "It's fine now. Will you be ok?"

"Yes. I'm not letting you undress me."

"I'm not suggesting that. I just don't want you to fall and hit your head."

"Ok, I get it. You're worried about my father's wrath."

"No. I'm actually worried about you. What would have happened if I didn't take care of you tonight? Where the hell was Aaron?"

"I don't know. I think he was getting us drinks."

"Well you don't leave a girl on her own in a club – ever," he spits out, glaring at me. His outburst causes me to jump slightly, and I'm unsure of how to react.

"Take your shower. Then I'll wash your clothes and take you home," he says calmly as he walks out of the door.

For a while I just sit there, feeling horrible and deeply regretting getting myself into this situation. I'm suddenly realising why my father was so against me going out – I've managed to make a total fool of myself.

As I shower, using Damien's Lynx body wash to clean my hair, and his mouthwash to remove the terrible taste from my mouth, I slowly start to feel human again. Turning off the water, I step out onto the floor mat and dry myself before getting back into my underwear – at least I didn't vomit all over that.

My dress however, is a total mess, and I feel so terrible for behaving badly. I pick up the navy blue cotton boxer shorts and hold them in front of me. Damien has really narrow hips. I'm not sure that his things will fit me.

Sliding them over my legs, I sigh as I feel the material pull tight around my thighs and buttocks. Suddenly that song about 'short shorts' starts going through my mind.

Dropping the t-shirt over my head, I pull it down, grateful for his broad shoulders – at least this fits me.

"Um… do you have any other pants I could wear?" I ask as I emerge from the bathroom, feeling incredibly exposed in the fitted shorts.

"What's wrong with those?"

"They're um… your underwear…"

"I only wear them to sleep."

"Ok, well… they're very… short."

"I'm the only one that will see you."

His eyes travel from my bare feet, up my legs and over my body, slowly, until he reaches my face, locking his gaze with mine. I don't breathe the entire time as a hunger toward him that I'm not sure I want sated, flares inside my body.

"Give me your dress," he says after a beat, holding out his hand.

"I'll wash it. It's kind of gross." I say in a rush, trying to sound normal.

He reaches forward and grabs it from my hand, sighing a little as he snatches it away.

"Just wait here. Drink some more water. I'll be back in a few minutes," he instructs.

Doing as I'm asked, I fill up a glass from the tap and drink. Although my stomach isn't too keen on the idea of having any more liquid introduced to it right now. So I slowly sip, walking around the apartment as I do.

"What the hell did you do with her?" I hear after a while, coming from outside the door. Holding my breath, I listen.

"I don't know what you're talking about, mate."

"Etta. Where the fuck did you take her? Is she in there?"

"She was drunk. She passed out. She's lucky I was there, because *you* certainly weren't taking care of her."

"Fuck you Damien. She was just having some fun – blowing off steam. We all do it. I just spent the whole night looking for her, then someone says they saw her leave with you. Where the hell is she?"

"Safe."

"In there?" Suddenly, he's banging on the door. "Etta?"

Oh god, please don't let Aaron catch me in here, I pray, realising how bad it would look if he saw me wearing Damien's clothes.

"Etta?" he calls out again.

"Satisfied?" Damien says. I hear a slight shuffling sound on the other side of the door and then, "Are you serious? You're calling her now? It's one o'clock in the morning."

Shit! My phone! Frantically, I look around the apartment to try and locate my bag, finding it sitting in the centre of the couch. When I grab my phone out, it's lighting up with Aaron's name and number, but it's already on silent – Damien must have done it while I was sleeping.

"Hello?" I whisper, creeping into the bathroom so he can't hear me through the door.

"Etta," he breathes. "It's Aaron. I've been trying to call you all night. Are you ok?"

"Yeah, I'm fine. I was just sleeping. I drank way too much. I'm so sorry. I'm really embarrassed about it all," I try to explain.

"It's ok. As long as you're alright… I was worried."

"I appreciate it. I really am sorry."

"It's ok – really. You can make it up to me another time."

I can't control myself as a smile creeps over my face. "So… I didn't scare you off?"

"Never. Sleep well Etta. I'll talk to you soon," he says in a soft voice, and I can actually hear him smile.

"You too," I murmur, ending the call before exiting the bathroom.

The moment I open the door, I suck in my breath. Damien is right there, like he's appeared out of nowhere. I drop my phone. He's right in front of me, his intense eyes boring into mine, making my world fall away as my heart pounds against my chest.

His eyes drop to my lips and without even meaning to, I lick them. When they flick back up to meet mine, I see the look. I know I'm in trouble.

Like magnets of opposite poles, unable to control their pull, our mouths collide. His tongue pushing and sliding against mine as our teeth clash and our breath mingles.

We pull at each other, like we're trying to draw the other inside ourselves. It's a strange feeling, one that I've never experienced before. I'm normally always in control, but tonight has been one of those times when I'm not. Although each time I've had something to do with Damien I've lost control…

Somehow, we end up on his bed, kissing like the connection between our mouths is the only reason we're alive. His hands slide over my curves, skirting around the edges of my clothing.

When his fingers brush lightly between my thighs, I moan, arching up to meet him as my body makes this decision for me – I want him. Suddenly, he freezes and breaks our kiss, pressing his forehead against mine, his eyes closed and his breathing heavy.

"This needs to stop," he murmurs, his voice thick and gravelly sounding.

"I…" I start, not really knowing what it is I should say.

"*Shit*," he hisses, sitting up on the bed, pulling away from me. He doesn't really look at me, just sits, leaning forward on his thighs as he rubs his hand back and forward over the top of his head. Eventually, he clears his throat. "Stay here. I'm going to check on your dress."

Suddenly I feel really cold, very alone and … rejected.

Taking the blanket from the end of the bed, I wrap it around my shoulders, then go and retrieve my phone.

What's going on with me? I never really go out and when I do, I end up making out with two guys and nearly sleeping with one of them. I like Aaron, I really do. He's a good friend, fun to be around, and so loyal to me.

Then there's Damien, who has really been nothing but a problem since the moment I met him. But somehow, he's the one I almost end up sleeping with. *Jesus*.

Moving over to the couch, I pick the remote up off the coffee table and power on the television, flicking through the channels until I find something that isn't an infomercial trying to sell me something.

Time ticks away as I wait for Damien to return. I find myself fidgeting impatiently, constantly looking at the door and wondering if I should just go and find him. Eventually though, he bursts through the door, causing me to jump.

"Get dressed. I'll take you home," he says, handing me my now clean dress.

A deep sense of hurt fills my chest. "Is the idea of sleeping with me that bad?" I ask, pausing in the doorway of the bathroom.

"No Henrietta. Not at all," he tells me, his voice calm, his gaze intense. "Just go and get dressed."

"Then why did you stop?"

"Get dressed," he repeats.

I briefly consider getting dressed in front of him, just to see what he would do. But I don't. Stepping through the doorway, I quickly remove his clothes and put my own dress, warm from the dryer, back on.

"Ready," I say, my voice small and quiet as I emerge.

He's already standing by the door, holding my bag, his keys in his hand. The sight hurts my heart.

Following him out, I glance toward Aaron's door. Feeling horribly guilty about everything that has happened tonight, as I make my way to Damien's car and we start the short drive home.

"So um, what was the deal with you fighting? Is that something you always do?" I ask after a good five minutes of silence.

"Not always," he states, focusing only on the road. I watch him as he drives, the lights of the streets flashing over his definite features as he traverses the street, not making an effort to further any sort of conversation with me until we arrive out the front of my house.

"Looks like someone's waiting up for you," he says, nodding toward the light coming from our lounge room window.

Glancing at the read out on his car radio, it's 3am. My father isn't going to be happy. I just hope that my mum kept her word and kept him calm.

"Well, goodbye," I say, opening the car door. "And thanks."

He just nods, keeping his eyes forward as he grips at the steering wheel, leaving me wondering what it is I've done wrong.

"I'll see you around Henrietta," he says, meeting my eyes briefly, a tiny grin pulling at the corner of his mouth. "I'll wait 'til you're inside."

Nodding, I shut the car door, and jog up to the entrance to my house. The moment I slide my key inside, the lock turns from the inside, and I'm face to face with my father.

"Who's that? Is that Damien?" he asks, looking over my shoulder.

"Yes. He gave me a lift home."

My father simply grunts his acceptance and nods toward the car. As I look over my shoulder, the rumble of the engine bursts into the atmosphere as Damien drives away.

8

The next day is spent pretending I don't have a hangover while I pack up my room, ready for the big move tomorrow. My father hasn't said a word about how late I came home last night, so I think my mother must have worked some pretty amazing magic.

"Do you want me to just stack these boxes in the lounge room?" he asks, pointing at the packed books and personal items that I want to take with me. I don't need furniture since the room already has some, but the guts of my room is coming with me.

"Yes please," I say, as I shove a drawer's worth of clothing into my suitcase. Once that's full, I move on to putting the rest of my clothes into another box.

"This house is going to feel very empty as of tomorrow," my mother comments as she brings over most of my hanging garments.

"Mum, I'm moving one train stop away. I'll be back for dinner regularly," I assure her.

"You'd better. Otherwise, I'll send your father out to drag you back here." Reaching out, she wraps her arms around me in a tight embrace.

"Mum?" I say over her shoulder, still hugging her. She hums in response, squeezing me a little tighter. "I know you'll never change Craig's room. But can you please reclaim mine? Turn it into a home gym or something."

"Sure I will," she sniffles, so I know she's started crying. "I might just knock down a wall and make a giant bathroom or massive wardrobe." She pulls away from me and wipes at her eyes, putting on a brave face.

"I think that would be a great idea," I smile, turning back to my packing. She's joking of course. I'm sure that my room will forever be mine. But I want her to know that she's free to change it if she likes.

Just as I start off the last box of stuff, my phone goes off from beside my bed, displaying an image of Aaron sitting on the grass at uni.

"Hey," I say in greeting as I answer.

"Are you free? I wanted to know if we could talk."

"Um… I'm kind of in the middle of…"

My mother starts to make frantic hand gestures as she whispers about leaving it with her. "Go, go" she yell-whispers, shooing me away with her hands.

"Actually, I'm free," I tell him, smiling and nodding at my mum, trying to hold two conversations at once as she starts telling me that I'd better come home for dinner since it's my last night and all.

Grinning at her, I place my hand on her shoulder as if it will silence her. Sometimes I wonder who the child is between the both of us.

"Great. Would you like to meet somewhere or would you like to come over to my place?"

"I'll come to you, I don't have long," I tell him, hanging up and promising my mum I'll be back before six.

***

I arrive at Aaron's at around four-thirty, ready to meet him for our 'talk'. I have a pretty good idea what it's about. I vaguely remember kissing him last night before I ended up outside with Damien. So I'm assuming he wants to DTR. Personally, I find defining the relationship to be a bit of a waste of time. I mean, we're at uni. We have our whole lives ahead of us still. As much as Aaron is a great friend of mine, I think I need to make it clear that anything that happens between us needs to be fairly light-hearted, especially after what happened with Damien last night. I'm obviously not in the right headspace to be serious with him right now.

Besides that, I'm moving out of home for a chance to set my own rules and do my own thing. I don't particularly want a steady boyfriend. I just want fun, so if he can agree to that, we'll be just fine.

As I take the stairs up to the second floor, my eyes stray immediately to Damien's door. The six has swung down again, so I pause and reach up to press it back in place.

Once again, I can hear music from inside, and I hesitate about moving on. Perhaps I should just thank him? I mean, he did kind of save my arse last night... Feeling as though it's the right thing to do, I bang on the door and wait. The music cuts out, and I hear shuffling on the other side.

"Put this on," he says to someone inside.

Realising he isn't alone, I take a step back from the door, suddenly feeling silly for stopping by.

"What's up?" he asks casually as he answers the door – once again shirtless. My eyes drag down his torso as I try to remember what it was I wanted to say.

"Don't you ever wear a shirt?" I blurt out.

"It's my apartment. I can walk around naked if I want," he states.

"Who's there Damien?" a woman's voice asks. I expect it to be that Bec girl again, but when she comes into view, it's someone a bit older, and all she's wearing is a sheet.

He shoots a look over his shoulder and narrows the door, blocking my vision with his body.

"What can I do for you Henrietta?" he asks calmly.

"It's Etta. And I um… just wanted to thank you for helping me last night. I think you saved me from getting into a lot of trouble with my dad."

"My pleasure," he nods. "You didn't have to come all the way over here just to say that. You could have called."

"Oh. I didn't. I came to see Aaron. I just thought – since I was here…"

His posture stiffens. "Did you drive here?"

Frowning, I shake my head. "I don't have a car. I caught the train."

"Come and get me when you're done. I'll drive you home."

"It's fine. You're busy. I'm used to getting trains."

"I will drive you," he insists.

Rolling my eyes, I step away from the door to end the conversation. "Whatever tickles your fancy," I respond, walking away from him while fully intending on leaving without telling him. It's not like he'll be able to hear over the music anyway.

As I reach Aaron's door and knock, I hear the soft click of Damien's door just before the music turns back on. I'm still looking over my shoulder frowning when Aaron answers.

"Hey," he smiles. "What's up?"

"Oh… nothing," I answer as I step inside. "I just don't get him." I say, putting my bag down on Aaron's couch.

"Who - Damien?"

"Yeah. I just stopped off to say thanks for driving me home last night and he was acting really weird."

"He's probably got one of his women in there with him," he snorts.

"Yeah. That's how it looked," I comment, not sure why I find it so annoying. I mean, it's not like we're dating. He's just this random guy who kissed me senseless and rejected me. When I really think about it, I should just forget him – he keeps getting in my way.

"There's a rumour that he's a male prostitute," he states as a matter of fact.

"Seriously? What makes everyone think that?"

"Because he seems to have a lot of money for a uni student. It's got to come from somewhere," he shrugs.

"Maybe he gets the money some other way?" I suppose, remembering that he was fighting for money last night.

"Where? From his fighting scam?"

"You know about the fighting?"

"Yeah, I've seen him hustle people a few times. Some of the guys like to take bets to see how many guys it will take to beat him."

"And how many guys is that?"

He shrugs. "I don't think anyone knows yet."

"Have you ever tried to fight him?" I ask.

"No, have you seen him fight? I'm not stupid. I know my limits," he laughs. "But don't worry yourself about him. If you stay out of his way, he stays out of yours." He shakes his head. "Anyway, let's forget about him. I want to talk about you," he says, moving toward me. "How are you feeling after last night? I'm sorry I got you so drunk. I feel so guilty over it."

"Don't be. I'm the one who was drinking them. You weren't shoving them down my throat."

"Well, I should have been taking care of you," he murmurs, slipping his hands around my waist. "I'm sorry." He tilts his head down slightly and brushes his lips against mine. "I've missed your lips."

"Is that a fact?" I smile.

"Yeah, I want more." Softly, he kisses me, gently pulling my bottom lip between his, humming as he breaks his mouth away from mine. Guilt washes over me as flashes of last night and Damien enter my mind. As much as I like Aaron, and as much as I enjoy kissing him, this just doesn't compare to whatever it was I felt with Damien.

"Do you think we could pick up where we left off?" he suggests, forcing my focus to return to him. "Now that you have your freedom."

"I think that we can maybe just see what happens. I'm not ready to jump into anything," I tell him, trying to let him down gently.

He steps back a little, breaking our contact, giving me some space.

"I guess I just thought that since your dad won't be looking over our shoulder, things could be different between us," he says, running his hand over his head and he rests the other on his hip.

"Aaron, I can't switch my feelings on and off. We've been 'just friends' for almost a year now. Let's just go out with the group, have fun, and see what happens. I just…I don't want to go from my parent's house straight into a relationship. I want some time to just be me. I don't want to worry about anyone else. Does that make sense?" I try to explain. I really don't want to hurt his feelings. He is, after all, one of my very best friends.

"So what you're saying is, I can make out with you on dance floors, but you won't actually date me?" he clarifies.

"It sounds silly when you say it like that. I guess I just shouldn't have let you kiss me at all…"

"No, Etta. It's fine. I've waited this long. I can wait a little longer."

"I care about you a lot Aaron. I just… I need to find me in here," I explain again, touching my head.

"I get it Etta. Really I do. And I'll be right here for when and if you need me ok?" he says, before his mouth turns up in a cheeky half smile. "I'm even available for booty calls if you'd like," he laughs, just as Jeremy bursts through the door.

"Who's taking booty calls?" he asks, walking straight into the kitchen and opening the fridge. He offers us a bottle of beer, but I shake my head to decline. I think my body has had enough alcohol for a few days.

"Etta," Aaron says simply.

"Awesome, I love redheads. I'll grab your number," he laughs, giving me a wink before tossing his head back as he takes a mouthful of drink.

"On that note, I'm going home. The big move is tomorrow," I explain.

"I know. Call me if you need help," Aaron says.

"Will do. See you Jez," I call to Jeremy, who's now rummaging in the cupboard for some food.

"See ya," he calls back.

I give Aaron a finger wave and smile as I mouth 'bye' to him and exit the apartment. I close the door as quietly as I can, not wanting to alert Damien to my presence. I just want to catch the train like I normally do. I don't need some guy who, as far as my friends are concerned, is some ninja sex worker. But as far as my father is concerned, seems to be the ideal solution for letting me leave the house – and I don't need, nor do I want, a body guard.

Luck doesn't seem to be on my side. When I pass Damien's door, it opens and he immediately follows me out.

"What are you doing?" he asks from behind me.

"Going home," I reply, taking the stairs quickly and pushing through the door to outside.

"I told you I would take you."

"I don't need for you to take me," I state, still walking ahead of him.

"Henrietta," he calls.

I stop. There's something about hearing my full name that always affects me. I guess that's why I hate it so much. *"What?!"*

He doesn't actually say anything. He just takes me by the hand and walks briskly with me toward his perfectly polished car.

Opening the passenger door, he guides me in, leaning across me to click my seatbelt in.

"I could have done that myself," I say.

"I know," he states, closing my door before walking around to the driver's side.

After a few moments of driving in white knuckled silence, he finally speaks.

"What's going on with you and Aaron?"

"I don't know. What's going on with you and that woman who was in your apartment? What's going on with you and Bec?"

124

"This isn't about me."

"I don't even understand why this is about me. Why are you so interested now? You lost interest pretty fast last night."

"You took my restraint as lost interest?" he asks incredulously, taking his eyes off the road momentarily to shoot me a look.

"No. I took your restraint as the act of a man who is too scared of my father to do what he really wanted to do."

"*What?!*" he spits out, suddenly pulling the car over to the side of the road.

"What are you doing?"

"The things I do in my personal life have absolutely *nothing* to do with your father. Am I more careful with you out of respect for him? Yes I am. But when I stopped last night, it had nothing to do with him and *everything* to do with the fact that I didn't want to *fuck* you – which is what we were about to do."

"You didn't want to fuck me? Um… ok… great. What part of that speech is supposed to explain how you didn't lose interest? Because not wanting me, sounds a lot like disinterest to me," I bite back, confronted by his outburst.

Slowly, he eases out the breath in his chest, as he looks out at the traffic on the road beside us.

"You fuck people you don't care about, Henrietta. There's a whole other word for what it's called when you do," he says quietly, flicking his blinker on before pulling back into the stream of traffic.

He cares about me? Swallowing hard, I sit in silence for the remainder of the drive, having no idea how I should respond or exactly what his words meant.

"Thanks for the lift," I say, as he pulls up outside my house. For some reason I feel as though I've just gotten into trouble, and I want to do something to make it better. "I didn't sleep with him," I blurt out suddenly. "With Aaron… just in case you were worried… or just wondering…" My voice trails off. I'm not even sure why I'm saying this. I don't know how to deal with what's going on in my life right now – especially Damien. I don't even know how to begin classifying what this is.

He looks me in the eye, his eyes darkening as he studies my face. I feel this great pull toward him and find myself wishing that he'd reach across and take me in his arms…

"I'll see you around," he says, clicking the red button on the seatbelt, releasing me - dismissing me.

"Of course," I whisper, once again feeling dejected at the end of our brief time together.

Getting out of the car, I head inside quickly, wanting to get out of his magnetic field, or aura, or whatever it is that he exudes. I need the space to breathe. As soon as I shut the door, I hear his car drive away and close my eyes, as I try to focus on calming down. *What the fuck is wrong with me?*

After a moment, I feel calm enough to push of the door and

head into the kitchen where my mother is chopping up a head of lettuce for tonight's salad.

"How was your friend, and will we ever be meeting her?" she asks.

"Is dad home?"

"Not yet."

"It was a *he*. It's that guy dad flipped out about me dating last year. We're still good friends though."

"Ha! I knew it! I saw his photo flash up on your phone's screen. Is he still just a friend or is there potential for him to become your boyfriend?"

"At the moment he's just a boy who's a friend."

"At the moment huh?"

"Yeah," I smile. "I'm just not sure if I want it to turn into something more," I confide in her, stealing a piece of already sliced carrot and popping it in my mouth.

"What's wrong with him? Is he shorter than you or something?"

"No," I laugh. "It's not that at all. He's actually a couple of inches taller than me."

"Well, that's definitely a plus. What's holding you back?"

"Well, it was dad. But now…I don't know. He's nice, I get along really well with him. But when he kisses me, I don't really feel that spark, you know?"

"That spark? What do you know about that spark young lady? Exactly how many boys have you been kissing lately?" my mother asks, a huge smile on her face.

"Only two."

"Henrietta Davis. I let you out for one night and you've already attracted the interest of *two* boys. Don't let your father know or he'll build a tower and lock you up inside."

"There is no way I'm talking to dad about that kind of stuff."

It's at that moment my father chooses to enter the house, calling out hello from the front door. My mother grins at me, her eyes sparkling mischievously from our shared secret as she holds her finger to lips and silently shushes me.

Not every eighteen year old girl has the same type of relationship with their mother that I do, and I'm grateful that she's someone I can talk to. Otherwise I think I would have felt dreadfully lonely in this world due to my strict curfew. While I was sitting at home, a lot of my friends were out, bonding and doing things that young adults do. Really, my friends are just Aaron's friends. It's been because of my history with him that I even have any sort of social life. It's not that I'm unlikeable, once again, I think it comes down to the age thing. It's really hard to fit in with people who are at an age where they are driving and drinking, when you're still a teen. So I've spent a lot of time with my mum – really she's like my best friend. I can tell her almost anything and know she'll understand me.

"Was that Damien's car I saw leaving our street?" my dad asks, as he enters the kitchen, heading straight over to my mother to give her a hug and a kiss in greeting.

"Um… yeah. He actually lives a couple of doors down from one of my uni friends. He drove me home."

"Why is he driving you home?" he asks. "You're not training. There's no reason for him to have anything to do with you."

"I don't know dad. I was hoping you could tell my why he's so interested in me."

He grunts. I'm not sure if it's happy, angry, thoughtful or just a grunt for the sake of a response.

"You can always call him off," I suggest. "Shockingly, none of the other girls have a bodyguard."

"What are you talking about?" he frowns.

"Oh my god, Dad. You're the one who has him following me around. Isn't he your guard dog – making sure your daughter never puts a foot out of line? I don't need to be taken care of Dad! You've got him thinking I'm a baby too."

"I've done nothing of the sort. He's come to that conclusion on his own."

I pause and give my father my best unimpressed look. "Can you just call him off please? Tell him that you don't want him to be my guardian?"

"I didn't tell him to watch you."

"What do you mean? I thought you sent him out on Thursday to keep an eye on me?"

"No. Why would I do that? You're eighteen now. I promised you I'd back off."

"That man!" I say pushing back from the table. "Mum, can I borrow your car? I need to go and speak to someone."

"Sure honey," she laughs. I don't understand why she is finding this all so amusing. "The keys are hanging by the door."

"Jan, this isn't funny," I hear my father tell her as I grab her keys off the hook.

"Just let her deal with it," she responds, as I slam the door behind me. Jumping in her car, I take off to confront Damien. What game is this guy playing? I just don't understand it. Why lead me to believe he's been asked to protect me. This is just ridiculous, and I need to get to the bottom of it.

I pull up outside his building and stomp toward the entrance, continuing my stomping as I climb the stairs until I find his door.

"Damien!" I yell, thumping on his door with my fist. "Damien!"

"I'm coming. Hang on," he calls from inside. "What is it?" he exasperates as he opens the door, water beading all over his body as if he's just been in the shower... my mouth goes dry and my thoughts leave my mind as my eyes drag over him – to his hand as it clutches the towel about his waist.

"I… um…" I stammer.

"Jesus," he hisses, grabbing me by the wrist and pulling me inside. "Just sit," he commands, heading back towards his bathroom, pausing only to grab some clothes from his bedroom before he disappears back inside.

I sit at the small table, listening as he finishes his shower and berating myself for not being able to keep a hold on my thoughts around him.

As I look around, I start paying closer attention to his pin board, remembering that the first time I was in here, it was turned around and had a bunch of drawings on it.

Listening to the still running water, I twist the board around. The entire surface is covered with small pieces of paper. Some are lined, some are white, some are yellow and a couple are green or pink. It seems that it's just been whatever has been on hand at the time and they're all overlapping each other so you couldn't possibly see each one without removing everything on top. On each piece of paper is a sketch. There's no distinct theme, I'd assume he's just drawn whatever has taken his fancy at the time. There are trees, chairs, hands, lips, eyes, people studying, people laughing, buildings, and at the very bottom – me…

"Seriously?" I say to myself, looking closer at the piece of lined note paper with my image on it. It's picture perfect and shows me, laughing as I tuck my hair behind my ear. I can tell by the clothing I'm in that he drew this on Thursday when I was at the Uni Bar. How did I not see him doing this?

The clearing of his throat behind me, snaps me to attention, and I spin around to face him, feeling immensely guilty. "Why is there a picture of me there?" I demand immediately.

"If I wanted people to look at this, I'd have it on display." He leans around me, smelling of soap and warmth as he flips the board back around.

"That doesn't answer my question," I whisper, leaning up against the wall – I kind of need it to hold me up right now.

He smiles, his hand resting just above my head as he searches my face. "Why did you come here?"

"I…" He's too close to me. I can't breathe, let alone think clearly.

"Do you need something?" he whispers, leaning close to my ear. His breath washes over me, causing my skin to prickle. I can't help it, and I turn toward him.

My words, usually so important to me, have evaporated into the ether, and I can't even remember what I was so annoyed about. All I want right now is him.

Softly, he brushes his mouth along my jawline, causing my breathing to increase as my heart thuds against my chest. My eyes flutter closed as my tongue sneaks out of my mouth, wetting my lips, wanting him to kiss me.

But as his lips travel toward my mouth, he brushes upward, skimming the corner and leaving me wanting. I whimper in response, turning my head slightly toward him.

"Henrietta," he whispers. "Open your eyes."

Slowly, I force my eyes open, meeting his.

"Do you want me to kiss you?" he asks, brushing his bottom lip right next to my mouth again.

Once again, I whimper, nodding my head in response, struggling to find my voice.

"I need you to say it."

"Yes," I whisper.

"Tell me what you want."

"I want you to kiss me," I admit, my voice barely audible as I force my voice to speak.

"Want or need?" he whispers, bringing his mouth to mine, gently grazing my bottom lip.

"Need," I breathe, my body pressed firmly up against the wall, frozen and unable to move with him so close to me. It's true, I do feel a need for him. I don't think I can even move without his assistance right now.

Sliding his arm around my waist, he pulls my body against his, kissing my mouth with a controlled passion that makes my head swim, and my senses scream. I want more.

His tongue snakes out, teasing my mouth, getting me to part my lips to let him in. Tiny whimpers escape my throat as his tongue slides over mine, smooth and minty from his mouthwash.

One of his hands cups the side of my head, holding me steady as he explores my mouth and I, in turn, explore his.

Our breathing grows heavier and somehow I manage to gain control of my body and find a way to move my limbs. My arms slide around his body, pulling him closer to me, gripping at his black shirt as my want – my need for him, increases.

Breaking the kiss, he pulls his head away from me, smoothing the skin on my cheek as he gazes upon my face. His eyes study me, as his thumb smooths, moving from my cheek, to my brow bone, down my nose and over my lips.

"I'll take you home now," he says finally.

"What?" I ask, confused – this is ending now?

"Come on," he says, moving to collect his wallet and car keys, pocketing them in his black jeans and holding his hand out to me.

I move toward him, as if in a dream, still feeling heady after our kissing, and collect my bag, slinging it over my shoulder.

Smiling approvingly at me, he takes my hand and gently kisses the side of my forehead, before leading me back downstairs and out of the building.

"Oh, you don't need to drive me. I borrowed my mum's car," I tell him, suddenly remembering how I got here. "It's just this one here."

He nods once, walking me toward the silver hatchback and takes the keys from my hand as I fumble with them, my mind a complete mess right now.

"Here," he says, pressing the button to unlock the car, opening the door for me. As I climb in, he reaches for the seatbelt, and I don't stop or argue with him. I want his arm around me, I want to inhale the scent of his skin as he leans in to click the buckle in place.

"Thank you," I whisper, meeting his eyes.

I'm rewarded with a smile, a beautiful heart stopping smile. "Drive safely and text me when you get home." He kisses me, just next to my mouth and my lips burn, wishing his mouth was there instead. "I'll see you in the morning."

Nodding, I can't keep the smile off my face as he shuts me in the car and steps back as I start the engine.

Forcing my mind to concentrate on driving, I turn around to reverse out of the car space, glancing again at the man standing on the footpath, watching as I leave.

He nods his head at me instead of waving, his mouth curled up on one side in an amused smile.

As I drive away, the fog that occurs when I'm near him lifts from my mind like a veil. Of course he was smiling, he just managed to make me completely forget what I was doing there. I didn't even get the chance to ask him why he lied about my father telling him to protect me. Moreover, why does he feel the need to protect me? It's not like I'm prone to getting attacked.

"Oh! That man!" I yell, slapping my hand on the steering wheel, feeling like I've just been made the fool and what the hell did he mean by *'I'll see you in the morning'*?

My annoyance returns tenfold by the time I'm home, and the last thing I want to do is let him know that I made it home safe. Instead, I switch off my phone and spend the rest of the evening studying before falling into a restless sleep. Tomorrow is the day I get my freedom. It's the day I move.

9

A loud thumping rattles the glass on my window, and tears me from my sleep. Glancing at the clock beside me it reads 2am. Scrunching my face up in confusion, I climb out of bed as the banging continues.

Cautiously, I pull the curtains to the side, my heart beating wildly in my chest as I wonder what's going on. But I relax a little when I see Damien standing there.

"Come outside," he tells me through the glass.

I sleep in a singlet and underwear, so I grab a pair of leggings and a t-shirt and put them on before heading to the front door to see what he's doing here.

"I hope you aren't planning on making me train or something?" I ask as soon as I open the door and step out onto the small landing.

"Why didn't you message me like I asked you to?" he responds, moving to climb the two steps that lead to my front door – to where I'm standing.

Holding my hands up, I step backwards, wanting to keep some distance between us so I can think properly. "Don't. I can't think properly if you're too close," I admit.

"I can't think when you're far away." My heart freezes, the strain in his voice conveying my exact feelings around him.

"What's going on Damien? My dad didn't ask you to watch out for me. Why are you so hell bent on protecting me? And from what?"

He runs his hand over his head, messing up his usually neat hair. "I don't know. I just need to. I don't know what it is. But you feel it too right? It's not just me."

"No. It's not just you. But I don't know how to deal with this. I mean, would we even work in a re–" I stop, not wanting to say the word 'relationship'. I have no idea what this thing is right now.

"I've never even been in one," he admits, stuffing his hands in his pockets as he stands on the concrete path at the base of the stairs. "I just… I need to know you're ok. It's been just over a week, and I'm constantly thinking about you, and what you're doing, and who you're with – it's driving me insane. I'm not sleeping, and I've just spent all day and most of the night trying to tell myself that it doesn't matter that you didn't text me. But it does Henrietta. I can't explain why. But it does."

"Why are you so worried about me?"

"I don't… I don't know. I just am, and I don't know if I can stop," he says, once again moving toward me, in the dim light, it's hard to make out his features, but I can see that something isn't right.

"Have you been fighting?" I ask, reaching up to gently touch his cheek where it appears as though he's sucking on a wad of cotton wool.

"I was distracted. They got in a lucky punch. I still won though."

"Why do you do it?"

"Fight? Because I'm good at it," he murmurs. "Normally, they don't even get a punch in." He shift his stance, seemingly agitated. "Don't you see? This is why I needed you to tell me you were home safe. When you didn't message, I tried to call you but your phone was off. Then when I went out, all I could think of was you, and I didn't see the hit coming."

A pain lodges itself in my chest as his own distress radiates off him, causing guilt to wash over me as I realise that my actions got him hurt. "I'm sorry," I whisper, leaning up to press a soft kiss against his cheek. "I should have messaged you. I was just being stubborn when I realised I didn't even get to yell at you for lying to me."

"I told him I'd look out for you. I didn't lie. I don't lie Henrietta."

"But you avoid the truth."

Sighing, he wraps his arms around me and pulls me against his chest, tucking my head into the crook of his neck. I breathe him in, his scent and his closeness is so intoxicating to me, making my head spin as my hormones release euphoric serotonin into my bloodstream, heightening my emotions as I wish to stay in his arms forever.

Finally, he releases me. Kissing me in my hair as he descends the steps backwards to stand at my feet.

"I'll pick you up at six," he informs me.

"I don't want to train Damien," I murmur, shaking my head from side to side. "Please don't make me."

"Please," he whispers, his voice thick and his expression pained. "I need to be around you and training with you is...it's calming. Please Henrietta. Be ready at six." He steps away, and the sight of him retreating makes my heart lurch. I don't want him to go. I want more of him.

"How about I go with you now? To um...your apartment – if you'd like me to of course. I mean, if I'm with you – at least you'll know where I am... and you can sleep..." I suggest boldly, biting on my lip nervously as I wait for his response. "But I still don't want to train."

Looking up at me, he nods, his hands on his hips as the moonlight washes over his face, showing a man who doesn't know how to handle this attraction we have. Hell – I don't know how to handle this. It's never happened to me before.

As I go inside to grab my bag, my shoes, and write a note for my parents, I wonder what this is. What is it about him that's making me so crazy to be around him? I've been attracted to men before – but not like this. This is something else.

Pulling the door closed quietly, I walk down the steps and take the hand he's offering me. Without speaking, he brings my knuckles to his lips as he leads me to his car, and buckles me in.

As we drive back to his apartment, we're quiet the whole time. It's as if we're trapped in a spell, neither of us really willing to speak for fear of breaking it.

Once inside, I follow him to his bedroom, my heart thudding the entire time, as he moves over to the bed, and strips off the sheets. I stand by, watching him move around, depositing one set into his laundry basket and pulling a new set out of the cupboard, making up the king sized bed neatly.

"You take the bed," he says, breaking the silence. "I'm happy to sleep on the couch."

"Oh. Ok," I say, a slight pang of disappointment landing in my stomach, as he effectively breaks the spell too. "I'll um… just use the bathroom."

When I left with him, I didn't really think about what I would sleep in. I'm still wearing the singlet and panties I had on for bed, as well as the leggings and t-shirt I put on top of them.

I relieve myself and wash my hands, splashing water on my face before I study my reflection in the mirror. I look pale, my dark auburn hair surrounds my light features, and my blue eyes appear larger than normal with dark circles from my lack of sleep, beneath them.

I remove my leggings, hanging them on the towel rail to put back on in the morning, but I leave my shirt on. It's long enough to be worn as a night shirt. So it will have to do.

When I emerge from the bathroom, I notice him sitting in a pair of boxer shorts on the two seater couch he's made up, with a spare pillow and blanket.

 "How are you going to fit on that?" I ask him.

"I'll be fine," he says, rising from his seat before he walks toward the bedroom. "Here, hop in," he instructs, as he moves to the bed, pulling the sheets back and waiting for me to slide between them.

Slipping between the cool soft cotton, I look up at him. "You know, it's a giant bed. We could probably both fit."

"I don't know." He frowns, his eyes travelling between me, the space I've made for him, and the couch that can be seen through the open door.

"You're far too tall to sleep on that couch. I don't mind sharing. We're just sleeping – right?"

He nods, shifting his bulk to slide in next to me, reaching his arm around my waist and pulling me toward him. I pull my long hair around my shoulder, to keep it out of his face, at the same time exposing my neck. Delicious chills roll through my body as he plants a soft kiss on the skin of my throat.

"Thank you," he whispers, his arm tightening around me as he pulls me closer, kissing me softly again.

Closing my eyes, I let out a peaceful sigh. I don't think I have ever felt more at home than I do right now – the curve of our bodies combined, the sound of his steady breathing as he relaxes into sleep, and the firm grip of his arm, holding me, protecting me. I didn't know how much I wanted it, or how much I needed it. Now I'm not sure how I'm going to cope without it.

It's not long before I'm drifting off to sleep myself, although I'm sure, that throughout the night, I keep feeling soft kisses against my shoulder – perhaps it's just a dream.

***

When I wake, it's to the aroma of bacon frying and coffee brewing.

"What time is it?" I ask, after stumbling out into the living area, bleary eyed from sleeping so soundly. I find it strange as I've never been one to sleep anywhere but in my own bed.

"Almost eight," Damien informs me from where he's standing at the stove, keeping a watchful eye on breakfast.

"Eight?! Shit, I'm moving today. I need to be home. We're going there at ten," I ramble, instantly awake and in a panic, knowing that my mum and dad will be up already and have probably been trying to call me. I race into the bathroom and pull on my leggings, running my fingers through my hair to neaten it. It's thick and heavy, so I very rarely wake up with it looking messy, but it doesn't hurt to check.

"You've got plenty of time to eat," he says.

143

"No, Damien. I don't. I have to go," I argue.

"Sit. Twenty minutes isn't going to kill you."

I stand in the doorway of the bathroom, wondering if I should keep arguing as I watch him move back into the kitchen and lift the pan, taking it over to the table and sliding eggs, bacon, and some cooked mushrooms, tomato and spinach.

"Coffee?"

"Um... ok." I give in. "White with one sugar. I'll just use the bathroom properly," I inform him, pointing toward the door.

"Of course." He nods, working his way around the kitchen, pouring mugs of coffee and setting small glasses of juice on the table next to our plates.

Inside the bathroom, I perform my usual ablutions and double-check my appearance before I go out to join Damien at the table.

"Thank you for breakfast. It looks wonderful," I say, as I lift my knife and fork, and dig in.

We eat in companionable silence for a while. I don't know why, but I don't feel the need to talk constantly while I'm near him. I just like to be in his presence. I find it calming – I guess it must be the same for him.

Eventually though, I look around the room, and my eyes land on his cork board.

"Why do you hide your drawings? I mean, aren't you doing a fine arts degree or something?"

"No. Our university doesn't offer a fine arts degree. I'm actually doing a Bachelor of Design, so most of my work is computer based. I still love to sketch though, and paint. But I do it for me. That's why I don't display them. It's sort of like a journal I suppose."

"I'm sorry for looking at them," I tell him.

"It's ok," he says, taking a mouthful of juice.

"They are beautiful though. You're very talented."

He nods in quiet acceptance. I guess people have been praising his talent for a long time, so it must be a normal thing for him now. I take a mouthful of my coffee, watching him, just like he's watching me.

My mind begins to sift through the snippets of information I have about him, raising questions that I feel fairly certain he won't give me answers to. But I ask them anyway. "So, if you aren't doing art – why was Bec modelling for you?"

"I do portraits. But it's all digital. I mainly get commissioned by women, and sometimes couples. It's kind of like what they do for book covers and movie posters but it's for their own personal use."

"Can I see some of your work?"

He drops his eyes as he places his coffee mug carefully on the

145

table. "No."

"Why? Are they naked?"

He smiles and shakes his head slightly. "They're not mine to show."

For the first time since coming here, I'm suddenly feeling uncomfortable. I want to know more about him, but he's not making this easy.

"Did you know there's a rumour about you and all those women you have over here?"

He rubs his hands, back and forth over the top of his short spikey hair. "I don't tend to listen to rumours," he glowers.

"Are they true though? Do these women pay you to... you know."

"Who told you this shit? Aaron?"

"Yes."

"Jesus," he breathes, shaking his head from side to side before he picks up his unfinished plate and walks it over to the kitchen sink.

"It's true though isn't it? I mean, I saw you with that woman. That wasn't just a portrait was it?" I ask, needing to know the answer.

"Why does it matter?"

"Because it does."

With his back to me, gripping the edge of the sink, I can see the muscles in his forearms flex and relax, as the silence drags on without any answer to my question. It's then that I realise it's all true, and I wish I had just kept my mouth shut.

"I think I should go," I whisper, pushing away from the table with the idea to go and get my bag.

"What do you want me to say Henrietta? I'm sure you're aware that I've had sex before. Is it really important that you know who it was with and why?"

"I don't know. I just…" I stop speaking, standing in the centre of the room, not really knowing what it is I want to say. This is all so new to me.

"Can you just accept that since I met you, I haven't been with anyone else?" he explains, moving toward me, reaching his hands around my waist, holding me to him.

"What about that woman I saw in here? What about Bec?" I argue, tears in my eyes as I push against his chest ineffectively. He's like fucking kryptonite when he's near me and suddenly I'm helpless against him as my hands rest against his chest, and my fingertips smooth over the soft cotton of his shirt.

"I don't lie. I didn't have sex with either of them. I promise you that."

"I just don't like the idea of you being in a room alone with a naked woman," I whisper, resting my head on his shoulder, already giving in.

"It's my job Henrietta," he explains, gliding his hand soothingly up and down my back. "If I don't have that income, I won't be able to afford this place. My course. My car. The fees to train with your father. It all costs money. I have two things that I'm great at – portraits and fighting. I can't make a huge amount of money back alley fighting without getting busted by the cops. So I do portraits. The fact that they're risqué is what keeps me in business. But I promise you, it will just be portraits – nothing else."

"What if they don't understand that? What if they think they can sleep with you?"

"Babe, I'm not a gigolo – it's not like they were paying me for my sexual services. And I didn't 'sleep' with any of them. You're the only girl I've ever literally slept with and when you're ready, you'll be the only girl I ever make love to. I want you to be mine Henrietta, and in return, I'll be yours."

10

"Do you want me to help you move?" Damien asks, as he drops me off at home after breakfast.

"I do. But it's all planned. My parents are helping, and I think it's important that it's just me and them. This is kind of a big deal for them – and for me of course. I just… do you understand?" I ask, stopping because I don't feel as though I'm making any sense.

"Of course I do. You go. Move into your new place and call me when you're done," he says, taking my hand and kissing my knuckles. "And can you actually leave your phone on this time?"

"Absolutely."

When I get inside, my parents are both dressed and ready, sitting together on the couch watching TV. As I enter the room, they turn their heads toward me, and I can tell they're expecting an explanation.

"Morning," I say, as cheery as I can, pretending like I didn't just spend the night at some guy's house.

"Shhhh," my mother hisses at my father. "She's eighteen." Her voice is low, but I hear her clearly as she admonishes my grumbling father. "Damien again?" she asks me, setting a smile upon her face.

"Yeah," I nod, giving her a small smile. I can tell she wants to ask me a lot of questions, but the stormy look on my dad's face means that they'll have to wait until we get a chance to be alone.

"Let's get this done," my father proclaims, as he gets up from the couch with a slight grunt that shows his age. Forever the gentleman, he holds his hand out to help my mother up. "We'll start with the boxes by the door. Hopefully it will all fit in one run. If not, I'll drop you and your mother off, and then come back for the rest."

"Sounds like a plan," I smile, trying to keep my excitement level even. I don't think it's appropriate for me to be keening about leaving them. Even though I'm fighting the urge to squeal and jump up and down yelling 'moving day!'

Piling into the Barina, we let dad do the driving to my new accommodations. The trip is no more than ten minutes, but it feels like it takes forever. I'm travelling toward my future, toward my freedom, and I can't wait.

I love my parents, I really do, and I will visit them as much as I can. But I can't breathe in that house. I need my space.

As we pull up in front of the townhouse, my heart beats excitedly in my chest as I jump out of the car and jog up to the front door, calling to my parents that I'll open the door to clear the path for the boxes.

"Happy moving day!" Jessica singsongs, as she opens the door for me. "Where's your stuff?" She looks at my empty hands and frowns, a flash of worry crossing her features.

"It's in the car," I smile, thumbing over my shoulder. "I was just going to open the door so we can bring it in.

"Great. Let me help you," she says, stepping outside and calling out to Kensi that I'm here.

I don't have a huge amount of boxes, but the Barina is tiny, so it didn't fit everything inside. Working together, we take all of my stuff upstairs and start unpacking while my dad returns home to get the last of my things.

"Can I get you something to drink Mrs Davis?" Jessica asks my mum. "Tea? Coffee?"

"That would be lovely. Tea please, white with no sugar," my mother returns, opening up a box and stacking items on my bed.

"Great, I'll just go and put the kettle on. Do you want something Etta?"

"No thanks, I'm all good."

As she exits the room, Kensi finally decides to make a very bleary eyed appearance in the doorway to say hi, before mumbling something about coffee and following after Jessica.

"Those two seem like polar opposites," my mother muses.

"They're nice though." I move to the wardrobe with my hanging clothes over my arm and begin positioning them in a tidy row.

"So… since we're alone. Do you want to tell me what's going

on with Damien?"

"I have no idea what's going on with Damien. I barely even know him. I just know that I'm drawn to him," I explain, glancing at her over my shoulder as I continue to work on packing away my things.

"Do you think it's wise to be spending the night with him so soon?" she asks, sliding clothes into my drawers.

"I didn't have sex with him mum. We just slept, that's all."

"You're an adult now honey. I can't tell you what to do. I just want you to be careful. Don't rush anything."

"I'll be careful," I assure her, moving on to a box full of personal items. "Mum? Why is dad so funny about him? He was happy when he thought we were training. Why does it bother him if I date Damien?"

She pulls a set of sheets out of a box and shakes it out, ready to make the bed she's just finished clearing. I stand across from her, taking a hold of the opposite corner to help.

"Oh, I think your dad would be funny about any guy, and I guess he didn't think Damien would make a move on you."

"Why? Because he's one of his students?"

"No, because he was friends with Craig. You probably wouldn't remember him. He was all pimply and had braces on his teeth back then – he wasn't the good looking man he is now, that's for sure," she chuckles, smoothing her hand over the bed before grabbing the top sheet. "They were in the same training group, and got along really well - if you have a look there's a few photos of them together at the dojo. Damien was there that night too. The night Craig fell in the river," she informs me, not making any eye contact as she continues making the bed. "Not that it was his fault, he was just one of the many kids that were there... I guess he feels a little responsible – or guilty – for not realising Craig had gone missing... I don't know. We don't blame him of course. You dad actually has a bit of a soft spot for him. The poor kid hasn't had the easiest life, he's been through a lot, so your dad's worried that his feelings toward you are a little misguided."

"What do you think?" I ask, suddenly feeling as though Damien might only want me out of guilt, or misguided loyalty.

"What do I know really? You're looking at a woman who married a man, who seems very much like Damien. Moody, demanding, hard to get along with. But together, we work. I think you just have to go with your gut in these situations. Aikido helps to keep them centred. So does a lot of love and understanding."

As I process this information, Jessica returns. "Tea's ready," she informs us. "And it sounds like Mr Davis has just returned with the last of the stuff."

While mum follows Jessica into the kitchen, I head outside to help my dad unpack the car. "Is this everything?" I ask.

"Yep," he replies, leaning into the car to pull out my lamp. "It's amazing how much you can fit in when you don't have two women in the car."

153

It takes a couple of trips back and forth from the car to my bedroom to get all of my things. All the while, I'm trying to think of a way to talk to my dad about Damien. In the end, I just come out with it.

"I didn't realise Damien was friends with Craig."

"Um… yeah, I teamed them up as sparring partners. Don't you remember him? They used to come first and second at a lot of the tournaments."

I laugh. "I never paid attention to what everyone came. I only knew what Craig came. I was too busy stuffing around with my friends."

"Yeah, I remember. You were always trying to get your mum to give you change for the vending machines. You were good though, you could have been great."

"I just liked doing the same thing my dad and brother were doing."

Pressing his lips together, he lets a burst of air out his nose as he plugs the lamp into the wall and places it on the square table next to my bed, checking that it's still working by turning it on then off.

"So… is there anything going on between you and him?" he asks, as he stands up straight. He's not really looking at me, so I can tell he finds this all a little awkward.

"Not yet," I tell him. "We're just getting to know each other."

Nodding, he places his hands in his pockets and looks around the room. "Just… watch yourself with him ok? He's um… a complicated kid."

"What does that mean? Should I stay away from him?"

"Don't be ridiculous. What are you saying to her?" my mother asks in a clipped tone, as she re-enters the room.

"I'm saying to be careful," he exasperates. "She's my daughter. I want her to be careful."

"I'll be careful," I promise. "Don't worry. I'll be fine."

***

After my mum and dad thoroughly inspect my new home, they reluctantly leave to let me settle in. Kensi and Jessica have been on their best behaviour, so I'm pretty sure my parents feel as though they've left me in good hands. Although as soon as we hear their car drive off, Kensi yells, "PARTY!" as she throws her hands in the air and dashes to the kitchen, returning with a bottle of butterscotch schnapps and three shot glasses.

"Seriously Kens? We're starting at lunch time?" Jessica laughs. "Didn't you drink enough last night?"

"The best way to beat a hangover is to just stay drunk," she explains, pouring the sweet liqueur into the glasses. "Plus, we need to celebrate." She hands us both a glass and holds hers to her lips. "To new friends and lots of drunken nights together," she toasts, lifting her glass upward slightly before tossing it

155

down her throat.

"Cheers," Jessica and I say, as we do the same. The thick sweet liquid is like mouthful of nectar as it slides down my throat.

"Wow, I think I just got a cavity from that," I laugh. "It's like drinking a liquid lolly."

"It is, I love it," Kensi laughs, sliding her tongue inside the shot glass to lick away the remnants.

"Are you finished unpacking?" Jessica asks.

"Almost. I just have a little more to do," I explain, prompting us all to head up to my room while I finish.

They help me a little, but mostly, they just keep me company while we chat and get to know a bit more about each other.

Kensi takes it upon herself to leaf through the things in my wardrobe, complaining that she won't be able to steal my clothes from me due to the huge difference in our heights.

"Oh, you have to wear this dress out tonight!" she exclaims, pulling out a royal blue body hugging singlet style dress. "It will look amazing with your hair and eyes," she says.

"I have it in a green as well," I tell her, flicking through my clothes to show her. "Where are we going anyway?"

"Oh, there's a party at number four," Jessica explains. "Cute boys, a BBQ and loud music. It's going to be fun."

"You should invite Aaron," Kensi intimates, nudging me lightly with her elbow as she re-hangs my dress. "And maybe he could bring Jeremy."

"You liked him huh?" I laugh, remembering how every time I saw her on Thursday night she was hanging off him.

"Very much. I need another chance. So call him – please," she begs, holding her hands together like she's praying.

"Who's that guy you went home with on Thursday, Etta?" Jessica interjects. "He came over to where we were sitting and demanded your bag. Then he just carried you out like you were a baby."

"Oh my god! That's right. He was HOT. But very unhappy," Kensi adds, turning her mouth downward. "Who was he? Please tell me he's your brother or a relative of some sort. Otherwise, there's no chance for the rest of us."

"I thought you were into Jeremy?" I respond, setting out my nail polishes on top of my dresser.

"I am, but if things don't work out…" She shrugs as if it's all no big deal. "I have to keep my options open."

"His name is Damien and he's my…" I shake my head and bounce my shoulders. "I don't know what he is at the moment. It's all very new."

"Well then, invite them both," Kensi shrugs.

"I don't know if that's a good idea," I start to say when we hear

157

a knock at the door.

"I'll get it," Jessica says, jumping up from where she's sitting on the end of my bed and bouncing down the stairs, her honey streaked, brown ponytail swinging happily behind her.

"I don't know where that girl gets so much energy," Kensi comments, shaking her head as she moves over to my chest of drawers and starts inspecting the nail polish. "Can I borrow this one?" she asks, holding up a black bottle with silver glitter mixed through it.

"Sure," I agree.

"We've got a visitor," Jessica sing-songs, as she reaches the top of the stairs. Looking out my door, I can see that she's followed by Aaron.

"Hey, happy moving day," he smiles, handing me a small wrapped gift as he leans in to kiss my cheek.

"Thank you. You didn't have to get me anything," I exclaim, pulling open the package to reveal a hook for my wall.

"It's to go with the key chain," he explains, tilting his head as he shrugs a little. "I'm just losing my keys all the time. So I thought this might save you from the same problem."

"This is great Aaron," I tell him, opening up the packet and removing the film from the adhesive side before sticking it on the wall near my door. After holding it on the wall for the required ten seconds, I release it and step back. "There.

Perfect."

"Almost," Jessica says, rushing out of the room and returning with my new house keys. "This one is the front door, and this one is for your bedroom door." She shows me each key before handing them over.

"Will you attach them to the key chain for me?" I ask Aaron, moving over to my desk where I had sat the key chain he gave me for my birthday.

"Of course." He takes them from me and bows his head as he pries the metal ring open and winds the keys in place.

"So, there's a party in our complex tonight. You busy?" Kensi asks Aaron, as she spins from side to side on my desk chair.

"Um, I was going to go out with some friends – you were invited by the way," he says to me separately. "But I can stop by later on if that's ok." He moves over to the hook and hangs the keys in their new spot.

I thank him as he and Kensi continue to talk. "You can come any time you want. We'll be here," she drawls. "You can bring your friends."

"Ok," he says politely, before turning his attention back to me. "Anyway, I just wanted to drop by and check you were all good. I might see you later ok?" he says, touching me lightly on my arm as he leaves, telling Kensi and Jessica that it was nice to see them again on his way out.

"Spill. We want to know exactly what the deal is with these men in your life," Kensi says, leaning back in my desk chair as she prepares herself to paint her nails by laying out a tissue and borrowing my nail file.

I shake my head slightly, laughing a little at how comfortable she is with other people's things and make a mental note to keep my door locked whenever I'm not home.

"I'd like to know this too actually," Jessica adds, as she once again sits down on the end of my bed.

Having nowhere else to sit, I join her as I wonder where to begin. I start by explaining that Aaron and I were friends first, and that we dated each other for only a couple of months before my father found out and put an end to everything.

"I'm lucky he's such a great guy, because he didn't make me feel weird around him when things cooled down between us," I say.

"So you've slept with him before?" Kensi asks, blowing on her now freshly painted nails.

"Yes," I confirm.

"Was he your first?" Jessica adds dreamily. I can tell she has a fairly major crush on him.

"No, I had one other boyfriend before him. But that didn't last long either." I explain how strict my father always was, and how it made it impossible to have a normal relationship with anyone.

160

"So how does Damien fit in to all of this?" Kensi asks.

As I explain how I met Damien, I start to realise that the only information I have on him, came from other sources. When he met me, he must have realised who I was. How could he not? He trains with my father, he knew my brother. He must have known who I was. Then why not say so? Why behave as though everything between us has been completely coincidental?

"Geez, sucks to be you," Kensi says, as she kicks off her slippers and starts to paint her toes in the same colour.

"What do you mean?" I ask.

"You're eighteen. You're less than a year away from finishing your degree, and you have two very good looking men interested in you, and all you have to do is choose," she lists.

"I'd choose Aaron," Jessica chimes in.

"Yeah, but did you see Damien?" Kensi replies. "He's gorgeous."

"Yeah, but what's with all the secrets? Aaron is just as good looking, and he's so thoughtful. Look what he did for her?"

As they continue to argue the pros and cons of each man, I stand up from the bed and move toward my bag to get my phone. The sound in the room seems to dull around me. It's as if I can sense it's about to ring.

Staring at the screen, I jump a little when it actually does, and Damien's number appears.

"Come outside," he says, without waiting for me to say hello, before disconnecting the call.

For a moment, I'm frozen with the phone still against my ear. I'm still a little weirded out be the whole sensing the call thing. And now he says he's here? But I haven't even given him my new address…

"What's up?" Jessica asks, looking at me curiously.

"I just… hang on," I say, pocketing my phone into the back of my jeans as I leave the room to go downstairs. When I reach the front door, he's there. Of course he's there, I can feel him.

"You going to let me in?" he rumbles, his baritone entering my ears and absorbing into my body, sending gentle ripples coursing through me.

Without saying anything, I unlock the screen door and let him inside.

"Ladies," he nods, directing his greeting toward Jessica and Kensi, who are both standing directly behind me, mouths open as he enters, the top of his head barely making it under the doorway.

"Oh my god. It's like Conan the Barbarian just came to visit Jean Grey," Kensi mutters.

"What?" Jessica giggles, scrunching her face up in confusion.

"Not the old Conan, the new one," Kensi clarifies. "And Jean Grey is the telekinetic chick from Xmen."

"Oh yeah, I would have pegged her as more of a 'Rogue' myself," Jessica joins in.

"Maybe, but I don't think Rogue is tall enough."

"But is Jean Grey?"

As they continue yet another debate, Damien takes my hand and leads me up the staircase. "Which one is yours?" he murmurs, as we reach the top.

"Just in here," I say, pointing to the first door on the left.

Our eyes connect momentarily, and he tugs me inside, closing the door behind us and flipping the lock.

"We don't need any more comic book references," he informs me as he moves toward me and takes me in his arms, burying his face in the crook of my neck as he inhales deeply.

My head seems to swim as I lean against him, feeling drunk on whatever it is that his presence does to me. He turns his head a little, kissing me gently on the skin behind my ear, on my jaw, my brow and my forehead, before stepping us toward the bed and guiding me so I'm laying down next to him.

"I just need to hold you," he explains, kissing me on my forehead as he pulls me against him.

I curve my body into his, my arm sliding around his firm waist. "Is everything ok?"

"It is now," he says, pressing his lips in my hair.

Closing my eyes, I listen to the steady beating of his heart, and the sound of his breath as it filters through his lungs, and before I know it, I'm fast asleep.

***

When I wake I'm still wrapped in his arms. For a while, I just lay there quietly, enjoying being with him as I think about the events of my day. Eventually, the questions that surround him fill my mind, and I want some answers.

"Damien," I whisper, twisting in his arms so that I'm facing him. "Why didn't you tell me you knew Craig?"

Sighing, his eyes open, an expression of sadness in them as he focuses on me. "Because… it's not my proudest moment."

"What do you mean?"

He sits up on my bed and shakes his head like he's trying to shuck the memories. "Do we have to talk about this?" he directs over his shoulder at me.

"Yes Damien. We do. This is important. I want to know why you didn't tell me you knew him. I mean, the moment I said my brother fell in the river and drowned, you must have known – especially after I told you who my dad was. Why have you kept it a secret?"

He grips his head with both hands and brings his knees up, leaning his elbows on them as he lets out his breath slowly. "Because he was with me, and I was too busy trying to get this

164

girl to take a walk with me to notice that he'd gone missing. If I had have been paying attention…" he pauses, his voice going hoarse as he shakes his head. "I just… I didn't think you'd want to know me if you knew." His voice is almost a whisper as he looks at me beseechingly.

"Oh Damien," I cry, reaching out for him and wrapping my arms around his broad shoulders. "Please tell me you don't blame yourself. It wasn't anyone's fault. It was just an accident."

He inhales sharply, pressing his finger and thumb to his eyes before releasing his breath slowly, trying to stay in control.

"Damien," I say again, moving so that I'm kneeling next to him. I reach out, smoothing my hand down the side of his face. "It wasn't your fault."

He lifts his gaze to meet mine, his eyes rimmed red with emotion. Suddenly, his arms are around me holding me to him as he continues to apologise to me for not noticing Craig had gone missing. I clutch at him in return, assuring him repeatedly that it wasn't his fault.

In between apologies, he plants soft kisses on my face, in my hair, on my shoulder – anywhere I have some exposed skin. I'm slowly going insane with desire. I want him to kiss me properly. I want to feel his mouth on mine.

"Why won't you kiss me?" I whisper, gripping my hands on either side of his face so he looks at me.

"Because I don't think I can stop if I do," he states, running his fingers through the length of my hair.

"Maybe I won't want you to stop," I return, my eyes moving between his eyes and his mouth, my body screaming for him to connect with me.

Just as his resolve seems to slip, and he edges toward me, Jessica calls through the door.

"Etta? We're going to start getting ready. Are you still coming with us to the party?"

"You're going to a party?" he asks, pulling back from me.

"Um, yeah," I call back, effectively answering both questions at the same time.

"Where is this party?" he responds, his brow furrowing as he runs his fingers through his now messy hair.

Jessica once again calls through my door. "Do you want a shower? I just need to know so we can work out our bathroom times."

"Yeah. I'll go last."

"Ok." Listening, I hear her move down the hallway and into her room, which is the one next to mine.

"The walls are thin," Damien notes as we can clearly hear her move around.

"They're thin at your place too," I comment, remembering how clearly I could hear conversations from within the hallway.

When we hear the shower turn on in the bathroom, he focuses his attention on me again.

"You didn't answer my question."

"Oh, the party. It's at number four. It's a BBQ or something. Are you going to come with me? Make sure I don't get into too much trouble?"

"Tempting. But I can't. I have plans."

"Oh," I say, now frowning myself. "I… I didn't realise. Sorry, I just…" I stop there, feeling as though I'm bumbling. A sinking feeling settles in the pit of my stomach as I realise that he made plans that don't involve me. "You've made other plans. Fine." I state, trying not to sound too bitter about it.

"I'll call you when I'm through though. Just don't drink too much this time. I won't be around to carry you home."

"I'll be fine," I bite out, annoyed at myself more than I am at him. I had envisioned spending the night with him after the closeness we developed just now. But instead, I'm attending a party, on my own, after experiencing the most emotional and sexually frustrating afternoon of my life.

Cupping my chin in his hand, he lifts my head. He wants me to meet his eyes, but I'm refusing to. I'm acting like a spoilt child. I know that. But I don't want him to go out. I see the way women react to him.

167

"What's wrong," he asks me, tilting his head to catch my eyes.

"I don't want you to go," I tell him quietly.

Sighing, he releases my chin. "Would you look at me please?"

Shaking my head in response, I keep my face turned away. My eyes are burning as I fight tears. Tears I shouldn't even need to fight. *Shit*. What the hell is it about him that has me acting like this?

"Henrietta. I need to go. This has been set up since last weekend."

"Is it a fight?" I ask.

"Yeah. It's in Darling Harbour. I can't take you with me."

"Why? I won't do anything. I'll just watch."

"It's not safe, and I won't be able to concentrate if I'm worried about you. Please stay here. I'll call you when I'm through."

"Maybe I won't answer," I tell him defiantly, attempting to worry him on purpose in the hope that he'll change his mind and stay.

"Maybe I'll take you to my place and deadbolt you inside."

"You wouldn't!" I cry, horrified at the idea.

"Try me."

We stare at each other for a moment, each one challenging the other. In my mind, I'm trying to figure out how to get my way. That's when it dawns on me.

Launching myself at him, I press my lips to his, urging him to respond as I wrap my arms around his neck, and suck on his lips.

At first, he places his hands on my hips as if he's about to push me away, but I feel his resolve melt away as his body relaxes and his hands slide around to my buttocks, pulling me into his lap as his mouth works voraciously against mine. Sliding my hand underneath his shirt, I run my fingers over the definite bumps of his abs, loving the smoothness of his skin versus the hardness of his muscles.

When he hums into my mouth, I take it as a good sign and boldly slide my hand further, tucking my finger beneath the waist of his jeans.

"Not yet," he murmurs, closing his hand over mine and bringing it back up to his mouth, sucking gently on my fingertips.

"But I'm ready," I pant, feeling like I'll die from the throbbing his kisses are creating between my thighs.

"Not yet," he repeats, sliding me off his lap and onto the bed. As he stands, there's a knock on my door.

"Shower's free," Kensi calls out.

"Come on," he says from the doorway.

My heart starts to thud in my chest as images of showering with him make my already aroused body light on fire. I can't wait to run my fingers, laden with soap over the top of his well-defined torso.

As I step inside the bathroom, I watch as Damien walks over to the shower and twists the taps to start the shower running.

"There you go," he says, testing the water before retreating toward the door.

"You're leaving?" I blurt out, all my fantasies evaporating before my very eyes.

"Yes. Have a nice shower." He smiles knowingly as he leans in and kisses my cheek, before quietly retreating from the bathroom. Leaving me on my own.

My cheeks flame hot, feeling embarrassed for assuming I could seduce him into staying. God, I'm behaving like some sex crazed lunatic. But I want him – bad.

I get that most people view sex as a big step in a relationship. I personally, do not. I don't see a problem with giving in to your desires. I see more of a problem in denying yourself, I mean, how can this be a good thing? He's just gone out with a hard on and I'm in here with a throbbing clit. If he'd just let me touch him, or if he'd just touch me, then this wouldn't all be such a big deal. Maybe we would get it out of our system and realise this thing between us is just amplified lust.

With a sigh, I remove my clothes, conceding my defeat as I step in the shower to get ready for this party. As the water rushes down over my body, I close my eyes and imagine what it would be like to have him touch me the way I want him to. I'm so keyed up that my own hands, acting as his, slide over my skin, cupping my breasts, gliding over my wet stomach and down to my mound.

A quiet gasp escapes my lips as my fingers connect with my swollen nub. The thought of him, enough to increase the throbbing I feel inside. With two fingers, I enter myself, pulsing in and out, massaging that sweet spot just inside before pulling out and swirling my juices around my clit.

Leaning against the cool tiles, I let the water rush down my back as my hand works, back and forth, urging my orgasm to burst out of me.

Holding on to the image of his face as he leans down to me, I concentrate on my nub, imagining it's him touching me. A slight whimper erupts from my throat as I explode around my fingers, my knees go weak and my body shudders as I slow my movement, holding pressure on my sensitive clit as the ripples of pleasure subside.

Slowly, I remove my hand, standing up straight and continuing my shower, being sure to soap myself up to remove any scent of myself on my hands.

When I turn the shower off, I wrap a towel around myself, and sit on the edge of the bath, feeling disappointed. I was so caught up in my need for release, that I didn't consider how imagining him doing that to me would make me feel when I opened my eyes and it was all a fantasy. Now I just feel lonely, and a little wanton.

Sighing, I stand up and move over to the mirror. Using my hand to remove the fog, I look at my reflection. This is one of those times when I actually see myself as beautiful. Something about having an orgasm causes my skin to glow and my lips to turn a deep red colour. I wish I could find a lipstick that made my lips like this, but I haven't been successful yet.

With my towel wrapped around me, I exit the bathroom to head back to my room and get dressed for this party. Not that I feel like going anymore. I kind of just want to sit in my room and wait for him to call – how sad is that?

"So where did Conan go?" Kensi calls, as I pass her room.

"*Damien* is going to the city tonight. He's got something going on in Darling Harbour."

"Oh, I love Darling Harbour. We should go there instead," Jessica calls out from her room.

"I'm in, it beats hanging out around here," Kensi agrees. "You in?"

A grin creeps over my face as it dawns on me that I don't need to do what I'm told anymore. I just moved out of home. I don't need anyone setting boundaries for me – especially not some guy I just met. Damien isn't my dad. He has no say in my life.

"Yeah, I'm in," I smile, feeling powerful and in control for the first time in ages.

"Yes!" Kensi hisses, pumping her first in the air. "Wardrobe change!"

She spins around and starts rifling through her wardrobe, and I leave her to it, considering I'm still in my towel and need to get dressed myself.

I decide to wear the emerald green singlet style dress. I've never worn it before and have always really wanted to. Based on all of the pictures I've seen of women with my colouring, green looks fantastic. And I really want to look fantastic tonight.

Kensi appears in my doorway, just as I'm finishing up with my hair. I've left it out, and run a straightening iron through it, so it falls softly over my shoulders and skims across the exposed skin on my back where the neckline scoops.

"Lookin' hot mama," she comments, waving her hand around like she's touched something hot.

"Thank you. You're looking amazing yourself." She's got this tiny little black dress on that has a ruffle of blue tulle around the base of it. She's teamed it with a few accessories, and killer electric blue heels that are a good five inches high.

"I know," she teases, giving me a wink as she moves to sit on my bed.

"Did you tell Aaron we aren't going to be at this party anymore?" she asks me.

"Oh. No. I'll text him from the train," I say, as I apply some plum lipstick then blot it with a tissue.

"Are you two ready?" Jessica calls from the hall before coming into view. She's wearing a really short sky blue dress that has a cowl neckline and is made out of reflective material – it kind of has a snake skin look to it when the light hits. "Oh good. Let's go. There's a train leaving the station in, like, twenty minutes."

We all file out of the townhouse and lock the front door, tucking our keys, ID's, phones and money into our bras for safe keeping.

Walking down the pathway, we head toward the station. I'm wearing the same strappy heels I wore to the Scarlett Party. With all three of us in heels, we're making quite the racket with our footwear as it hits across the pavement.

"We should have drunk the rest of the schnapps," Kensi says as we pay for our tickets and wait on the station. "The train ride is going to be so boring sober."

"Kens, you think everything is boring sober," Jessica laughs.

It takes us a good hour on the train before we're walking along Cockle Bay Wharf, trying to decide which club we want to go to. Eventually, we just choose the one that has the loudest music, and the most people.

"Looks like fun," Kensi notes, dancing to the beat as we push our way through the crowd toward the bar. "OK, now we each need to get four drinks each or we'll spend all bloody night at the bar," she yells over the music.

174

"How the hell am I going to carry four drinks?" I yell back.

"Watch and learn."

Leaning across the bar to yell her order at the average looking barman, she takes a straw from the dispenser and holds it between her teeth.

"Thank you," she yells, picking up one glass in each hand with her forefingers and thumb then lifting them up and grabbing the other two cups with her remaining fingers and palms.

"And how do you drink them?" I ask. This is when she gives me a look that tells me I shouldn't ever underestimate her. With the straw in her mouth, she rapidly downs the contents of one and flicks it on the floor, scattering ice all over the place. She keeps the straw in her mouth and just moves it across to the next drink.

"Kensi!" I admonish, looking down at the floor. "Someone will break their neck on all that ice!" I kneel down and pick up what I thought was a glass, but turns out to be a plastic cup and place it on the bar, ordering only two drinks because I don't feel like doing the juggling act Kensi is doing.

"Chicken," she laughs, as I turn around with my drinks.

Childishly, I poke my tongue out at her and stand to the side while Jessica orders hers. She turns around with three bottles of those vodka mixes we all love so much.

"It works out to four," she immediately says to Kensi. "Besides, I am not having a drinking competition with you tonight.

175

Otherwise poor Etta will have to carry both of our drunken arses home!"

"Party poopers – the both of you!" she calls out, returning to the bar and ordering four more. I can't believe she's finished them already. I've barely made it half way through one.

This time she returns with shots. "No, no, no," I say as she attempts to thrust one in my hands.

"Yes, yes, yes. Drink two, then we'll go dance, and I won't make you drink anymore. I promise."

"Fine," I say, finishing off one drink and returning my cup to the bar before I accept the shot glasses from her. "How am I going to do this?" I ask, holding one cup in one hand and two stacked shot glasses in the other.

"Seriously, you are such a night club virgin," she scolds me. "Here. I'll hold this one." She takes my cup of bourbon and coke from my hand so I'm free to do the shots.

Wincing at them, I take a deep breath before tipping my head back and quickly downing the both of them.

"Holy shit," I exclaim, shaking my head quickly and coughing a little, as the burn constricts my throat. "What the hell was that?"

"Absinthe."

"That was mean," Jessica giggles, taking a leisurely drink of her Cruiser.

Kensi hands me back my other drink, and I take a gulp of it, just to wash the taste of the absinthe away.

"Let's go dance," she calls over the music.

Taking me by the hand, she pulls me after her as she forces our way to the dance floor, securing a position she feels is adequate, before she raises her hands above her head as begins to dance.

The music seems as though it has a pulse, as the coloured lights dart around the dimly lit dance floor. Bodies are pressed against bodies, as they gyrate to the beat as it vibrates our very cells.

Mimicking their moves, I lift my arms, swaying my hips to the music, letting the throb dictate my moves. The air is thick with human warmth, but filled with energy as we sway. It doesn't take long before we start to attract the attention of some would-be suitors. They seem to slip in amongst us seamlessly.

The guy next to me, slightly shorter than I, with fashionably messy short brown hair, leans into my ear to speak.

"I love redheads," he says, yelling over the music.

"Good for you," I yell back, holding my thumbs up to congratulate him. He doesn't take my disinterest as a hint though, and continues his attempt to dance with me.

I look in the opposite direction, attempting to give him the cold shoulder. When I turn back, he's gone, and so are the other two guys that were after Kensi and Jessica.

"Over there," Kensi says in my ear, looking over my shoulder.

Following her line of sight, I notice Damien, and a couple of other guys, leaning up against a pylon, watching us dance. Pausing, I place my hands on my hips and stop moving.

Extending his index finger, he beckons me forward, a slightly unimpressed look on his beautiful face. Walking toward him, I try to look as unfazed as possible, pretending that I am an incredibly confident woman who won't be told what she can and can't do.

As I get closer, he glances toward the two other guys, tilts his head, and effectively dismisses them.

"What are you doing?" he asks.

"Dancing," I state, my hands placed firmly on my hips. I've heard that this is a confident stance, and since I'm starting to feel a little lightheaded after those drinks, I'm also feeling a little bold as well.

"You're supposed to be at a party."

"Change of plans."

His eyes skim up and down my body as he slowly nods his head.

"Besides, I thought you were here for a reason. Why the hell are you standing here watching women dance?" I accuse,

178

taking a step closer to him as I poke him in the chest.

"There's only one woman I want to watch dance Etta, and that's you," he says in my ear. The fact that I'm in his direct proximity has made me even more light-headed. I need to learn to keep my distance when I'm angry with him, or I'm never going to get my way.

"Here," he says, reaching into his jeans. Out of his pocket, he pulls a small Bluetooth ear piece, and attaches to my ear, moving my hair so it covers it. "Give me your phone."

Reaching into my bra, I slide my phone out from the side of the cup and hold it out to him. His eyebrows are raised as he accepts it from my hands. Using it, he calls himself, activating the ear piece. Reaching up, he presses it to answer the call, brushing his thumb lightly against my cheek. "Dance for me," he says into the handset.

"Here?" I ask.

"No. Out there. I want to watch you."

Walking backwards slowly, I keep eye contact with him, loving the way he watches me as I dissolve back into the crowd.

"Stop there," he commands, as I reach the edge of the dance floor. I do as he says, watching him and waiting for what comes next.

"Now close your eyes. Listen to my voice, and feel the music. Move your hips. Imagine you're moving only for me."

His voice caresses me as it enters my ear, the only clear thing in a throbbing sea of pulsating bodies. I follow his instructions, feeling the music vibrate through me, imagining that only he and I are in the room as I sensuously roll my hips from side to side, letting my hands slide up my body, from my thighs until I reach my hair, lifting it, letting it cascade slowly over my fingers.

A body brushes up against mine, and I flinch, thinking it might be another unwanted suitor, but no sooner do I open my eyes than the offending toucher is mysteriously absent.

"Just focus on my voice," he says. "Dance for me. You look so goddamned sexy in that dress. If you were ready, I could take you right now," he tells me, causing my insides to clench. "Jesus, I'm getting hard just looking at you. Everybody here wants you. Every man in here is looking at you, hungry, thinking that he needs you. *Fuck.* Henrietta, get the hell back over here. I need you. I need you by my side."

Opening my eyes, my focus goes immediately to where he's standing, the look in his face is so full of hunger that I can't even think straight. All I want is him.

As I step toward him, I'm stopped by some random guy, stepping in front of me, grabbing at my waist and telling me how gorgeous he thinks I am.

Panicked, I look to where I last saw Damien, only to find he isn't there. I push the guy away from me, telling him no.

"Come on darlin', just one dance. That's all I want," he says, pulling me closer.

"Get the fuck off her," Damien growls, towering over the other guy who is too drunk to realise when he's met his match.

"Find your own woman," the idiot yells back, keeping his hand on my waist.

Damien reaches out and grabs his arm, twisting it uncomfortably, whispering close to his ear. I can't hear what he says, but the guy's face goes as white as a sheet before he rapidly makes his retreat.

"What did you say?" I ask, as he pulls me against him.

"I told him it's not nice to try and snipe another man's woman," he informs me with a grin, just before he takes my mouth in his, swaying with me to the music, our bodies pressed up against each other as our lips lock. It's so erotic that my body screams out for him to touch me more intimately.

His hands slide over my body, cupping my butt firmly in his strong hands, pressing me against him. I can feel his need for me growing between our bodies as we melt into one another. His hands slide down, to the bare skin on my thighs, skimming under my dress and back up to my arse.

"What's this?" he asks.

"Lace panties," I reply.

"We should have a rule about underwear," he says in my ear.

"You're the only one who was ever going to see them," I murmur.

A grin creeps over his face as his hands move either side of my face, pushing my hair back as he looks into my eyes intently.

"What is this?" he asks suddenly. "This thing between us."

"I don't know," I reply, "But it feels like everything."

"Everything," he repeats, just as his mouth meets mine.

11

"I'm sorry I ruined your fight," I say, as Damien walks me to my door. Kensi and Jessica are already inside. Actually, they're spying on Damien and me through the window while they share a tube of Pringles.

"No, you're not," he chuckles, taking me by the hand and pulling me to the side of the house, out of the sight of my prying roommates.

"I don't want to say goodbye," I whisper, tilting my head up toward him, holding my mouth a hair's breadth away from his.

"Then don't," he returns, letting his lips brush lightly against my own.

His eyes darken as he moves toward me, holding out his hand for me to take. He pulls me toward him, and my hands fly up to brace myself as our bodies collide.

Holding me firmly against his body, he dips his head, taking my mouth in his. Every single cell in my body sings in joy as euphoric feelings swirl within me, increasing my want – my need – of this man.

Suddenly, he breaks the kiss and bends his knees, picking me up over his shoulder. Squealing, I kick my legs. "I'm taking you with me," he informs me, as he deposits me in his car, leaning in to kiss me as he clips me in safely.

"We could just stay here. I haven't even slept in my new room yet."

"Your bed is too small."

"Last night, we slept on top of each other – we don't need that much space," I point out.

"Are you always going to argue with me?" he asks, as he starts the car and pulls away from the curb.

"Are you always just going to do whatever suits you?" I return.

"Yes," he grins.

"Then yes, I'm going to argue."

His apartment is even closer to my new place than my parent's house is, so we're there in less than five minutes.

"Do you want a drink or anything?" he offers as we enter his apartment, and he drops his keys on the bench. I lean against the front door, watching him move about. Without waiting for my answer, he takes out two glasses and fills them with cold water from the fridge. "Here."

He stands in front of me, watching as I take the glass and drink down the water. I don't know why, but the way he watches me, makes me very warm. As soon as I've finished, he takes the glass from me, brushing his fingers against mine as he drinks his own water. My breathing quickens as I watch him in return.

I feel like I'm a deer, caught in headlights. I can't stop watching and waiting.

Placing the two glasses on the table beside us, he entwines his hands with mine, moving his fingers sensuously against my own. Slowly, his hands travel the length of my arms, and up over my shoulders, causing my skin to prick as his fingertips brush lightly against my skin until he's cupping my face either side, his fingers sliding into my hair as he smooths his thumbs against my cheeks.

"You are so beautiful," he whispers, his eyes travelling over my face like he's studying every curve and hollow – every line. "I just…want to kiss you. Nothing more."

His mouth closes over mine as I willingly part my lips, granting him entry, moaning as his tongue slides over mine. My hands travel up to his waist and under his shirt. I've been making out with him all night, and I want to feel his skin. My body wants more. I want more.

Pressing against him, I feel his own need for me growing and pressing into me. My hands pull, and my fingers curl into his skin, bringing us closer, as I moan and move against him, loving every deep sound that escapes his throat. His hands drop from my face and reach down to grip my butt, pulling me even closer.

Pulling at his shirt, I lift it up, urging him to take it off. Dropping it on the table beside us, I run my fingers all over his bare chest, loving every bit of his soft skin as my hands travel over the hard planes of his body.

185

Breathing heavily, he drops his face, breaking our kiss and pressing our foreheads together. His hand still rests on my arse cheek, and I slide my hands down to his, pulling him back against me.

"I think we should get some sleep," he murmurs, causing my heart to drop with a thud into my stomach as he steps out of my reach. "I'll get you a towel and something to sleep in."

I can't even move right now. We've just gone from being all hot and heavy to getting ready for bed, and it's taking me a moment to let the whole situation sink in.

Once again, he turns the shower on for me, and leaves me with a towel and a t-shirt. I shower quickly, and wrap myself in the towel, frustrated that he isn't responding to my advances, wondering if I'm doing something wrong.

Realising I don't have a toothbrush with me, I open the medicine cabinet, hoping to find a spare one in there. Lucky, I do. He has one of those five packs of Colgate toothbrushes sitting in there. There are two toothbrushes remaining, and I can't help but wonder who used the other three. It wasn't him. He has an electric one.

Jealousy swirls within my stomach as I vigorously brush at my teeth. I try to tell myself that it isn't important, that it doesn't matter. But he said that he didn't sleep with people. Why then, are there toothbrushes here? That seems like he has regular sleep overs to me. As I spit the foam down the sink, I decide I want to go home. I don't want to be here anymore. I don't like the way he's making me feel.

186

Pulling the door open, I stomp into the bedroom, holding up the toothbrush. "I just used this one. Do you have a marker so I can write my name on it? I wouldn't want any of the other people, that packet of toothbrushes is there for, to mix their spit up with mine."

"What?" he responds, his brow knitted tightly in confusion as he stands up from the bed, now shirtless and wearing only a pair of boxer shorts. I have to force myself to focus on my anger, or else I might just run over to him and wrap my arms around his body, just to feel his skin against mine.

"I thought you didn't have sleepovers." I glare at him, gulping as he strides toward me, while I still hold the toothbrush up as my evidence.

Taking it from my hand, he walks past me, into the bathroom and over to the vanity, placing the toothbrush inside the rinsing cup. He then opens the mirrored cabinet and removes the packet containing the last remaining toothbrush and turns back to face me, leaning his weight against the bench top.

"This has been in there for a while you know. When I bought it, there were five – all different colours." He sets the package aside and holds out his hand, counting on his fingers. "They were blue, green, and orange. You chose the purple one, which just leaves the pink one. If these were here for my 'sleep overs' – as you put it – then don't you think the girl colours would be gone?"

My face drops as I realise what an idiot I've just been. "I'm sorry," I whisper. "I just… the thought of you and other women is kind of making me crazy. Especially when…"

"When what?"

"When you're refusing me."

He stands up from the vanity and strides over to me, sliding his hands either side of my face and tilting my head up toward him, so we're staring directly into each other's eyes.

"I want you so badly Henrietta. I'm struggling to control myself. But I have to. Because once I have you, I am never going to let you go. I need to make sure you're ready for that."

"What if I told you I am? What if I told you that *I* can't let *you* go?"

He runs his fingers through my wet hair, tucking the damp strands behind my ear, his eyes soft as they wander over me as I lean against the doorframe, still wrapped in only a towel. "Not yet Henrietta. Not yet," he whispers, pressing his lips against mine, igniting the fire inside me all over again.

My arms curl around him, and I pull him against me, absorbing his hardness into my softness. Despite his protests, he grows instantly hard. I press my thigh against it, delighting when he releases a groan into my mouth. He shifts his weight slightly, and I take his hand, guiding it between my legs.

My other hand slides down his back, gripping onto his arse cheek as I pull him closer still, rocking my body against his, rubbing myself with his hand. I can feel his fingers twitching –

he can't stay passive for much longer.

"Stop," he growls, panting as he pulls his mouth and hand away from mine.

"Please," I beg, taking his hand, damp with my juices again and pressing it between my thighs. "Just give me this." I gasp, clinging to him, grinding against him, completely lost in my need to be near him.

"Oh god," he groans, his own body moving against mine. "You're going to make this happen too soon. Oh… fuck." He pulls his hand away again. My heart jumps with disappointment but instead of stopping, he reaches his hands up and pulls my towel open, taking a long look at my body as he exposes me. "Jesus Etta, just look at you. You're making me crazy."

"I want this. I need you Damien," I whisper, sliding my hand down his torso until I reach the tent in his boxers, gripping his shaft, long, thick and rock hard, rubbing my hand up and down it. He lets out a slow breath as I work him with my hand, moaning and whimpering as my pleasure builds.

"Touch me," I whisper. "I want you. I need you. Touch me." I'm begging him, the need inside me seems too all-encompassing. I don't want to wait.

His breathing quickens as I slide my hand up and down his shaft, and he gives in to me, slipping his hand between my thighs, rubbing between my folds, circling my engorged clit as I grind against him, desperate for release.

"Etta, we need to stop this. We aren't ready," he murmurs, as his fingers move inside me, slipping back out, wet and slick to caress my sensitive nub.

"I am ready," I gasp. "I don't want to stop this. I'm so close…oh god!" I explode, lights flashing behind my eyes as I throw my head back and moan, bucking against his hand, my own hand gripping his cock firmly.

"Fuck. Etta." he moans, as he shudders against me, dropping his head into the crook of my neck, breathing me in, softly kissing my flesh, his arms wrapping around my body holding me against him.

Gasping, my chest filling with emotion as we just stand together in the doorway, clinging to each other. I slide my arms up his back and rake my fingertips through his hair soothingly, kissing his temple, wondering how the hell this is happening. I know I'm inexperienced when it comes to relationships, but this… this is something else. My chest literally aches, and I can't move. I can't stop holding him.

Eventually, he reaches his hands beneath my buttocks and lifts me off the floor. Normally, I'd squeal if something like this happened to me – I'm not the lightest girl in the world – but he does it with such ease, and there's an intensity in him that's sucking me into his aura, making this a very serious moment.

We don't speak as he carries me into the bathroom and reaches over to turn on the shower again. He somehow manages to remove his boxers while still holding me, then steps us both into the shower, pulling the curtain with a sweep of his arm.

He aims us underneath the spray and lowers me down so I'm standing in front of him. Our eyes lock as he reaches for the shower soap and a sponge. He starts from my shoulders and works his way down, getting on his knees to make sure that every part of me is covered in suds.

He then positions me under the jet stream as he quickly soaps over his own body before joining me under the spray. I stand there as he rinses me off, as if I'm unable to do it for myself, somehow knowing that this is exactly what he wants from me.

When he's satisfied that we're clean, he switches off the water and steps out of the tub before reaching out and taking me by the waist. I place my hands on his shoulders and bend my legs up as he lifts me out and places me on the floor mat in front of him.

Securing a towel around his own waist, he takes another and rubs it over my body, drying me from head to toe. When he's done, he wraps the towel around me, securing it at my chest. He then lifts me again, and sits me on the vanity next to the sink where he proceeds to brush his own teeth. When he spits, he reaches for mouthwash, pouring a small amount in the lid and holding it to my lips.

Opening my mouth for him, I let him pour the hot mint liquid onto my tongue. He repeats the same action for himself and watches me as I swish it about in my mouth and spit it in the sink along with him.

He then scoops me up again and carries me over to the bed, standing me beside it as he removes my towel, then his, hanging them both neatly over the back of his desk chair.

Leaning forward, he pulls the sheets back, guiding me so that I'm sitting down, before helping me slide my legs in. Everything is so strange, yet so right, this isn't something I would have thought I'd go along with. But here I am. Letting him take care of me, when all I've wanted for years, is to do that for myself.

Pulling me close as he nestles in beside me, he plants soft kisses on my shoulder and up my neck, sending warm ripples curling through my body, lulling me off to sleep - wrapped up inside of him.

12

An overwhelming sense of warmth and bliss urges me to consciousness. My eyes flutter open slightly, met with the darkness of the room. The only light coming from the streetlights, as they shine brightly behind the blinds.

"Are you awake?" Damien whispers, kissing the curve of my thigh, just next to my entrance. I hum, reaching down between my legs and sliding my fingers into his hair as I adjust my body beneath him.

"Do you want this Etta?" he asks, running the tip of his tongue, softly around my clit, being careful not to touch it.

I shudder, pulling at his hair, rocking my hips toward his mouth.

"Uh, uh, ah," he tuts, pulling his mouth away and kissing the inside of my thigh instead. "I need to hear your answer. Do you want this?"

"Yes," I gasp. "I want this."

"Tell me exactly what it is you want," he commands, kissing over my folds, driving me mad as my insides start to throb.

"I want…" I pause, not knowing exactly what to say.

"You want what Etta? Tell me." He takes a finger and runs it every so lightly over my folds, causing a surge of need to grow inside me. "You obviously want something, you're dripping," he murmurs, taking his finger into his mouth and sucking the end of it. "Mmmm, I like the way you taste."

He continues to run his fingertips between my legs, but never exactly where I want them.

I lift my hips. "Please," I beg, wanting him to touch me more.

"What do you want?"

"I want your tongue on me. I want your fingers inside me."

"Are you ready for me Etta?" he murmurs, leaning down and brushing the tip of his tongue lightly on my engorged clit.

"I'm ready," I pant, as his mouth comes down around my clit and he sucks me into his mouth, the added pressure has me gasping and calling out his name within seconds as my orgasm builds strongly within me.

Holding on, I grip his head with my thighs and his hair in my hands as he enters me with his fingers, pulsing back and forth, swirling his tongue, sucking with his mouth.

I can't take it for long, the pressure builds inside me until I'm soaring, erupting from within as I spasm beneath him, my calls echoing out into the quiet of the morning.

Lifting his head, he kisses up my body, keeping his fingers inside me, pulsing gently, bringing me back to earth.

"I want you inside me," I whisper, as his kisses reach my neck. My arms pull him against me, clawing my fingers into his flesh. It's as if I'm trying to merge with him. I want him that much.

Withdrawing his fingers, he leans his arms either side of me, hovering over me, the weight of his erection, leaning against my thighs, leaving a damp trail of arousal as he rubs it against me.

Moaning, he dips his head, taking my mouth in his, kissing me languidly. My juices, mixed with the taste of his mouth, only leads to my wanting him more.

"Please," I beg, lifting my hips toward him.

"Tell me what you want," he whispers again.

"I want you inside me," I say immediately, not willing to beat around the bush this time.

He moves his tip over my thigh, sliding it through my juices, his voice rumbling erotically in his throat as he touches himself to my slick wetness.

"You're not asking the right way," he growls, his voice thick with arousal.

Desire smothers my mind like a thick fog. I want him inside me, my body screaming internally for him to fill me. "Just fuck me Damien. Please," I gasp out, tilting my hips up, trying to coax him inside me.

"Wrong," he says suddenly, rising from the bed, striding straight to the bathroom and slamming the door. The movement and change in demeanour, so sudden that I flinch, my heart thumping in my chest as I stare after him and wonder what the hell just went on.

I sit up, suddenly feeling way too naked and reach over to the desk chair to grab a towel. Wrapping it around myself, I walk over to the bathroom door and listen for a moment before knocking gently.

"Damien?"

The door bursts open, revealing a now clothed Damien, a calm controlled expression on his face as he gives me a cursory glance and moves straight past me, heading for the couch where he picks up my bag.

"What are you doing?" I ask, suddenly feeling as though he's about to tell me to go home - that he doesn't want me anymore. Tears spring to my eyes as the thought of not having him squeezes my heart. I don't know what it is, but in such a short time, I feel so connected to him. The thought of not being around him seems soul destroying.

"Get dressed," he says, throwing me my dress and underpants from last night.

"What's going on?" I try again, as I catch it.

"Get dressed," he repeats, more insistent this time.

Looking at the dress in my hands, and back to him, I ask, "Can I at least have my bra?"

"No. Get dressed Henrietta," he tells me again, the use of my full name again like a slap in the face after being called 'Etta' all night.

"Ok." I nod, moving to go to the bathroom to change.

"No. Get dressed right there."

"But – " I start, wanting to say that I need to use the bathroom, my bladder is full.

"Right there Henrietta," he demands, folding his arms over his torso as he stands by the couch watching me.

For a moment I just stand there, not one hundred percent sure on what I should do.

"Why are you being like this?"

"Get dressed. Please."

The intensity with which he watches me, overwhelms my senses, and I find myself capitulating, opening my towel, I let it fall to the floor, dropping the dress over my head before sliding my underpants on.

When I'm dressed, I meet his eyes again. "See, that wasn't so hard. Now you can use the bathroom."

I step into the bathroom, my mind reeling as I place my hand on the door, ready to close it so I can relieve myself in private, but he places his hand against it. "Leave it open," he tells me quietly.

"What is your problem?" I cry. "I'm sorry ok! Whatever the hell I did – I'm sorry!"

"You said you were ready," he reminds me, obviously seeing my discomfort.

"I'm just… I'm a bit confused."

"Use the bathroom, Henrietta. Leave the door open. I won't be watching you," he states, as he steps away.

I contemplate shutting the door anyway, but I reason that with the angle of the bathroom, he isn't likely to be able to see me. Besides, couples do this stuff in front of each other all the time right? It's just happening a little sooner than I'd like here.

Forcing myself to relax, I relieve myself, wash my hands and face, then brush my teeth. When I leave the bathroom, he's standing in the kitchen, drinking a glass of water.

"Better?" he asks, as he sets the glass aside. I nod, watching him warily as he reaches into the fruit bowl and removes a banana, breaking the stalk with a satisfying crack before peeling the skin away and dropping it in the bin.

Moving toward me, he holds it out. "Eat this," he says gently, holding it up to my mouth. Meeting his eyes, I relax a little as I reach up and lean forward to bite the tip off it and remove it from his hand.

He returns to the fruit bowl and grabs a banana for himself, before heading toward the door, grabbing my bag along the way. The action causes a pang of pain to thud in my chest as the sweet fruit I've just swallowed threatens to rebound out of my stomach.

"Let's go," he murmurs, his voice so soft that I take it as sadness. He's kicking me out. Great. I don't understand what he's so annoyed about. Everything was going fine, and then…this happens.

Forcing myself to swallow the last bite of banana, I walk out the door, attempting to take my bag from him on my way past. He keeps hold of it however, and just inclines his head, telling me to go ahead of him.

"You're being a jerk," I tell him, tugging again at my bag.

"It's time to go," he says, still refusing to let go. Rolling my eyes, I shake my head in annoyance and walk ahead of him to where he parked his car last night.

Getting into his car, he of course clicks me in. As he reaches across me, I turn my head to the side, not wanting his scent to cloud my head any further, feeling hurt by his actions and just wanting to go home so I can bury my face in my pillow and cry for a while.

Sitting quietly, I look out the window. The sun is starting to come up and glow pink and peach in the sky as it rises above the houses we drive past. Weaving through the streets, I realise we're not going toward my house. Instead, he takes a different route and turns down the street where my father's gym is then pulls into the parking lot.

"We're training?" I ask, turning my head toward him, confused. I was sure he was taking me home. He seems annoyed with me. "I told you I don't want this. And I'm not really dressed for it."

"You need it," he states, his voice still calm and soft. "Besides, you won't be dressed for it if you ever need it in a real fight, will you?"

"I guess not," I say, rolling the hem of my dress between my fingers as I contemplate my situation, running the events of last night and this morning over in my mind. "Damien? What is going on with us?" I ask suddenly, laying my head against the seat as I turn my head to meet his eyes.

"You said it yourself – it's everything," he whispers, reaching his hand out and brushing his knuckles down my cheek. The tenderness of his gaze, the softness of his touch, has all of my worry melting away as I close my eyes and sigh.

"I thought you were done with me. I thought you were taking me home."

"I'll never be done with you Etta," he murmurs, leaning toward me, kissing me softly. All I want is to be in his arms. It's all I can think about as I move my mouth against his, my hunger for him growing.

Dropping his chin, he breaks the kiss, our breathing heavy, the air around us thickening. "Come." He unclips my seatbelt, gets out of the car, and walks over to my side, opening the door before holding out his hand and leading me inside.

Holding fast to his hand, I follow him through the gym as he flips all of the switches and disarms the alarm. As we move down the hallway, I notice photos of tournaments and see Damien in more than a few, looking as he does now. But as my eyes drift over the older ones featuring my brother, I notice the boy he used to be.

"Is that you standing with my brother?" I ask, pointing out one as he unlocks the door to the dojo.

"Yeah. He always beat me," he smiles.

"Well, you've met his dad," I reply, reaching up and lightly touching the image. "I'm glad you knew him."

He leans against the door jab, watching me, as I go over the photos, pausing to study them and drink in the images of my brother. Smiling. Serious. Proud.

"I've always felt like he never left. I mean, everything is still the same. He's here, he was at home. I've spent the last six years expecting him to walk back through the door. But he won't. It's all just memories..." Letting out a forlorn sigh, I turn my attention back to Damien who is still listening to me quietly. "Do you still compete?"

"No. Not anymore." He moves to the side, then follows me as I head inside the dojo and remove my heels before I step on the mats.

"Why?" I ask.

"It just doesn't interest me anymore. I don't care about the trophies."

"I'll bet my dad isn't too happy about that."

"He wants me to compete, yes. It's good for the school. But there are others capable of competing at a high level. I'm not the only one."

"So you're fourth dan – Yondan – isn't it?" I ask, referring to the highest grade for his age and skill level in Aikido.

"I am," he nods, a small glint in his eye. I can tell he's impressed that I remember the grading system.

"It's all still up here," I say, tapping my forehead. "Are you going to continue your grading?"

"Most likely. The next dan isn't until I'm twenty-five. So I have a while to train for it."

"But you won't compete?"

"No, I won't compete."

"Hmmm. That's a lot of training I have to catch up on. I guess I have a long time before I reach your level and have a chance at beating you," I smile.

"Does that mean you're willing to train until you do?" he asks.

"Perhaps. We'll see if you can change my mind."

"Fair enough," he says, standing in front of me. "Attack," he commands.

I ready myself, trying to decide the best way to attack him without getting thrown on my back.

Faking to one side, I quickly move to the other, hoping to push him through as he reacts. However, he's too fast, too well trained and reads my move too well, sending me off balance and falling toward the mats. Grabbing at him, I refuse to let go, pulling him down on top of me.

Breathing heavily from the fall, I lay beneath him smiling triumphantly, looking up into his eyes. Slowly my grin disappears, as our gaze locks and his eyes darken. Reaching up, I run my fingers over his face, feeling his skin beneath my fingers before pulling him toward me, kissing him with everything I have.

"I feel so much around you Damien," I whisper. "I don't understand what's happening between us. But I know that I never want to do anything to make you stop being with me. I'm sorry I upset you this morning."

He pulls back and searches my face, for what, I'm not sure. But it's then that I realise what upset him this morning.

"Make love to me," I whisper, my fingers smoothing back and forth over his head. For a moment, I don't think he's going to respond, but he lets out his breath, relieved that I figured it out, and brings his mouth to mine.

His hands slide up to either side of my face as he kisses me slowly, sensuously. I can feel the passion pouring from inside him and into me as his mouth moves against mine.

The room is silent but for our breathing and kissing, it echoes out in the vastness of the training area as his hands leave my face and travel down my body. We moan together, as he grips my breast through the fabric of my dress. He rolls his fingers around my protruding nipple, causing me to whimper in response.

Sliding down my body, he lifts my dress, high enough to expose my bare breasts, his warm breath washing over me as he takes a nipple in his mouth, sucking back, grazing his teeth gently over it as he massages the other with his hand. Pulling me up to sitting, he lifts my dress higher, carefully helping me out of it, planting soft kisses on my chest, on my neck, then my mouth before dropping my dress on the floor beside us.

"You are so beautiful Etta," he coos, running his fingers along my arms and down my back, before guiding me to lay on the mat again. Studying me intently, he drags his fingers down my torso, hooking them into the waistband of my panties and pulling them down my legs in a slow, sensual motion.

Nothing he's doing is quick, but everything is passionate. Every touch, every kiss – there's so much emotion behind it.

"Just lay there. I want to look at you," he murmurs, pushing up on his strong legs so he's standing, his own erection pushing against his pants, demanding to be set free.

As he looks down at me, I stay as still as I can, not wanting to do anything to ruin this moment. My insides ache with want, I need him inside me – right now it feels like I need him to breathe.

"Take your hair out," he instructs.

Reaching up, I do as he says, pulling on the elastic and freeing my hair, letting it splay out beside me on the mat.

"Open your legs."

For a moment, I hesitate, but when I see his cock jump as his eyes graze over my body, a bolt of arousal shoots through me. I love how much he wants me. This dark, beautiful man – wants me. It makes me feel as though I can do anything.

Slowly, I bend my legs at the knees, parting my thighs to show him my core. Immediately, his cock jumps again, and a deep rumble reverberates in his chest.

"Beautiful," he growls. "Perfect."

With our eyes locked, he removes his own shirt and pants, standing gloriously naked before him as he rakes his eyes down my body once more.

"Tell me what you want."

"I want you to make love to me," I tell him immediately, my voice soft and breathy. My intention clear.

Dropping to his knees, he climbs over my body, planting soft kisses along the way until his eyes, once again meet mine, and his cock presses lightly at my entrance.

"Say it again," he murmurs, gazing down at me with rapt attention as he takes his weight, effortlessly on his arms.

"Make love to me," I whisper, running my fingertips lightly over his back.

"Are you ready Etta?" he asks, pushing himself slightly inside of me. I know that this time he's asking me if I'm ready for him. For everything that being with him will entail. And right now in this moment, I know I would do anything to be with him.

"I'm ready," I respond.

He slides himself inside me, stretching and filling my depths. I gasp out at his size as I adjust around him, and he starts to move through my slick juices.

"Oh, Etta. You're so wet."

Rocking my hips along with his thrusts, I take him in over and over again, my mind spinning as the arousal inside me builds. This is so much more than anything I have experienced before, and I understand why Damien objected to fucking me. This could never be classed as a fuck, the emotion, the movement. The way our bodies connect so perfectly – everything – is so much more.

"Damien," I pant, as my orgasm threatens to burst, gripping at his biceps as he skilfully thrusts, in and out, slow and perfect.

I'm blown away. Every cell in my body is buzzing, and it's as if the air has thickened as emotion rolls around us, wrapping us in our own private cocoon.

"Etta," he groans, pushing deep inside me, continuing to thrust as I whimper, gripping him tightly, so close to the edge. "I want you to come with me inside you," he whispers.

I was already on the brink, but the need in his voice pushes me over the edge. "Damien!" I call out, my hips jerking as my orgasm rips through me.

"Look at me baby. Look at me while you come."

My eyes fly open and find his as I shudder beneath him, my insides pulsing. I'm just in time to watch his face soften as he spills his own release inside me, our eyes connected in our most carnal moment. He's beautiful above me, and I feel our bond grow so much deeper in that shared moment.

His thrusts slow down, as he dips his head and takes my quivering mouth in his. The power of what we just experienced, causes me to shake. I've never imagined sex could actually feel this…transcendent.

We lay there together, naked and wrapped around each other, on the blue mats of the dojo, for an immeasurable amount of time, kissing and touching, lavishing the other with our passion, so raw and primal that neither of us seems to want to end this moment.

Finally though, we have to. Eventually the gym is going to open to the public, and the last thing we want is for my father to come in here and find us like this. Eighteen or not, it might be enough for him to lock me up and throw away the key.

With the strength of a man twice his size, he lifts us together off the mat. I keep my legs wrapped tightly around him, not wanting to break our connection until I have to. He carries me to the shower room and turns on the water, waiting for it to turn warm before stepping us under the spray. He moves to lift me off himself, but I wrap my legs even tighter around him.

"Stay," I murmur, gripping him with my internal muscles.

With a grunt, he leans me up against the tiled wall. I feel his erection stiffen again, pressing against my walls as he moves inside me. His movement this time much faster than before. My body jolts with each thrust, his pubic bone pressing right up against my clit.

"I could be inside you forever," he growls. "You're so tight. So perfect."

My body once again explodes, and I moan, shuddering as I spasm around him.

"Etta," he moans out, pulsing inside me.

When the shudders die down and our breathing returns to normal, he tries to move back again. But once again, I cling to him. "I don't want this to end."

"Etta, you've got me. This is never going to end. I'm never going to let you go. You are mine and I am yours. There is nothing that can change that now." He kisses me softly, the water still pouring down over us. "But you need to let go. I need to work today."

"Oh," I respond, feeling a little dejected. I had hoped that we could spend the day together as well.

Releasing my grip around him, I allow him to lower me to the ground and remove his shaft from inside me. I feel empty now without him. I want him back.

"Are you doing someone's portrait?" I ask, as he starts to rub soap over my body.

"Yes," he responds, rubbing his hands over my stomach, gently kissing my shoulder.

"Can I come and watch you some time?"

"No." His hands slide between my thighs, washing away our combined juices as they spill out of me.

My eyes flutter closed and my breathing thickens again, but I fight to keep my mind clear. "Will you do a portrait of me then? I want to see what you do."

"One day."

"One day?"

He nods, obviously not willing to continue the conversation as he angles the shower nozzle to hit me more directly so he can wash the suds off my skin then his.

"Stay warm," he says, stepping out of the stream. "I need to get our clothes and some towels."

When he returns, he follows the same routine he did last night, although this time he helps me dress. Even going so far as to help me into my shoes.

You'd think it would be strange having someone else dress you. But there's something about the way he does it. It's not as if he thinks I'm incapable. He does it because he wants to, it's an act of love.

Love… there's that word again. We made love, there are acts of love… but is this thing love? Or is it just an intensified version of lust?

I know that I feel a great need to be around him. But, I don't know exactly what my feelings are right now – it's all too much to qualify at this stage. All I can do is enjoy the ride, and put a name to it when these initial feelings die down. Even though right now, it doesn't feel like they possibly could.

13

"What are your plans today?" Damien asks, as he pulls up in front of my house.

"Well, I had planned to spend the day in your bed with you. But…" I shrug, lowering my lashes as I turn my head to the side.

"Etta," he croons, his voice rolling through me like a favourite song. "That's not possible."

"I know… work, right?"

"Yes."

Sighing, I move to unclip my seatbelt, although I'm stopped when his hand clasps over the top of mine.

"What are your plans?" he repeats.

"I'll probably just hang out here and study, I suppose."

"Alright. Make sure you have your phone with you. I'm going to call you later."

"Of course," I whisper, glancing down at his hand, still covering mine.

He lifts my hand up to his mouth, pressing it to his lips, inhaling deeply. "Wait there," he tells me, getting out of the car.

He walks around the car and opens the back door, removing my bag, before opening my door and reaching over me to unclick my belt.

Taking my hand again, he helps me out of the car, pausing for a moment to kiss me gently, tenderly.

 He then leads me to the front door, digging into my bag for my keys. "This is nice," he says, turning the oval shaped key ring over in his hands as he reads the inscription. "Was it a gift?"

"It was," I tell him, not really wanting to admit who it's from.

He looks at it for a moment longer, before unlocking the door for me and pushing it open. "I'll call you. Ok?" he reminds me.

"I'll be waiting," I tell him, rising up on my tiptoes to plant a kiss on the end of his nose.

Immediately, his hands slide around my waist and he pulls me close to him, burying his face in my hair.

"Not that I'm complaining. But, don't you have to work?"

Groaning, he releases me, kissing me one last time before leaving me to head back to his car.

"I'll call you," he says again.

"Ok," I laugh, standing at the door and watching him until he has driven out of sight.

"Someone seems very happy with herself," Kensi says as I shut the door behind me. I can't seem to stop smiling. "Have a good night?"

"I did. The best." I grin, moving toward the couch where she's sitting. "Oh, hello," I say as Aaron, who's sitting on the opposite couch comes into view. Suddenly I feel like I've been caught out, as if what I just did with Damien was wrong.

"Hey. Can we talk?" Aaron asks, rising from his seat.

"Sure," I say, a nervousness flitting through my stomach as I take him outside to sit in our small courtyard.

"I tried to call you last night because I wasn't going to make it back here for that party, but I couldn't get through."

"Sorry, I…"

"I know – you decided to go to the city. Kensi told me when I dropped around this morning to apologise for standing you up."

"Aaron. I'm sorry. I was supposed to text you while we were on the train."

"No big deal I guess. In a way, we stood each other up."

An awkwardness settles between us as we sit in the sun of the late morning, listening to the birds chirping around us. My eyes drift over to Aaron, my friend, and a man who holds a sizeable chunk of my heart, as the sun lights his features, glowing off his light hair.

He wears a pair of khaki cargo shorts, and a white t-shirt, displaying a black and white image of a skull in a moon, with a pirate ship in the foreground. Crossing one leg over the other, ankle to knee, he lets out his breath before returning his gaze to me.

"I know you were at Damien's, Etta," he states.

I freeze. Not sure what it is I should say to him.

"Jeremy saw you get home with him."

"Oh…" My chest seems to clench as my head starts to ache. I don't want to hurt Aaron. I couldn't bear it if he exited my life. He means too much to me.

"Are you… seeing him now?" he asks, although I'm pretty sure he'd rather it if he never knew.

"Uh… yeah… I am. I'm sorry Aaron. I know you thought…"

"That you and I would finally have a chance? Yeah, I did. But it looks like I've lost out to him yet again," he states.

"What do you mean?"

"You know Bec? That girl we saw him with when I moved in. She and I dated for a while during first year and well… Damien decided he wanted her. Some guys just take what they want, while the rest of us are left standing there wondering what the hell just happened."

"Did they start dating?" I ask, wondering if once again, Damien has misled me.

"No," he says, shaking his head as he creases his brow. "Damien doesn't date. They seemed to become fuck buddies. She really changed though, became a little promiscuous. I don't know... she wasn't like that before. There's just something about that guy. He ruins people."

"I don't think he means to."

"Just be careful Etta. I've never known him to have a girlfriend. It's just a whole string of women whom he uses and moves on from. I can't tell you how many of them I've found crying in the hallway because he won't see them anymore." He shakes his head. "I just don't get why women like him so much. I mean, he just seems like such a jerk."

"He's just... different," I try to explain. Although at the same time, I feel that doubt creep back inside my soul as I worry that Damien isn't being honest with me – that ultimately, he's just going to move on to the next pretty girl who turns his head.

"You don't need to explain, Etta. It's the story of my life. Maybe I should start being the bad guy for a change."

"No Aaron. You don't have a mean bone in your body. Don't talk like that."

He shrugs a little and looks the other way, squinting into the sun.

"Are you angry with me?" I ask after a while, worried about our friendship.

"No. Never. We'll always be friends Etta."

"I can't tell you how glad I am to hear you say that," I breathe.

We sit together quietly for a moment longer, neither of us really knowing what to say.

"Well," he starts, breaking the silence. "I did come around here feeling guilty, prepared to take you to a movie to apologise… it's still on the table if you want to go with me? I just don't feel bad anymore so… I reckon you should buy the ice creams."

Laughing, I nod, relieved that he isn't going to let my dating Damien get in the way of what we have. "Yeah, I think I can handle that."

***

"So have you done much about that research assignment? I've got all these papers to read through, and I have no idea what I'm going to do with them all," Aaron tells me, as we leave the movie theatre.

"No, I've been so caught up with my birthday, and the move that I haven't done much at all."

"You want to come and go through my stuff? It might give you some ideas on what you want to do," he suggests.

"Yeah, I wouldn't mind that actually," I respond, climbing into the passenger seat of his Lancer.

For a moment I just sit there, wondering what the pinging noise is when he puts the key in the ignition. "You need to do your seatbelt up," he reminds me.

"Oh!" I exclaim, laughing at myself inwardly – how easy it is to get used to having someone do things for you.

Once we reach his apartment block, I can't help but notice the music coming from Damien's place. I know that he's working, so I do my best to keep myself from knocking on the door. But I really want to see what's going on in there.

"That was playing when I left too," Aaron says as he slides the key into his door.

My eyes stray toward it, wishing I had x-ray vision.

"Do you know exactly what he does?" I ask, remembering the earlier conversation we had.

"I only know the rumours, and what I see," he tells me as he pushes the door open.

"What do you see?" I ask, following him in.

"Lots of women Etta. Lots of women."

"He said the rumours aren't true. They're not paying him to sleep with them. He does their portraits."

"And you believe him?"

"Yes, I do."

He looks at me for a moment, studying my face. "It's your life Etta. I can't tell you how to live it, or who you can see. But you know I don't think Damien is a good guy."

Shifting uncomfortably on my feet, I look over his shoulder to anywhere in the room but at him. "How about you show me those papers?" I suggest, in an obvious subject change.

He stands in front of me for a moment longer, before conceding. "They're in the filing cabinet in my room," he tells me, his speech more like a sigh of disappointment than an actual sentence.

I follow him down the hallway towards his room and stand in the doorway as he rummages through the beige metal filing cabinet, muttering to himself about where he put them all.

"Aha! Here you go," he says, handing me a three-inch-thick manila folder. "That's everything I have. You can borrow it for the weekend if you like."

Flicking through the folder, I note that the papers cover a wide range of advertising principles. Some question morals in advertising, while others talk about the use of subliminal messages. "Wow, you've really pulled a lot of different topics," I comment.

"Yeah, I just have no idea which area to focus on," he says, shrugging his shoulders as he wrestles the drawer closed.

"Thank you Aaron," I say, as I continue to peruse their contents. "I really appreciate this. You've always been so wonderful to me."

Pressing his lips together in a tight smile as he nods his head, placing his hands on his hips. "It's no trouble Etta. Just know that I'm always here for you. Okay?"

I nod, closing the folder as a feeling of warmth blooms inside me for this man, who has been a great friend to me for so long. I understand the disappointment he must be feeling right now. I mean, the only reason we broke up was because of my father's rules. I also know, that if Damien hadn't entered the picture, Aaron and I would most likely be dating again.

Stepping toward him, I wrap my arms around him briefly. "I know, Aaron and thank you. I'd hate to think of my life without you."

"Not going to happen," he promises, returning my embrace.

"I'd better get going," I inform him, pulling away. "I've obviously got a lot of reading to do." I wave the folder, gently from side to side to demonstrate.

"You don't want me to drive you?" he says.

"No, it's only a short walk, and it's a nice day," I point out. "Thanks for the movie too. It was fun." With a promise to meet up for lunch or another pool competition soon, I bid him farewell and thank him again for his help.

Making my way into the hallway, I can once again hear the music. It's not some heavy metal rock beat - it's jazz. It's the kind of music that makes you want to move your body. Standing outside his door, curiosity gets the better of me, and I press my ear to the wood and listen.

I can hear his voice, soft and coaxing as it says, "Open them for me. That's it. Good girl. Now show me how you touch yourself."

Sucking in my breath, I jump back from the door, sure that I must've heard wrong. With shaky breath, I lean in again, just as I start to hear a woman moan.

All of a sudden, my world stops. That fucking bastard! And to think, I almost thought I was falling in love with him.

With anger pumping my blood around my body, I drop my bag and the folder where I'm standing then throw myself at the door, banging on it with my fists.

"Let me in, you fucker!" I scream. As I take another breath, the door bursts open, and Damien stands before me, his eyes wide and his brow furrowed.

"What the hell are you doing?" he growls.

"Putting a stop to whatever the hell is going on in here," I yell, pushing past him and into the living area.

That's when I see Bec, standing in the middle of the room, nothing but a swathe of burgundy fabric covering her body.

"What's going on?" she asks Damien, an edge of panic to her voice as her eyes dart from him to me.

"Get out!" I screech. It's like that satiny fabric is the red flag, and I'm the bull. I don't know what comes over me, but I charge her, screaming like some sort of banshee as I grab her by the hair and drag her out, kicking and screaming about her clothes and her bag.

Depositing her in the hallway, I return to the apartment, spot her things and throw them out on the floor next to her.

"Damien!" she shrieks, her eyes wide as she looks to him for help.

"Stay the fuck away from him," I growl at her. It's then that I notice Aaron has stepped out into the hall.

"Etta?" he says quietly, looking as though he can't really believe his eyes.

"Just… don't," I say, holding my hand up to him as I pick my bag up and gather the papers I dropped.

"She's a fucking pyscho!" Bec yells, scrambling to stand up and keep herself covered.

"And you're a fucking whore!" I shout back, completely enraged at what I just heard and witnessed. I don't care if that's how he makes money. I don't care. I can't handle this.

"Henrietta," Damien warns, reaching down to take the papers from my hands.

"Don't touch me!" I yell, throwing the papers about the hallway as I push to standing. "I heard her moaning Damien. Moaning! And I heard you asking her to–" My voice catches in my throat, and I need to take a breath to calm down before I can speak

221

again. "Don't call me. Don't fucking come near me – we're done!"

Turning on my heels, I rush out of there. I'm hanging by a thread and need to get home before I lose it entirely in front of everyone.

I run the whole way home, the fight to keep my tears at bay, causes my chest to ache and my eyes to burn. I find myself fumbling with the lock on our front door as I try to get inside. Into the sanctuary of my room.

"Etta? Are you alright?" Jessica asks me through my locked door.

"I...I'm fine," I choke out between sobs.

"Do you need to talk? Are you upset?"

"No. I'm just tired. It's been a long day," I lie.

For a moment, she doesn't respond, and I wonder if she's going to call me on my fib. "Ok, well we're just about to head out. Do you need anything at the shops?" she asks.

"No, I'm fine. Thanks," I call back, as cheery as possible, relieved when I hear her move away, so I can rebury my face in my pillow.

After a good hour of sobbing, my phone starts to sing from inside my bag. I know it's Damien.

Rising from the bed, I retrieve my phone and switch it off. I don't want to hear his excuses – I heard enough this afternoon.

I do everything I can to try and keep busy, to try and stop myself from turning my phone back on to see if he's still trying to call me. I try to be strong, focusing on what I heard and the fact that Aaron – the nicest guy I know – thinks Damien is no good.

My resolve lasts maybe ten minutes before I'm powering my phone on again. The moment the screen loads, it bursts to life in my hand with Damien's name and number displayed on the screen. I send him straight to voicemail and a moment later, a message comes through telling me I have fifteen messages.

With a shaking hand, I dial through to my message service.

The messages all follow a similar vein. They start off calm. *"It's me. We need to talk."*

Before becoming more demanding. *"Answer the phone Henrietta." "Answer the phone!"*

And then he becomes frustrated. *"Fuck!"*

"Shit," I hiss, as I hear the last message. - *"I'm coming over."*

As soon as I switch off the phone, I rush over to the window and look out, I can hear his car coming.

"Shit," I hiss again, jumping back from the window, running my fingers through my hair as I try to decide what I want to do.

"Henrietta?!" he calls from outside, banging on the door.

"Go away," I call from the other side. "I don't want to do this anymore Damien."

"You can't back out now Henrietta. This isn't ending."

"Yes it is. I thought I could handle it, but I can't. I heard you, and I heard her. I can't..." I stop, my heart constricting in my chest as I remember the moans. "You said I could trust you. You said it was just portraits."

"It is. Open the door."

"Portraits don't moan Damien!" I sob.

"Henrietta!" he yells, trying the door knob then slamming his body into the door. "Open the door or I'm going to break it!"

Stepping back, I cover my mouth, watching the door rattle with each thump. I don't want to open the door, but god help me if my housemates come home to it broken in.

"Alright!" I screech, my breath catching as I turn the tumblers to unlock the door.

The moment it opens, he slams his body against mine. I don't even get time to react before I'm pressed up against the wall, and his mouth finds mine, kissing me aggressively.

I push my body against him, my hands on his shoulders as I try to fight. But it's Damien, and the moment he's in my headspace, I can't seem to say no to him. Slowly, my body starts to relax and my hands curl into fists, gripping the fabric of his black t-shirt, as I attempt to pull him into me.

224

Small whimpers begin to escape my throat as his hand slides down to cup my buttocks, pulling me closer to him. His erection presses firmly into my hip, and I find myself rubbing against it.

"You are mine, and I am yours Etta. Don't forget that," he growls, as he grabs the waistband of my panties and drags them down my legs.

With a swift movement, he has his arm under my thigh, lifting my leg as he frees his cock, deftly slamming it into me.

"Oh god!" I gasp, as he fills me, pumping his hips skilfully, driving his shaft back and forth, frantically inside me.

"You don't get to end this," he growls, thrusting into me forcefully, causing me to explode. Gripping on to him, I moan, rolling my head back as I feel him pulse inside me.

Calming down, he kisses me softly then pulls out of me, moving his hand to cup between my legs.

"You're the only one I do this with," he whispers, as he pushes his fingers inside of me, rubbing our combined orgasm between my thighs. "You're the only one I think about. The only one I see." His fingers circle my clit, causing me to pant, to whimper. "The only one I want. Come home with me. Stay with me. I want you by my side. I want you in my bed."

Moaning, my body takes over my mind, clouding it with whatever pheromones Damien produces.

"Do you want me, Etta?" he asks, his voice warm and soft, like

225

gentle fingertips, caressing my mind.

"I want you," I gasp, rocking against his hand as his fingers move around my clit, sliding into my opening, then pulsing back again, over and over.

"Then why did you come to my apartment? I told you to stay away," he growls, his fingers pumping faster as he adds another.

"I...I..." I gasp, unable to find my words while my body and mind are screaming with arousal.

"You said you would be here. Studying. I need to be able to trust you, Henrietta. This thing won't work without trust," he whispers, his fingers pushing inside me, rubbing against that spot that makes my eyes roll back, and my body ready to explode. "Why were you at my apartment?"

"I was...I was..." I pant, as he adds another finger, filling me further. "Oh god!" I cry out, shuddering around his hand, struggling to stay standing.

Languidly, he continues to move his fingers inside me. "Tell me."

"I was with Aaron," I admit.

"What were you doing with him?"

"He had... oh god, I can't think with you doing that," I gasp, my orgasm building inside me again.

"What were you doing with him?" he repeats, ignoring my struggle as he pushes his hand in deeper.

Whimpering, I try my best to form an answer. "He had... some papers for me. I went and saw a movie with him."

"Did he try to fuck you?" he asks, with an upward thrust.

"No. He'd never... it's not like that with us..." I pant, my head feeling drunk as he removes his hand and starts to roll his fingers around my clit again.

"When you tell me your plans. I want your plans. They don't change Henrietta. I need to know where you are," he whispers, slipping his fingers into me once more. "Do you understand?"

"I... oh god... yes, I understand," I gasp as his whole hand slips inside me, pressing firmly against my g-spot.

Lowering his mouth to meet mine, I struggle to move my mouth against his. I'm so overwhelmed with the sensation of his hand moving inside me that I can't even see straight. "Good girl," he whispers as I explode again, my orgasm ripping through me, causing me to fall against him, exhausted.

Slowly, he removes his hand from between my legs, and bends down, scooping me up into his arms to carry me up the stairs. I lay limply against his chest, every ounce of my energy spent. I can't even remember why I was upset anymore. It all seems so trivial. Being in his presence seems to make everything ok. When he's near, I don't care about anything else – just him, and what he does to me, body and mind.

As he carries me to the bathroom, I stay quiet, laying my head against his chest, listening to his heartbeat and his breathing. Once inside, he settles me on the edge of the bathtub and runs the taps in the vanity sink.

Using a washcloth, he cleans between my legs, his movement gentle yet deliberate. Feeling a swell of emotion toward him, I run my hand over his head – through his hair and down his face to cup his cheek. Closing his eyes, he inhales deeply, kissing my palm.

"We need to start using protection," I tell him. "I'm not on any birth control."

"We'll be fine," he says, continuing our clean up.

"How do you know?"

"Because I do." It's all he says, before he lifts me up again and walks me to my room. Setting me down on the bed, he begins to rummage through my drawers, pulling out clothes and setting them on the bed beside me.

"What are you doing?" I ask. I thought he was just getting something for me to wear – I'm still in the dress I wore last night and nothing else, my underwear probably still on the floor near the door.

"Packing," he states simply, moving to my wardrobe and opening the doors. Reaching up, he removes my suitcase from the top shelf and drops it on the floor by his feet, going through my hanging clothes and dropping items in.

"Damien. I don't know about this…" I start. "I only just moved in."

"It's alright. I'll bring you back. You're not moving out. You're just… staying with me. I need you with me. Here," he says, walking over to me, a pair of jeans in his hands.

"Do you have something against underwear?" I ask.

"On you? Yes," he states, reaching down and pulling my dress off my body. He selects a fitted navy blue singlet top and slides it over my head, before helping me into my jeans, holding his hand against my mound as he pulls up the zip, to protect me from any accidental catches. "There," he finishes, sliding his fingers through my curls as he removes his hand from my pants.

"What am I supposed to tell my roommates? I haven't even spent the night here yet," I ask, as he places the last of the clothing, and a few toiletries in the bag.

"That you'll see them on Friday." Zipping my suitcase, he lifts it and holds his hand out to me expectantly.

I take it. Of course I take it. Can I do anything but say yes to this man? Something tells me that I can't, and for the life of me, I wish I could explain why.

14

"What are you doing?" I ask in a whisper, watching as Damien draws an intricate floral design over my outer thigh. I'm lying on my side, naked on his bed after spending hours in his arms, lost in his body, in this feeling we share.

It's almost 3am, my body is buzzing from a night filled with love making and refusing to sleep, for fear I could miss a single moment with him.

"Branding you," he murmurs, planting a kiss, just next to where he's begun drawing a butterfly.

"It'll wash off, won't it?" I ask, grinning as I watch the concentration on his face – the gentle crease of his dark brow, the slight narrowing of his light brown eyes, the pull of his lip by his teeth. He's beautiful.

"Eventually." He smiles slightly, as he blows gently over my skin, drying the ink.

"What kind of a pen is that?"

"Don't move. You'll ruin it."

"Damien," I complain, but I stay still anyway. I wouldn't dare risk ruining this – he's drawing flowers and vines curving down my thigh, and to my knee. He's adding butterflies to it at the

230

moment that look like they're about to set down upon the flowers.

"Yes Etta?" he asks, glancing up at me, his mouth curved into a half grin.

My eyes drag over his body, lean and carved, as it flexes and ripples with his movement. "It's beautiful," I whisper, causing his grin to broaden.

"Not as beautiful as you are," he informs me.

"*You* make me feel beautiful," I confide, my voice soft and intimate.

"Don't you think you are?" he asks, placing the cap back on his pen.

"No actually, I don't. I've always felt... big. I mean, I know there's nothing wrong with my weight or anything – I'm fit, but I'm big. I wish I was dainty like a lot of other girls, I wish I was hourglass curvy. But I'm not. A lifetime of being called an 'Amazon' makes you feel like people see you as this towering angry woman."

"You see being called an Amazon a bad thing?"

"Well, isn't it? It makes me feel like a bit of a freak, then the red hair to top it off..." I roll my eyes and huff out my breath, turning onto my back. "We don't need to go through my list of insecurities."

He climbs on top of me, and kisses me gently, my lips swollen and tender, but never having enough. "Most men find the idea of Amazon women very sexy," he murmurs, planting soft kisses between my breasts. "They're tall, strong, beautiful, intelligent – everything wonderful in a woman. They can take care of themselves, and don't need men. So to capture the heart of one, is very special indeed. To be the man who protects a woman who is capable of protecting herself... you'd be hard pressed finding a man who didn't find the idea of that hot."

"You're making all that up," I giggle, but loving every word.

"Am I?" he asks, rolling off me, and the bed. "Come," he says, holding his hand out and helping me up, leading me to the bathroom. "Now, look in the mirror. I want you to see what I see."

"I only see you," I smile, my eyes locked with his as I drink him in, every line, every detail of his beautiful stubbled face.

"Look at yourself. I'll tell you what I see." He sweeps his hands through my hair, smoothing it out and settling it over my left shoulder. "I see beautiful, soft milky skin." He traces his fingertips over the curve of my neck, and I can't help but admire his long fingers as they drift over my flesh.

"Not me Etta, look at yourself," he whispers. I force myself to focus on my skin, instead of his fingers as he continues. "Your hair, is like a silken blanket, soft and warm as it falls about your face, accentuating the rose that blooms in your cheeks and over your lips when I touch you."

My breathing quickens, and my skin heats beneath his

fingertips as he runs them down my back and over the curve of my behind. "Your body, soft, and firm in all the right places, tight and warm where it counts," he whispers, his own breathing growing heavy as his hands slide between my thighs. "Wet, every time I touch you." His fingers slide through my folds, my juices silken beneath his touch. "Look into your eyes Etta. See what I see."

As his fingers dive into my depths, I try to keep my focus locked on my own reflection. But it's hard. My eyes want to see him – the object of my desire. "Your eyes," he reminds me, a slight reprimand apparent in his tone. "Don't look away."

Pulsing his fingers inside me, he continues to whisper in my ear. "Do you see it? Your skin flushing, heating up because of what I'm doing to you? Look into your eyes, watch yourself come."

With my hands leaning on the vanity, I do as he asks, watching as the blood rushes into my face, and fighting to keep focus when my vision clouds with ecstasy. Guiding my legs apart, he tilts my pelvis back and enters me from behind, reaching his hand around front to tease my clit.

"Oh!" I call, my eyes rolling back and losing focus as my orgasm mounts.

"Keep watching Etta. See what I see," he commands, thrusting himself inside me.

I force myself to look in the mirror again, my eyes shining, my face pink, my lips red, and I shudder, my orgasm bursting forth as I moan and grip him internally.

"There is nothing more beautiful to me than your face when you come," he whispers.

Watching myself as I come, I think I see what it is he sees. In the moment, I am completely free, there is no holding anything back. It's just sheer bliss and raw emotion. You can see exactly how I feel, and the realisation of it hits me hard – this is all happening way too soon.

15

"I need to talk to you about Bec," I say, the next morning when we wake up. It seems that whenever I wake, my questions and doubts are sitting at the forefront of my mind. "What's going on between you and her?"

He turns onto his side to face me, running his fingers up and down my arm as he takes his time responding.

"I'm not having sex with her if that's what you're asking," he says, his voice low and soft as he moves his hand and repositions my hair so it's hanging behind me.

"It didn't sound like you were having sex with her. It sounded like you were watching her masturbate," I state frankly.

Taking a deep breath - that I'm coming to realise means that he's keeping information from me - he sits up in the bed.

"I think we should get ready for training," he tells me over his shoulder.

"I don't want to go to training. I want you to tell me what's going on."

Standing up, he opens his drawers and starts pulling clothes on. "What do you want me to say, Henrietta? You know what you heard, and I'm not going to lie. But I'm not going to talk about it either. She doesn't mean anything to me."

"Have you had sex with her before?"

"Please don't start asking me those kinds of questions. I'm not interested in who you've been with before me."

"I don't want you seeing her anymore," I tell him. The idea of them spending any more time together is eating me alive.

"She's in my class. I can't make that promise."

"Then just don't bring her here!" I demand aggressively. "Don't do whatever the hell it was you were doing with her. I don't want *your* eyes on *her* naked body! Is that clear? I don't want to see, hear, or even suspect that you are around her for any reason other than school work. Or I swear Damien, I'll..."

"You'll what Etta?" he asks softly.

"I don't know. But the thought makes me crazy. God only knows what I'll do if it's a reality," I whisper hoarsely, realising that I'm shaking.

Sitting back down on the bed, he takes me in his arms and shushes me gently. "If it makes you feel better, I'll tell her no more portraits. But you have to understand that you are the only girl I want. The only one I care about. You have nothing to be upset about."

"Just keep her away from me." I wrap my arms tightly around his chest, clutching at him as I bury my face in his warmth.

"Alright. I'll keep her away," he concedes, holding me a moment onger before moving back from me to lift my chin so our eyes meet. "As long as you come training with me." A grin pulling at his mouth as he tries not to smile.

Slapping him against his chest, I then fold my arms tightly against mine. "I'm being serious Damien. Don't try and blackmail me."

"I'm serious too. If you're going to keep attacking every girl you see me with, I want you to be trained well enough to do it quickly," he tells me as seriously as he can.

"You're a dick," I say, trying not to smile myself.

"Don't call me that. I wouldn't call you a vagina," he points out, extending his arm toward me.

I take his hand willingly as he pulls me from the bed and into his arms, his hand sliding over my bare skin as I lean into him. "I think the opposite word for dick is a bit ruder than vagina."

"Really?" he laughs. "And what is this rude word you speak of?"

"I'm not saying. It's too rude," I murmur, feeling a little embarrassed over something as simple as a swear word.

Gently, he pinches my skin, tickling me, causing me to squirm against him as he continues to tell me that I need to say the word.

"Stop! Stop!"

"Tell me the naughty word Etta," he laughs. "I'm not stopping until you do."

"Cunt! The word is cunt! Just stop!" I giggle, laughing as he lifts me off the floor and sends us both tumbling on a heap onto his bed.

"You're right. That is a horrible word," he whispers, holding himself above me as he leans down to kiss my neck, his hands travelling over my skin as his kisses move down my body, and over my mound. Opening my legs, he slides off the side of the bed onto his knees on the floor, pulling me so my legs hang over his shoulders.

I feel his breath, warm against my core, and hold mine, waiting for his mouth. "Etta?" he murmurs, causing me to open my eyes and lift my head to look down at him.

"Hmmm?" I respond, expecting that he wants me to tell him what I want.

"Get dressed. We're going training."

"That. Is. So. Mean," I say, as I lay there, spread eagled on the bed as he stands in front of me. "So. Mean."

"No, Etta. It's a promise of things to come."

My insides clench as I close my legs and sit in front of him. "Are you really going to make me wait?" I pout.

"If you come training then after I will make love to you until you can't stand it anymore."

My pout turns into a grin. "I have class after lunch. We have until then."

238

"Then we'd better not waste any time. Come on."

He pulls me up from the bed and hands me some clothes to train in, a pair of grey tracksuit pants and one of his black t-shirts. I inhale as I pull it over my head, even though it's clean, it still has a smell that reminds me of him. Although perhaps it's just the washing products he uses…

In around five minutes, we're already getting into his car and heading to the dojo to train. Secretly, I hope our training session ends up much like our last one – one move and then sex on the mats, and in the shower. I can handle that kind of training. However, Damien has other ideas.

"Henrietta, would you do this properly? This isn't a joke," he says calmly.

"Come on Damien, we've been here for nearly an hour already. This is your thing. It's not mine."

"I seem to recall it being very much your thing. You were very good when you were here."

"You remember me from when I used to train?"

"Of course I do. You're the Sensei's daughter. Everyone knew you. Plus, who could miss that hair of yours," he grins.

"Well, I wasn't good because I wanted to be. I was good because I was trained more often than anyone else in the club. But I quit remember. Besides what we've done lately, I haven't trained properly in years."

"I'm sure your father didn't just let you sit around learning nothing all these years. Did he?"

"No. He didn't," I admit. "But I have been very resistant to learning."

"I'll bet you know more than you're letting on. Otherwise you wouldn't be able to handle the advanced stuff I've been making you do. How about disarming someone attacking you with a knife. Did he show you that?"

I stand there with my hands on my hips, tired from a lack of sleep, and the training we've already done, chewing my lips as I decide if I want to answer. If I give in now, and really train properly, this opens up a whole new door. It means I have to trust him enough to let him be my teacher. It means that I have to stop looking at this as a bit of temporary fun that could end up with us tumbling on the mats.

Closing my eyes, I take a breath. "Yes, he did teach me that."

"Then show me," he says, moving over to the wall and removing the plastic training knife. He walks over to me, tossing the knife from hand to hand. "I want you to take this seriously Henrietta. We're not here to play."

He lunges at me with the knife, keeping his distance so he can assess how I respond. A grin curls over his mouth as I flinch, preparing myself to deflect his arm.

"I knew you remembered more than you let on," he smiles, lunging toward me again. Once again, it's a tease.

"I'm rusty. I'm not inept," I reply, concentrating on his movement, knowing that if I'm not ready, he'll get me with the blade – even though it's plastic, it can still hurt when it jabs you.

He lunges at me with the knife, aiming for my stomach, and I dodge, pushing against his arm, as I grab hold of his wrist, twisting my body around so that I'm controlling his movement and the weapon.

A slight grin curves on his mouth as I direct the knife toward his throat. His role as the attacker is to behave as though the knife is real and try to keep it away from himself. So, the movement knocks him off balance, and as he falls, I manipulate his wrist, forcing him to roll his body and give up the weapon.

He lets out a chuckle as I put my knee into his back and remove the knife from his hand. "You've been holding out on me," he says, as I slide off his back and sit down on the ground next to him.

"Now will you take me home and make love to me until I can't stand it anymore?" I ask seriously, looking down at him as he rolls over onto his back and meets my eyes, smiling triumphantly. "What are you grinning so broadly about?"

"You're training," he states.

Rolling my eyes, I stand up and head toward the door. "I'll meet you in the car then?" I say, refusing to discuss the fact that I just had my first proper training session in a very long time. There were no games, no sexual escapades, just pure training, and I have to admit it felt good.

Before I can make it to the door, Damien rushes up behind me and scoops me up, flipping me over his shoulder like I'm a rag doll. Just like I did the last time he did this, I squeal – of course I do. He caught me completely by surprise.

"Put me down you brute," I laugh.

But he just gives me a tap on the butt, causing me to squeal again and beat my hands against his arse as he carries me toward the door.

"Well... at least the view is nice from here," I state, giving up my fight and relaxing over his shoulder as we exit the gym.

"What's going on?" I hear a very familiar voice ask.

Damien slides me off his shoulder and sets me down on the gravel, an audible crunch sounds as I find my footing and straighten myself and my hair. I hesitate for a moment before turning around. "Hi dad," I say. as the looming figure of my father stands before us, hands on hips as he waits for an answer.

"We were just training," Damien explains, his voice calm and collected. I find it amazing that he can act this way around my father when I'm having a short panic attack.

"Keep it that way," my father says, looking pointedly at Damien. "Henrietta. Can I speak to you inside for a moment?"

"Um, sure," I answer, leaving Damien outside as I follow him into the reception area.

"How are you settling in to your new place?"

"Fine. It's nice. I like it there."

"Come to dinner at the house on Wednesday. Your mother misses you."

"Of course."

He leans behind the counter and pulls out a plastic binder, thick with paperwork before he looks up at me again.

"Look after yourself ok?" he says, letting me know he's said all he needs to. Although I find it strange that he isn't saying anything about the fact that he just found out I was training again.

"You too dad. I'll see you Wednesday."

"Is everything ok?" Damien asks, as I walk outside.

"Yeah," I nod quickly. "He just wants me to have dinner with him and mum on Wednesday."

"Fair enough," he says, opening the car door for me to get inside. "What time is your class?" he asks on the way back to his apartment.

"Two," I tell him, as I admire the muscles in his forearm when he changes gears in the traffic, feeling my insides clench just thinking about all the things we could be doing until that time. "What about you? Do you have anything on today?"

"Just you." He looks at me momentarily, the heat in his eyes is enough to send my heart racing.

The moment he parks the car, I unclick my belt myself and jump out of the car, before the engine is even turned off. "Hurry," I call out to him, giving him a knowing grin before I spin on my heel and run for the foyer door.

He's fast, and by the time I'm in the stairwell, I hear him coming up behind me. Glancing over my shoulder, I laugh as I quicken my pace, noting the hungry look in his eyes as he pursues me up the second flight of stairs.

"Gotcha," he growls, his hands gripping my waist and lifting me off the ground, spinning me so I face him. Squealing with laughter as we collapse on the staircase together, I can't help but notice how he holds me to him to soften my fall. "I've got you," he says again, but in a whisper this time as he brushes his lips over mine, his arms sliding around my body as he lifts me off the stairs and takes my mouth with his.

I wrap myself around him, legs and arms as he carries me up the last few steps, kissing me fervently as he slides his key in the door and lets us inside.

"I want you Etta. I can't stop wanting you," he murmurs, as we each tighten our grip around each other, it's verging on being painful, but I can't stop pulling at him. I dig my nails into his back through his shirt and just pull.

"Make love to me Damien," I gasp. "Make love to me right now and don't stop. I want you inside me. I want to feel you. Please."

244

He drops us to the floor, dragging my pants down my legs and pushing them to the side before sliding his hands underneath my arse and moving me like a doll so that my legs are over his shoulders. My back curves upward as he lifts my hips off the floor and drives his tongue between my folds then sucks firmly on my clit.

"Oh god," I gasp out, my arms splayed on the floor in support as I push down on his shoulders with my thighs, rocking myself against his mouth as he dines from my depths. His tongue swirling fiercely around my nub as he sucks and licks at me, holding me in position.

My whimpering increases as my orgasm builds, and I find myself bucking against his face as the sensation increases, setting my senses on fire. Just as I'm about to explode, his hands slide underneath my shirt, his long fingers curling around my ribs as he withdraws his mouth and lifts me toward him, repositioning his arms as I slide down his body and he captures my mouth in his, feeding me the taste of my own arousal as his tongue drives into my mouth fiercely and I feel as though I'm about to be devoured by him.

I don't think there's anything in this world I want more.

I slide my hands under his shirt, urging it upward as my fingers desire the contact of his flesh. "Take it off," I whisper, as I pull at the fabric and graze my teeth over the stubble on his chin.

"You too," he says, lifting his own shirt as his eyes smoulder looking at mine.

Together, we remove our shirts, each one drinking the sight of the other in. I crawl toward him, dipping my head as he starts to lean back and running my tongue from the line between his abs, all the way up and between his pecs, tasting his salt as I continue up his neck, my licks turning into soft, sucking kisses. Once again, I graze my teeth over his chin, loving the feel of his stubble as I make my way to his mouth, kissing him hungrily before pausing to look down at him.

"How is this even happening?" I whisper, as I hold myself over him, looking down into a set of eyes that seem to mirror that exact emotion in mine. This feeling is so much – maybe too much for such a short amount of time. My chest actually hurts from the desire I experience around him.

He reaches a hand up and lightly touches my face, before pulling at the elastic that secured my hair, so it falls like a curtain over one side of my face.

"I don't know. But it is," he says, rolling us over again so he's on top, shifting his weight to remove his pants and settle himself between my legs. As he pushes inside me, our eyes are locked and they stay that way as he thrusts back and forth languidly. I'm scared to blink, I don't want to miss a second of this… this thing we're sharing.

It's not love. I know it's not love. It feels more like… a compulsion – something I don't think I could stop. Even if I wanted to.

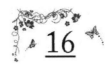

16

"Shit. I'm late," I say, getting out of the car when Damien drives me up to the uni. "I've got to run." Bouncing on my toes, I aim to kiss him on the cheek and then run toward the lecture halls where my class has already started.

"Not so fast," he says, gripping me by the waist. "Let me walk you."

"Damien, I need to run. I'm late," I insist, attempting to pull away.

He leans down and kisses me, "Relax. You can walk with me," he says, taking my hand in his before beginning the short walk from the car park to the main building.

Resting my head on his shoulder, I sigh as I walk beside him. "You're going to have to stop kissing me every time I object to something. It's not fair."

"I'd rather die than stop kissing you Henrietta," he says, taking my bag off my other shoulder and slinging it over his. The thought of this coming to pass causes my heart to clench painfully in my chest.

"Then don't ever stop," I whisper, pausing where we are on the footpath to press my lips to his, inhaling deeply to drink in his scent. I have this need to etch everything there is about him into my memory. I don't know why. Perhaps it's because I don't feel as though this could possibly be real. I mean, how does this even happen? Damien is so far out of my league, and so not the kind of guy you go crazy for…

"Would you still carry that if it were bright pink?" I ask, as we enter through the main doors of the building, heading toward the large curved staircase to ascend to the second floor.

"Of course," he smiles, as we come to a stop outside the correct room.

"This is it," I tell him quietly, noting that the door is closed, meaning that the lecture is well and truly underway.

"I'll meet you out front when you're done," he murmurs close to my ear, pressing his lips against my temple.

"Ok," I reply, quietly opening the door and slipping inside, refusing to take my eyes off him as he leans against the wall, his light eyes watching me hungrily, until the door clicks shut.

"Nice of you to join us. Will you hurry up and take your seat please?" the lecturer, Professor Aldricht asks curtly, pushing at the bridge of her dark framed glasses as she glares up at me, causing the entire class to turn around and take note of my tardiness.

"Sorry," I say, hurrying to my seat next to Aaron. "Hey," I say in greeting, as I sit down beside him.

"Hey," he says in return. It all seems normal enough, but his demeanour tells me he isn't very happy with me. For a moment I wonder what his problem is, but when I see the thick folder that I threw all over the hallway sitting on the seat beside him, I remember that he witnessed my whole 'Bec' outburst.

"Listen, I'm sorry about what happened the other day. I lost my cool," I whisper.

He pauses taking down notes from the lecture and looks at me frowning before leaning in to whisper as well. "You lost your cool? Etta. I have known you for nearly three years – not once have you behaved anything like that. That was… I don't even know what to call it. But it wasn't you. It wasn't the girl I know and care about."

"Would you like to come up and present this lecture Mr Stevens?" Professor Aldricht says, her hands on her hips as she pauses yet again.

"Sorry Ma'am," he says, clamping his lips together as he resumes his note taking.

We sit quietly and listen for a while, my mind ticking over, trying to find a way to justify my actions.

"It's not like she was the innocent party," I add, when Professor Aldricht turns her back to the lecture hall to demonstrate something on the whiteboard.

Aaron just looks at me, his eyebrows raised as he shakes his head but doesn't speak.

"What? She was in there *moaning* with *my* man," I expound, expecting that to somehow make him understand.

He drops his pen on the desktop, unable to keep quiet anymore as he whispers. "Oh my god. Did you actually hear what you just said?"

"That's it you two. Leave," Professor Aldricht demands. "Talk on your own time. Not everyone else's."

Gathering our things, we make our way out into the hall before continuing our conversation.

"Etta. I don't know what to say to you. You've been going out with this guy for what? A week? Maybe not even, and already I've seen you attack a girl. Not to mention the fact that you were late for class today. You are never late for class."

Placing my hands on my hips, I look over the railing and down to the first floor where some other students are milling about in the foyer, to distract myself from the disappointment in my friend's face.

"What do you want me to say Aaron? I already apologised. I know I lost it."

"You don't have to say anything. I'm just worried about you. I want you to be careful," he tells me, placing his gentle hand on my arm. When I turn back to him to meet his gaze, all I see is concern. Concern for me.

A pit forms in my stomach, just before all the hair on the back of my neck stands on end.

"Aaron," Damien nods, as he appears beside me, sliding his arm around my waist in propriety.

Aaron simply nods in response, before turning his attention back to me. "Listen, I'm going to go to the library. I brought the papers with me if you still want them. Look after yourself Etta. You know where I am if you need me." He hands me the folder, which Damien takes for me.

"She'll be fine. There's no need for concern," he says, locking eyes with Aaron as their testosterone levels begin to rise.

Aaron breaks the stare and focuses on me. "See you around." He turns toward the stairs and both Damien and I watch him as he descends and leaves the building.

"What are you doing out so early?" Damien asks.

"We got kicked out for talking," I admit, as he relieves me of my bag, once again, then leads me down the stairs.

He nods, worrying me that he's annoyed about seeing me with Aaron.

"Aaron is a bit upset with me for the way I reacted over Bec," I explain, hoping to gain a little empathy. "He doesn't think I'm acting like myself."

He slides his arm around my shoulders, pulling me against him as he drops a kiss on my head. "What we have is very rare. I'm pretty sure it doesn't exist in the realm of 'normal'. Not everyone is going to understand us Henrietta. We can't expect them to."

Minutely, I shake my head in confusion. "I don't even think I understand it myself."

17

"Why won't you let me see in the room?" I ask Damien on Wednesday afternoon, as I get ready to go and visit my parents for dinner.

"What room?" he asks nonchalantly, as he sits on the couch, his head bowed as he scratches a pencil over the pages in his A5 sized sketch book.

"Very funny smartarse. The room with the great big bloody padlock on it," I say, pointing at the door of the second bedroom.

"Just pretend it isn't there. All of my work gear lives in there. It's not important." He twists his book around, holding it horizontally as he tilts his head to study his sketch before scratching away again in a different place on the page.

"It will be important the next time you get a commission," I point out, sliding my feet into a pair of red Converse skate shoes. I'm wearing my faded blue jeans, my shoes and a bra right now. "Where is my shirt?" I ask, disappearing back into the bedroom. He keeps cleaning everything up, putting my things in with his so I have trouble finding it all.

"Just wear one of mine," he suggests, as he leans against the doorframe after following me in. "It will make me feel like I'm still with you." He reaches into the open drawer and hands me one of his more fitted black shirts.

Taking it from his hands, I drop it over my head, loving the soft cotton as it rests loosely against my skin. "You're not getting out of this conversation by the way. I really hate that there's a room with a padlock that I can't go inside. It makes me feel like you're hiding dead bodies or something."

"I'm not hiding dead bodies. I promise you that," he assures me, as he flips the sketch pad around for me to see.

"Oh…" I breathe, stepping closer to him to examine the drawing. It's me. I'm not smiling like I am in the small picture he drew of me. In this one, I look thoughtful, sensual. "It's beautiful," I tell him. "How do you make me look so beautiful?"

He places the book aside before sliding his hands around my waist and pulling me against him. "Do I need to take you into the bathroom and show you again?" he murmurs, his need for me growing obviously as my own pulses between my legs.

"You'll make me late," I return, although I'm not moving away from him. I want him. I always want him.

"I don't even want you to go." He crushes his mouth against mine before I can respond, my head swirling as I whimper into his mouth, melting beneath his touch.

His hands work quickly to unbutton my jeans as I shuck my shoes off to the side before he pulls the denim down my legs. At the same time, I remove the shirt I just put on and drop it on the carpet, just in time for him to stand and lift me off the floor.

"Stay with me," he whispers, walking us into the bedroom and laying me on the bed.

"I want to," I breathe, my arms reaching out to him as he removes his clothes and climbs on top of me. "I really want to."

He lets out a slow moan as he sinks himself inside me, his eyes locked with mine, and a look of pure bliss on his face. "I need you Etta. You're everything to me."

As he moves inside me, he continues to whisper about how he feels when he's around me, how he needs me, and doesn't want me to leave him. His words fill my heart with such emotion that it feels as though it may very well burst along with my insides as I burst around him.

"You're all I have," he murmurs, as I moan through my orgasm, his thrusting increasing in pace as my climax continues, and I start to shriek, the intensity becoming more than I can bear.

"Oh god! Damien! Oh!" I yell, blood pumping through my ears as my mind reels with the increasing sensation of what I think is about to be another orgasm.

He reaches between us, rubbing at my clit as his thrusts continue. "Don't ever leave me Etta. Don't ever fucking leave me."

"I won't," I gasp. "I promise you I – oh god!" My hips buck up again as white spots burst from behind my eyes, and my core clenches, tightly around him. He thrusts into me, as deep as he can go, shuddering and spilling his juices inside me.

Breathing heavily, he dips his head down, kissing me slowly as our connection pulses between our legs. His tongue enters my mouth, and slides against mine, exploring every texture my mouth contains.

I wrap my arms around him, feeling as though his kisses are feeding me the life I need to live as he rolls us over, so I'm on top. Pushing through my arms, I separate our mouths and look down at him lovingly, before dropping soft kisses over his face - similar to what he does to me. I kiss him on the arch of his dark brow - on the line in between them that forms when he frowns. He closes his eyes, and I kiss him on his eyelids, his cheekbones, his dark stubbled jaw, and the tiny hint of a cleft that can be seen in his chiselled chin.

I'm amazed by how much I feel. I know I'm young. I know I only have a couple of relationships to compare this to. But, this feeling… I struggle to describe it. It's wonderful, yet frightening. Is this level of connection even normal?

The intensity creates an ache in my chest that makes me want to claw at my skin to get it out. I don't know what it is. It's making me crazy, elated and scared – all at the same time. I. Just. *Want*. Him. But, I feel perplexed by my want. It seems irrational, yet irrevocable.

Placing my hands on his chest, I sit back and remove my bra, dropping it on the floor beside the bed as I slide up his shaft and lower myself down languidly, sending us both once again into the oblivion that seems to exist between us.

***

Opening my eyes, I blink twice in the dark of the room. Damien's

255

arm rests snuggly around my waist as he curls his body around me, his face tucked into the back of my neck.

My stomach grumbles loudly, and I realise that we were so caught up in each other that we skipped dinner. Which reminds me. "Oh no, my parents!" I gasp, flinging Damien's arm off me as I sit bolt upright in the bed.

"What?" he asks sleepily.

"My parents. I was supposed to go there for dinner. Oh my god. They're going to kill me."

"Relax. I messaged them for you. They said to come on Sunday instead. I'll go with you if you like."

"What do you mean? When?" I ask, reaching over to click on the bedside lamp so I can see him.

He flinches his head back, squinting against the light as his eyes adjust to the bulbs bright intrusion. "When you were in the shower. Can we go back to sleep now?"

"No Damien. We can't go back to sleep. Are you telling me that you messaged them before I even got dressed to go out, and told them I couldn't go without consulting me? What were you going to do if you couldn't convince me to fall into bed with you? Tie me up?"

"You're overreacting. I did you a favour. You very obviously wanted to stay."

"You can't just keep using sex to get your way, and you can't

256

go making decisions for me. They're my parents. You shouldn't be cancelling my dinners with them and then luring me into bed to keep me away."

"As I recall, I didn't have to try that hard to get you into bed," he says, sitting up beside me and kissing the bare skin of my shoulder.

"I might have to start making it a lot harder," I say, annoyed that he was so presumptuous. "You know what? I'm going to start staying at my place instead of yours. This is bullshit." I whip the sheets away from my body and stand up to go and find my clothes so I can leave.

"That's not going to work," he says calmly from the bed.

"Isn't it? How do you figure that?" I say, as I lean down and scoop up my bra before turning to leave the room and get the rest of my clothes from the living room floor.

I don't even make it to the door before he springs out of bed and comes up behind me, wrapping his body around mine, pressing us up against the wall. "Because every time I touch you, this happens," he growls in my ear, causing my heart to drop and my chest to constrict. I hate that he's right. I hate that he holds so much power over me.

My body screams out for him as his hand slides over my stomach and between my legs, his fingers gliding between my folds, already dripping with my arousal. His cock presses against my butt cheek as his fingers push inside me before gliding out and circling my clit with their silken touch.

"Oh god," I moan, my anger evaporating. I don't understand why this is happening, but I'm loving every second he touches me. "I hate you for this," I gasp, writhing against him, struggling with the power he seems to hold over me at the same time. How is it that one man can enter your life and take over it completely in such a short time?

Using his feet to spread my legs, he tilts my hips toward him, impaling me from behind as his fingers continue to work on my nub. Gasping with each upward thrust, I press my hands and face up against the wall, all thoughts and protests leaving me as I go spiralling toward ecstasy like this man is some sort of drug to me. I'm totally addicted.

18

"What are your plans for today?" Damien asks me a week later after training. He's got me going every day at the moment, and despite having reservations about it at first, now that I'm giving into it, I'm finding that I'm really enjoying it.

I still haven't gone and had dinner with my parents. Once again, I cancelled. But at least this time I did it on my own. I told them I had some uni work to catch up on for my Monday class when really, I was too busy luxuriating in Damien's attentions. I just can't seem to get enough of him.

We're sitting in the waiting area of the gym, eating a breakfast of blueberry muffins. He actually made them – they're just a packet mix, but the effort he went to while I was still sleeping is very touching.

"I guess I'll try and catch up on some uni work and veg out at your place?" I suggest, wondering if he'll let me stay there on my own.

"How about, I drop you off at the library - I have a class at ten, then I can pick you up afterward, and we can go home together?"

"Sounds perfect," I smile, although I'm slightly disappointed. He speaks of trust, but won't trust me with things that are important to him. I don't think he trusts that I won't start going through his things, or try to get into his spare room. I suppose he's justified in thinking that way. I probably wouldn't trust me either – I really want to know what he's hiding in there.

I watch him, wondering why he's so secretive as he gathers our things. What else is there going on with him? I know that he knew my brother, he back alley fights for fun and profit, plus he works on nude portraits of random women. I don't understand why I'm not allowed to see or be a part of any of it. Does he think I'm so fragile that I couldn't handle the reality?

Granted, I flipped out when I saw Bec half-naked in his apartment, but that was Bec – the woman who acted like she owned him when I first met him. Of course I wasn't going to be ok with her. But perhaps, I could be ok with his other clients if he'd just show me what it all entails. Perhaps I could understand. Right now, I just feel like he's protecting me from absolutely nothing. I'm not a child. I can handle knowing.

He takes my hand, his touch breaking through my thoughts as the connection of our skin heats my body. Leading me by the hand, the cool air of the morning touches the bare skin on my legs as we step out into the sunshine and get into his car.

I'm wearing one of those really short khaki coloured skirts that look like they're trying to emulate cargo pants, and a fitted black singlet with a pair of iPanamas and my hair piled up in a bun on my head. It was all Damien's choosing. I expected that the gym bag would contain my usual t-shirt and leggings combo, but today, he went and changed things on me.

"I can't believe this pen hasn't washed off my legs yet, it's been a week and a half and it's only faded a bit. What the hell did you use?" I ask.

"It's a tattoo pen, it'll wash off eventually," he tells me casually, as he pulls out onto the traffic on Northern Road.

"Eventually? That doesn't help me much." I run my hand over the intricate design. It's edges starting to blur with wear, but it's still beautiful. "Why do you have a tattoo pen?"

"Why *don't* you have one?" he counters with a grin.

"Do you have it because you like tattoos? Are you thinking of getting one of your own?" I shoot at him.

"Yes, and no."

"What made you buy the pen?"

He just glances at me, and suddenly I realise that there might be another girl – maybe more – out there who have had him do the same thing. Pressing my lips together, I pull my skirt lower, trying to cover it.

"No. I haven't done that before," he says suddenly. When I look at him in question, he explains, "Laid in bed with a beautiful woman and drawn on her – you are the first."

Sighing my relief, I release the hem of my dress.

"You're a jealous little thing aren't you?" he asks.

"Have you seen you?" I retort, as if that should explain everything.

261

"No, I only see you," he replies. My breath catches in my throat, and quickens in my chest. With just a few simple words, he's got me all hot and bothered again.

"I want you Damien," I murmur, feeling a little bold, sliding my hand over his thigh.

"How do you want me Henrietta?"

"Right here. You need to pull over."

"Where?"

"Up there." I point, squirming in my seat.

He pulls over on the dirt strip beside the busy road. "Now what?" he asks with a grin. He seems to be really enjoying this.

"Slide your seat all the way back."

He does as I ask, clicking the lever at the side of his seat and letting it roll all the way back. "Get on," he tells me, taking the lead back from me.

Glancing down, I can see his cock, straining against the linen of his black pants. I climb out of my seat and onto his lap, pulling on his drawstring and sliding my hand inside, nursing his cock in my hand.

"I love your cock," I whisper, stroking my hand up and down his shaft.

"My cock loves you," he grins, grabbing onto my hips and lifting me up. My hands fly up to his shoulders to steady myself so I don't hit my head on the car roof. He pulls my panties to the side and positions himself at my entrance. "Slide down," he growls, pressing down on my hips, as I ease myself over him, joining us to the hilt.

Moaning, I start to move on top of him, pushing through my thighs, dragging up his long, thick shaft, and slamming back down, grinding at his base. As my excitement grows, my speed increases, rocking the car with our movement.

"Oh god!" I call out, digging my fingers into his shoulders, my insides bursting like a dam at the same time that he shudders beneath me, spurting himself inside me, his own fingers digging into my hips. As our breathing calms down, I start to laugh.

"What's so funny?" he whispers, dropping a kiss on my shoulder.

"Just this. Us. Look at what you're making me do."

"I'm making you? Who's the one suggesting road-side quickies?" he chuckles.

"I can't help it. Just looking at you turns me on," I whisper, leaning down to kiss his earlobe. My hips start to roll again, and I feel him harden inside me, always ready, just like I am.

Whoop Whoop

I sit up quickly. "Shit. Cops," I hiss. A flurry of motion ensues as I jump off his lap and return to my seat.

Damien slides his seat forward and rights himself, at the same time grabbing for his phone. He presses it to his ear, pretending to have a conversation as the police officer walks up to the driver's side window.

"Sorry mate. I'll have to go… yeah… thanks," he pretends, tapping his finger against the screen and powering his phone off. "Yes officer?" he asks innocently.

"You are aware this is a clearway?" the policeman points out, looking from Damien to me suspiciously. "You can't stop here." I squeeze my thighs together as hard as I can, hoping that the officer can't see any of the evidence from our dalliance as it leaves my body.

"I'm sorry officer, I didn't realise. I got a phone call and since it's illegal to talk and drive, I felt it safer if I pulled over to take the call," he explains, straight faced.

"Why is your seatbelt off miss?"

"Oh… um… we were pulled over, and I… um… was trying to find some…gum in my bag – it's in the back seat." I don't do as well as Damien does, but the police officer – even though he looks as though he doesn't believe a word of it – nods his head.

"Well, I guess that explains why the car was rocking. All that rummaging for gum?" he asks pointedly, although I can see a tiny grin pulling up the corner of his lip.

"Yeah," I laugh uneasily. "I still haven't managed to find it."

He lets a burst of amusement out of his nose before tapping the roof of the car. "Alright you two. Just get this car on the road and stay out of the clearways in future."

"Yes sir," Damien says with a nod, as the policeman returns to his vehicle.

Leaning over me, he grabs my seatbelt, meeting my eyes as he clicks it in place. His are full of amusement, whereas I'm sure mine are filled with worry. He then starts the engine and pulls back into the stream of traffic as it flows past us.

"Holy shit," I breathe, my heart thudding wildly in my chest. "The first time I get a little adventurous, and I nearly get us caught."

"Babe. That was hilarious. I'm going to be smiling all day," he chuckles, reaching in the back seat to retrieve the gym bag, keeping his eyes on the road while he rummages around inside. "Gum," he laughs, giving his head an amused shake as he pulls out a travel pack of tissues. "Here," he says. "To… you know."

"Thanks," I say, gratefully accepting them and pressing a couple between my legs. "What about you," I start, when I've finished cleaning myself up. "Pretending to talk on the phone. What if it had have rang in your hand?"

"I had it on silent, it wouldn't have mattered."

"Hey, I thought you didn't lie," I laugh.

"Etta, do you really want to get hauled in front of a judge for indecent exposure?"

"I guess I'll let it slide," I smile, settling back into my seat as I watch him drive. He's far more interesting to me than the scenery outside, and going by the way he frequently glances at me - he likes it when my attention is one hundred percent on him.

"Do you need your laptop?" he asks, as we near the university campus.

"No, everything I need is on the Cloud. I can access it pretty much anywhere."

Pulling into the entrance, we find a car space and walk together, hand in hand toward the library.

Leaning down, he kisses me gently before whispering in my ear. "No flirting with strange men. I'll see you in two hours."

"I'll do my best," I grin as he kisses me on the forehead. I stand and watch him walk toward the design building, noticing as a few other girls watch him with interest. My chest aches as I fight a great urge inside me to rush over there and tell them all to keep their 'come hither' looks to themselves.

Swallowing hard, I drag my eyes away and head inside, aiming for the research computers. I still haven't gone through all the papers Aaron gave me, and the thought of him causes my stomach to flip – I haven't spoken to him since that day. And he must be really annoyed or upset with me, because he hasn't texted or tried to call, but I've been avoiding him too. I haven't been to class all week. I'm embarrassed by what he saw and the conversation that followed. He's right – that crazy jealous woman isn't me. I'm normally so much more logical than that.

"Holy shit! Is that a tattoo on your leg?" spits Jessica in greeting, her eyes wide as she sees part of the drawing on my thigh.

"No," I laugh. "It's a tattoo pen. Damien was having a bit of fun." I wave it off as if it's nothing and turn back to my work.

"So how is Damien?" Kensi asks. "Is he the reason for the short skirt, and the absent bra?" she whispers, a conspiratorial grin on her face.

I shrug, nonchalantly, not willing to give anything away. I know a lot of girls love to share their sex tales with one another – I'm just not one of them. I'm selfish. I want to keep him all to myself – every last, delicious detail.

"She's not going to share," Kensi pouts, both her and Jessica tilting their heads together as they focus their puppy dog expressions on me.

"It's not going to work," I laugh.

"Fine. We just came to say hi, and ask you if you were still living with us."

"I am. I most definitely am," I laugh. "I'm sorry, I've just been…"

"Too busy hooking up. We know. But you might want to talk to Aaron, he stopped by last week. He seems really worried about you," Jessica informs me.

"Yeah, I'm sure he is," I admit, biting on my lip.

"He's at the coffee shop," Kensi tells me, standing up from her seat. "Oh, and we're going clubbing on Friday. You wanna come? You can even bring lover boy with you."

"I'll see what he wants to do," I reply. Waving briefly at both of them as they excuse themselves for class.

Logging off the computer, I make my way to the coffee shop to see if I can find Aaron. I owe him an apology. Or an explanation – something anyway.

I find him sitting at a table with his laptop out, drinking coffee and chatting with Carl.

"Hey," I say, placing my hand on the seat beside him, not so sure if I'm welcome to sit down.

"Hello," he says evenly, as Carl greets me normally. He obviously has no idea about my psychotic episode. "I thought you might be dead. But the moans over at Damien's place kind of sounded like you, so…"

"I'm sorry Aaron," I tell him. "You were right to be worried. I don't know what came over me."

"I might leave you two to talk," Carl says, pushing his seat back as he stands. "Nice to see you Etta," he says.

We wait for a moment as Carl walks off before continuing. "Why haven't you been answering your phone? I've called you and texted you because you haven't been showing up to class but… nothing," he shrugs.

"I don't have any calls from you," I tell him, pulling out my phone and showing him my call history.

He scrolls through my very short list, a frown creasing his brow as he looks through my settings. "What a fucker," he says suddenly, shaking his head as he sits back against his seat.

"What?" I take my phone from his hands, trying to see what he was looking at that upset him.

"Damien."

"Why?"

"Give me your phone back," he says, taking it from my hands and calling his phone with mine. The read out on his says 'Private Number'.

"There must be something wrong with it," I suppose, taking my phone back and swiping at the screen, looking for something to explain it in my settings.

"There's nothing wrong with your phone, look," he says, showing me the read out on his phone as he selects my name and dials. Pressing the speaker phone option, I listen as the call connects and rings, but nothing happens on my own handset.

Scrunching my face up in confusion, I look between the phones.

"I think someone's switched out your sim card," he says.

"But... why... why would he do that?"

"Why do guys like that do anything Etta? They do them because they can."

"I don't understand."

"Etta," he says, his tone and his eyes serious as he places his hand on mine. "I'm not saying this because I have feelings for you. I'm saying this because I'm worried. Damien is not a good guy. Get away from him before this all gets out of hand."

I open my mouth to say something, but I can't, my words are all caught up in my throat. The thought of not seeing Damien again is physically hurting me, my throat constricts and my breathing becomes shallow. It's irrational, I know. I should be freaking out about the sim card, but instead, I'm freaking out because I might have to give him up.

Aaron takes my emotional state as a reaction to the phone. "It's ok. You won't have to go through any of it alone. I'll be here, you've got your mum and dad, and your housemates."

"No," I gasp, snatching my hand away from him. "Just…oh god, I hate feeling like this," I gripe, gripping my sides as my stomach clenches. As I sit back up, I pick up the phone. "There has to be an explanation for this."

"There is Etta, he's trying to isolate you."

Shaking my head, I stand, trying to think of a reason to explain why Damien would do it. "No, he's not like that. I'll get to the bottom of this."

Aaron's features crease with concern as he watches me retreat. "Call me if you need me," he calls out, just before I push through the coffee shop's doors.

Returning to the library, I force myself to work, making nonsensical notes about my project as time ticks slowly by. I manage to sense him before he's even near. It's as if my skin prickles, knowing that he's in the same room. I lift my head as the feeling grows more intense, my heart beats firmly against my breastbone, and my breathing quickens as I anticipate him finding me.

He stops behind me and runs his fingertips down the back of my neck and over my shoulders, sending glorious ripples of pleasure over my body, causing my nipples to harden and protrude obviously through the stretch cotton fabric of my top.

Leaning down, he brushes his lips against the edge of my ear, kissing me on my jaw.

"I've missed you," he murmurs, moving to sit on the chair next to me. "Where have you been?"

"Why do you think I've been somewhere?" I ask, looking around to see if I've been watched.

"Just answer the question."

"I went to the coffee shop," I tell him, feeling as though I'm in trouble, even though I know I haven't done anything wrong. He has.

"Who was there?" he asks, staring in my eyes, although it's more of a glare. I'm pretty sure he knows exactly where I was.

"Do you have people watching me?" I ask suspiciously, still looking around the library.

"Just answer the question."

"You obviously know already Damien. Otherwise you wouldn't be looking so shitty with me. Although it's you who should be answering my questions right now. What the fuck did you do to my phone?" I demand, glaring right back at him.

His left eye narrows slightly as he leans back against his seat and drapes his arm over it.

"Didn't think I'd find out did you? Why the hell would you do that? Why would you switch out my sim card?"

Standing up, he picks up my bag and holds out his hand to me. My face burns hot with my aggravation as I slap his hand away and hiss, "Just answer the goddamn question!"

He grabs my hand anyway, hauling me out of my seat so fast that he has to catch me against his body, knocking the air out of me as our chests collide.

"Because I care about you," he whispers, taking my face in his hands and pressing his lips against mine. It takes seconds before I'm putty in his hands again, breathing like I'm some dramatic actress of the 20s.

"You can't kiss everything away," I gasp, as our mouths part.

"I'm just trying to understand you."

He wraps his arms around me, and curls me into his chest, engulfing me with his big arms as he sighs. "Because, I can track you if you're on my account," he admits.

"Jesus Damien, what the hell do you think is going to happen to me?"

He tucks his face into my neck, his breathing shaking as his arms tighten around me more. "I don't know. That's what scares me. I just know that if I know where you are and what you're doing, then I'm ok. Just… feel my heart Henrietta."

Taking my hand, he presses it to his chest where I can feel the quickened beat of his heart as it thumps against his ribs.

"Is this because I went to the coffee shop?" I ask quietly, although not understanding why it upset him so much.

"I left you at the library. You need to stay where I leave you," he whispers, the worry evident in his face as he looks at me beseechingly. He wraps his arms around me again and pulls me against him again. "You can't wander off. Something could happen."

I pull back a little, wanting to look him in the eye. What he said was so quiet, I'm not even sure if I heard right, but he pulls me back toward him, just holding me against his chest. As we stand in the middle of the library, wrapped in each other's arms, I start to realise that my brother's death may have had a greater impact on Damien's life than I had initially thought. While I knew that he felt responsible for not watching out for his friend, it's only now that I'm linking his need to know where I am with that event all those years ago. Unless of course there's something else… something he's not telling me. But what?

"I need you," he murmurs in my ear, his warm breath washing over my neck, sending delightful shivers down my spine that chase my questions away.

"I need you too," I admit, capitulating to him yet again. It's possible that I always will – the need feels that imperative to me, that I may very well forgive him anything.

Hand in hand, we leave the library, ignoring the inquisitive stares of others after our public display. We walk to his car, driving back to his apartment block as fast as we can safely go. The air between us palpable, as I wonder if this feeling – this need, inside me is ever going to go away. It seems that the moment he is near, I need to touch him and to have him touch me.

This feeling is far more than attraction, and it's bigger than lust. I can't call it anything else but need. I need him, just like I need air to breathe and water to survive.

The moment we get inside his apartment, he kicks the door shut and drops my bag on the floor. Reaching down and lifting my singlet over my head, he throws it over his shoulder before pushing my skirt and underwear down as well, leaving me in front of him, completely naked.

"Take your hair out," he instructs, standing back as he studies me. It's amazing how a man looking upon your body with an intense hunger can make you feel like the most gorgeous woman in the world.

Reaching up, I pull the pins and elastic that were securing my bun in place, and let my long hair fall about my shoulders. Suddenly, I'm a sex goddess. I'm starting to understand how beautiful I am to him – he makes me feel amazing.

He circles my body, running his fingertips over my skin. Every sense is on high alert as I listen to our steady breathing, waiting for what comes next.

When it finally does, it's a flurry of movement that ends with us both in sweaty heaps, craving more. Always craving more…

***

"Open," Damien says, in that soft coaxing voice of his as he holds a fork full of steak and mashed potato up to my lips.

Locking my eyes with his, I wrap my mouth around the morsel and slide it off the tines.

"Would you like some of mine?" I ask, when I finish the mouthful, cutting into my meat.

"No, it's all yours. I just like doing things for you."

"I like it too," I smile. I love the caring he shows toward me. He's such a large, strong man. He's the kind of man many would find intimidating. So seeing him gentle and caring is wonderful.

We exchange knowing smiles as we continue our meals, Damien occasionally offering me another mouthful from his plate.

"Oh, what are you doing Friday night? Kensi and Jessica want to go clubbing and invited us along."

Suddenly, his features harden and his jaw sets. He narrows his eyes, setting down his cutlery as he reaches for a napkin and wipes his mouth.

"No," he says, as if he has the authority to do so.

"No? What do you mean no?" I ask, dropping my own knife and fork, suddenly not hungry anymore.

"I mean – I have a fight on, so after last time – you need to stay home. I'll put someone on guard duty if I have to."

"You can't tell me what to do."

"I can, and I will. You're not going."

"Fuck you Damien. We've been seeing each other for what? A month at most? And you think you can stop me from going out with my friends. No. Sorry. I'm going."

"Henrietta. You're being unreasonable," he growls, raising his voice a little. "I need to work, and to do that. I need you to be safe, in your own house."

"My *own* house? I have been here, with you the whole time! You are my home Damien!" I yell, upset at him for restricting me as well as casting me aside. "I'm coming with you. Wherever you're going. I'm going too. You don't get to do this shit without me." I fold my arms across my chest and stick my chin out stubbornly.

"No. I don't want you involved!" he yells, slapping his hand on the table, causing the plates and glasses to jump and clang.

"You're being unreasonable, and you can't stop me. I'm sorry, but I'm going. I didn't move out of my parent's house, just so you could tell me what to do," I screech, my emotions running high as I stand my ground.

"You're not fucking going," he roars, throwing the plates in the sink with an almighty crash that sends pieces of food bouncing up out of it.

The volume of his roars and the crash of the plates, shocks me frozen. I don't know what else to say. Frankly, I'm scared shitless right now.

"Oh my god," I whisper, a cold hard realisation hitting me hard in the chest as I force myself to articulate my feelings. "I...I can't do this with you. I can't keep feeling like this. You're trying to put me in a cage. I'm not... I need to go." Pushing away from the table, I head for the bedroom, grabbing my suitcase and throwing it on the bed.

Suddenly, I'm seeing that with him, my world will be even more restricted than it ever was when I was at home. As much as my body wants him near me, I'm smart enough to see that this isn't going to work. Aaron's right – I need to get out.

"What are you doing?" he asks from the doorway, his voice flat and emotionless.

"I'm going back to my place. I'm not fighting with you over my right to make my own choices."

"Put your bag back in the closet," he commands. It only serves to make me more furious, so I pack faster.

"I said, put it back," he growls, grabbing the case from the bed and upending it, dumping my things on the bedspread. "You're not leaving."

"Give it back," I demand in return. "Fucking, give it back."

"No."

"Fuck you. You don't own me!" I screech, my hands balled into fists at my side.

"You. Are. My woman! And you'll fucking do as I say!" he roars, throwing my suitcase against the wardrobe door, causing me to jump as my blood turns cold, afraid of what he's going to do to me. I know from training with him that I have a zero percent chance of winning any sort of fight against him.

We lock eyes for a moment, the air charged between us as we stand on either side of the bed. Sliding my gaze toward the bedroom door, I estimate that it's only a step away from me and decide I need to make a break for it.

I bolt, pulling the door shut behind me to slow his advance. It gives me enough of a head start as I dash through the living room, grabbing my bag and his keys as I make for the front door.

"Henrietta," he roars behind me.

Thinking fast, I pull a chair out and throw it in his path, grabbing the handle on the front door and finding my freedom in the hallway. My only thought is to get to his car and drive away.

Running at top speed, I take the stairs, two, sometimes three at a time, my heart beating rapidly as my blood whooshes through my ears and I pray that I don't trip and fall.

Fuck, how did I manage to get myself in this situation?

My heart thuds, wildly in my chest, as I hear him coming behind me, calling after me as I dash out of the foyer door and onto the street. I'm not even wearing any shoes as I take off down the footpath as fast as my legs can carry me.

Suddenly, I see salvation step onto the curb in the form of Aaron. "Etta? What's going on?" he starts, as he sees me running toward him, and Damien in hot pursuit. "Holy fuck! Get in the car!" He opens the back door and jumps into the driver's seat.

I dive in, headfirst, yelling, "Go! GO!"

But we're not fast enough, Damien grabs my ankle and hauls me out of the car, kicking and screaming.

Aaron, jumps out and tries to help free me, but with Damien's skill level, he's quickly turned away and pushed aside.

"Stay out of this Aaron. I don't want to hurt you," Damien warns, his chest heaving from the chase. I struggle against the grip he has on my arm as he holds me steadily at his side.

"Let me go you fucker! I don't want to be with you anymore."

"Let her go Damien," Aaron demands, stalking toward him.

"Back off," Damien warns again.

Aaron makes a move as if he's about to attack Damien, and knowing that this can't possibly end well for him, I yell hysterically, "Stop! Aaron – I'm fine. I'm fine. I'm sorry. I'm fine. You don't need to do this."

"What!?" he bursts out, his face disbelieving as he stands in front of me. "No Etta."

"Just. Stay," I cry, resting my hand on the warmth of his chest, taking a deep breath to steady my voice. "I overreacted. I'll call you later. It's ok."

Damien relaxes his grip on my arm and slides his arm around my shoulders, hugging me to him. The moment I inhale his scent, it reacts with my mind, and I'm right back where I was. Ready to do anything to be with him, and hating that I feel this way.

Aaron drops his stance a little, his eyes wide as he looks between Damien and me incredulously. "I'll be right down the hall if you need me," he promises, his eyes filled with concern.

In this moment, I feel utterly defeated and completely

incompetent. I know this is wrong. I know this thing I have with Damien isn't ok. But that doesn't stop me from wanting it. It doesn't stop me from clinging to him for dear life, right after I was just fighting to get away from him.

What the hell is wrong with me? I hate this feeling. I hate not being in control.

"She said she's fine. Now, fuck off."

Sliding his arm down to my waist, Damien steers me back toward the building. Inside me, there's a voice still screaming at me to run. But I don't listen. There's something about this connection we have that makes me force that little voice down as I realise that running from him would be pointless - he's just going to chase me down and, as disappointing as it is, every time he catches me I'll probably go back to him. I don't know if I'll be able to help myself.

"Etta!" Aaron calls after me, but I keep looking forward. I don't think I can handle seeing the disenchanted look upon his face as I walk away and begin to accept that my life is nothing without this big, domineering man beside me, who I feel *so* many things for.

When we enter the foyer, Damien leans down and scoops me up in his arms to carry me up the stairs. His quiet strength and caring toward me after I was just so horrible to him, overwhelms me and causes me to drop my head against his chest and sob.

"It's ok," he murmurs into my hair, kissing the top of my head. "I love you Etta. We can work this out."

My heart and chest ache so much right now that I'm not even sure I can breathe. God, how can being near one person make you so fucking crazy with lust, then fear, then anger, then need and love. *Fuck!* That's what I hate most - I'm in love with him. I don't want to be. *Fuck. Fuck. Fuck.*

When we reach his apartment, he carries me into the bedroom and sits with me on the bed, cradling me on his lap like a child.

Tilting my face up to meet his, he smooths his thumbs over my cheeks, wiping my tears away as he shushes me. "I'm sorry for scaring you," he whispers, bringing his mouth to mine, brushing his lips upward.

My body begins to quiver as I cling to him, continuing to cry as he continues to wipe my face and apologise.

"Please don't run away from me. I couldn't bear a life without you in it. I love you. I love you more than my body and mind can handle. My love for you hurts Henrietta, its hurts so much that it's a constant thud in my chest, pushing against my ribs as if it's trying to escape. But I don't want it to, I want it to hurt me forever. I want you forever. Do you understand that? I need you. You. Are. *Everything,*" he whispers, his voice as pained as his eyes as he attempts to express what this is, and he's right. It does hurt. It hurts so, so much.

"Make love to me. *Please.*" It's the only thing I can think to do. It seems to be the only way to express this emotion. The only way to ease this addiction.

A groan escapes his throat as he closes his mouth over mine

282

and shifts his weight, laying us on the bed as he kicks the pile of my clothes off and onto the floor.

I feel his erection, instantly hard against my thigh as we entwine our limbs, touching and kissing like this might be the one and only time we ever get the chance to be together. But it's like this every time, and scares me – it's more than I can handle.

"I need you Etta," he whispers, his kisses raining down upon my jaw, flowing down my neck and over my breasts. He takes a nipple into his mouth, sucking back on it, grazing his teeth over the tight hard peaks. "I love you."

"I don't…" I start, struggling to find my words as my feelings take over my mind. "I'm scared of this. I'm scared of us. It's too much. You make me feel too much," I cry, squeezing my eyes shut as a tear escapes my right eye and slides over my skin in a bright trail of pure emotion.

Spreading my legs, he rolls his tip at my entrance, distributing my juices before he pushes in, causing me to gasp as he fills my insides completely.

"I will do anything to protect you Etta, anything you want. Just don't leave me. Stay. I love you. I love you," he murmurs, sliding himself back and forth inside me.

"This can't be love," I gasp out, wrapping my legs around him, pulling him to me with my arms, kissing him against his shoulder. I want to absorb him, and carry him with me always. "I love you. But it's something else. Something more."

Turning his head, he kisses my neck, my jaw, my mouth, before taking his weight on his hands, looking down on me as he continues to thrust. "It's everything," he qualifies.

19

I don't go out with Kensi and Jessica on Friday night, and Damien doesn't go out to 'work' either. Instead we embark on a month of feeding off each other, shutting ourselves off from the world almost completely. We spend almost every waking moment together. Ignoring everything and everyone.

But eventually, we need to come up for air. We've each missed so much uni that it's likely we're going to have to redo this semester, and I haven't seen my parents since I moved out of home.

Now, they're demanding that I go and see them, even going so far as to guilt me into it by using my brother's death against me.

"We already lost Craig, Etta. Don't distance yourself so much that we lose you too."

It's not that I've been staying away from them to hurt them, I've just been so caught up in Damien. When it's just the two of us, everything is perfect. Everything is right.

"You could probably come inside for dinner too if you'd like?" I suggest to Damien as he drops me off at my parent's house.

"As much as I would love to, I've organised a meeting with a possible new commission for tonight. I need to go and see them," he explains.

My stomach sours, as the memory of Bec and her 'portrait' session flashes through my mind. "Do you have to do them?" I plead.

"Babe, this woman has been emailing me for ages, and I've been fobbing her off to be with you. But I'm running out of money. I need to do something."

"I don't like it. I don't want you with someone else. I don't trust any of them around you. Find another job – anything."

"And have to work so much to earn the same amount of money that we never get to see each other? Is that what you want?"

"Well… no, I don't bu–" I start before he cuts me off.

"Then trust me. Ok," he says, reaching over to me and brushing my hair away from my face.

I fight the urge to close my eyes and lean into his hand as it touches my skin. He knows that once he touches me I have trouble thinking straight. But this is important, and I force my mind to stay sane.

"I want to meet her."

"Excuse me?" he asks, confused.

"The woman. I want to meet her before you start working with her. And while you're working, I will be sitting in your apartment, listening through the door of the fucking room you're so secretive about, and if I hear one hint of a moan, I will go so crazy that what happened with Bec will seem like watching

286

kittens at play. You feel me?" I state, my eyes wide and serious as he watches me, calmly listening.

"It's the portraits or the fights. And fighting can get me thrown in gaol, so what will it be?"

I sit there, my eyes locked with his as he challenges me, knowing that I'd rather he did neither.

"You choose Henrietta. I can call her and cancel then call the guys to go and hustle a fight. Or I can meet her and maybe get enough money to keep us going for another month."

I bite my lip as I try to decide. "Take the meeting," I tell him, my voice flat as I move to get out of the car, annoyed that he sprung this on me now.

"Hey," he says, reaching out to grab my arm and pull me back toward him. He takes a hold of my face, and presses his lips to mine, kissing me tenderly, feeding me the life I need from him. "Don't leave me angry. Just love me. Trust me."

"I do love you, and it's them I don't trust. If they feel even a grain of sand's worth of my attraction toward you, they'll be all over you."

"I'll keep it professional. Call me when you're done, ok?" he says, kissing me lightly as I agree and head toward the front door where my father is already waiting for me.

He nods toward Damien as we both watch him drive off. "Is everything alright? Why isn't he coming inside too? I'd like to talk to him."

As I open my mouth to respond, my mother pushes in front of him and wraps her arms around me. "Etta! Finally. I've missed you so much. Ignore your father. He's just upset that he hasn't seen you properly for over a month."

I hug her back, feeling odd being back here again. It's strange. It was my home for so many years, but it doesn't feel that way. My eyes drift back over my shoulder, to the space where I just saw Damien, missing him already.

"Come in, your Dad's been cooking his special roast potatoes. He might not seem it right now, but he's been looking forward to having you visit."

My father leads the way toward the kitchen and dining area where everything is set and ready.

"So why did Damien leave without coming in?" he asks again.

"Barry," my mother admonishes.

"What? He's been monopolising our daughter's time for weeks now. So we never see her. I want to know why he can't spare a few moments to come in and say hi."

Before my mother can respond, I say, "He's got a business meeting to go to."

"A business meeting? What kind of business is he doing? I thought he was a university student, just like you," my father says, placing his hands on his hips as he looks to me for information.

"I don't know exactly," I lie, avoiding eye contact as I move to sit at the table across from my mother.

"How do you not know?" My father asks, as he collects a tray laden with food, and walks it over to the table, setting it between us all.

"Can I get anybody a drink?" my mother says, trying to steer the conversation elsewhere.

"Because it's none of my business," I state, staring at my father defiantly.

"I thought it might be nice to have a glass of red with the lamb," my mother continues, ignoring my father and me. "How are your classes Etta? Have you decided on what you're doing for your research assignment yet?"

"Well, you should make it your business," my father continues. "You spend enough bloody time with him. You should know every freaking thing about him."

My mother lifts the bottle of wine and pours each of us a glass. Her cheeks starting to flame red as she becomes flustered by our refusal to change the subject.

"Is this why you wanted me here? To question me about Damien? It would be nice if you could spend some time being interested in me for a change, and just me. Not my relationship. Not my training schedule or my grades. Just me. It might help if you actually took the time to try and find out who I am as a person. Then I might want to come around a little more often. I moved out for a reason dad. You don't get to start demanding information from me the moment I walk in the door – especially when you're the one who insisted that I come here."

Glancing down at my wrist, I see the Ki bracelet he gave me for my birthday. I've worn it every day without fail because I felt it was such a touching gesture. But suddenly, I don't want it anymore. I undo the clasp and push away from the table, dropping the bracelet on the table.

"You know what? I'm not hungry anymore."

"Etta!" my mother calls as I head for the door.

"I'm sorry mum. I just didn't come here to be brow beaten over Damien."

I pick up my bag and pull the door open, heading toward the train station on foot so I can go home.

"Etta," my mother calls, just as I step over the property line. "I'll give you a lift."

Stopping, I look back at my mother as she aims the electronic key at her Barina and presses the doors open. I press my lips together and walk over to the passenger door and get inside.

"I'm sorry mum," I say, as she reverses out of the driveway.

"So am I Etta. Honestly, I'm disappointed in both of you. You certainly aren't the innocent party here. You've barely called, you've cancelled dinners. And whenever we've stopped by your place, your housemates tell us that you're out with your boyfriend. I've had a hard enough job stopping your father from storming down to the gym every morning to give you a piece of his mind. What you've done. It isn't fair. You've gone and moved out and practically removed yourself from our lives as well. Don't you think we've lost enough? Don't you think we deserve better than a cursory text or phone call to let us know you're alive?"

"Yes. You do. I'm sorry mum. I'll try and be better to you."

"Don't try Etta. Do."

Before I know it, we've pulled up outside the townhouse, and she's reaching into her pocket for something. "Here," she says, handing me back the Ki bracelet. "Put it back on, and tomorrow, I want you to call your father and smooth things over."

"But mum," I start to argue, taking the black cord from her hands.

"Just do it. I'm not interested in being caught in the middle of you too. I can only handle one strong headed person at a time."

I look down at the bracelet in my hands and roll the cord between my fingers. "Ok, I'll talk to him."

"Thank you, and Etta, I want to see you properly too. I miss you. I know you're young and you're caught up in the glow of a new relationship, but you need to remember your family and friends."

Leaning toward me, she holds her arms out for an embrace. I of course, lean in and wrap my arms around her small frame.

"Thank you mum. I'm sorry dinner didn't work out."

"It's ok. Although I wish you could have stayed, you look like you could use a good meal. Are you not eating properly?" she cups my chin in her hand and studies my face. "You look tired too. Too many night clubs huh?"

"Something like that," I smile, dropping my eyes from hers. I can't really explain the truth. How do you say to your mother that you've been so busy being ravished that you have begun forgoing food and sleep, just to stay in his arms.

"It might be a good idea to ask Damien to check in with your father too. He hasn't been attending the usual training sessions and your father is starting to develop conspiracy theories."

"Ok," I laugh, shaking my head slightly. "I'll see what I can do." I bid my mother farewell and climb out of the car, heading to the front door of the townhouse while I dig around in my bag for my key.

Just as my hand clasps around the smooth metal of the keychain, the front door bursts open. "Etta! You're here," Jessica exclaims overly enthusiastically, blocking my way slightly.

"Well, I do pay rent for my room," I say, trying to move past her.

"Yes. Yes you do." Something about the way she's talking and moving beside me, makes me think that she's trying to herd me up the staircase instead of letting me through to the lounge room.

"What's going on?" I ask slowly, narrowing my eyes at her as I sidestep her and head to the living area. "Oh. I see."

Sitting on one of the couches are Kensi and Jeremy, she's half draped over him in propriety, so I know that she obviously landed her prize. On the other couch is Aaron.

"Hey Etta. How are you?" he asks kindly.

"I'm not dating him," Jessica says behind me, quickly and quietly. "You know – girl code and all that…"

"What?" I ask, not fully understanding what she said at first. "Oh! Girl code. Ok, I get it. It's cool. You can all hang out with or date whomever you choose."

"I'll um… leave you all to it." I nod, backing away from everybody before heading up to my room, where I can call Damien in private and grab a few things to take back with me.

Sitting on my bed, I pull out my phone and select Damien's number before holding it to my ear to await the connection. Although it goes straight through to voicemail.

"Dammit," I say to myself as I listen to his short and abrupt message.

"I'm unavailable, leave your details and I'll get back to you."

293

"Hi, it's me. Don't get all upset at me, but I'm not at mum and dad's place. Dad was picking a fight with me, so I left and mum dropped me off at my place. I'm just going to pick up a couple of things, and if I don't hear from you soon, I'll walk over to your apartment and wait for you there."

As I disconnect the call, there's a gentle tap on my door. "Etta?" Aaron says from the other side. I realise that the last time we spoke, was when I was trying to run away from Damien.

Opening the door, I smile at him. "I guess I should explain what our last interaction was all about."

"No. You don't. I just want to see how you are. I haven't heard from you. You haven't been in class. I just need to know that you're ok and if you need any help." He keeps his voice quiet as he stuffs his hands into his pockets and studies me with concern in his eyes.

"Why would I need help? We just had a fight and I over reacted. I shouldn't have forced you in the middle of it," I tell him defensively, not liking what he's insinuating.

"If you say so. You just don't seem yourself. It's unlike you to fall so far behind in your studies, and it's unlike you to avoid your friends to spend all of your time shacked up with some guy."

"You wouldn't be complaining if it was you I was shacked up with," I retort, taking offense to his supposed knowledge of the inner workings of my mind.

He presses his lips together and just nods his head, keeping his distance from me. "Ok." Is all he says before he starts to turn away from my door. He takes two steps toward the staircase before stopping and turning back to me. "I know I keep saying this. But when you're ready – when you need me. I'll be there for you."

"That's really nice of you, Aaron. But I won't be…"

"You will. Eventually you will. I have no doubt in my mind that you will one day call me, and I promise you that I will do whatever it takes to help you."

"Why?" I ask, wondering how he can be so sure and so unwavering.

"Because I love you Etta. How can you not know that?"

As he turns again and walks quietly down the stairs, I'm left with my mouth open and a pain in my chest as I watch after him. He's right – how could I not know that? He's been waiting for me this whole time. Ever since my father broke us up.

Feeling physically shaken after Aaron's revelation, I sit on my bed and look around my room, paying attention to all of the things I have adorning the surfaces, all of the things that represent me.

Damien's apartment doesn't have anything in there of me at all. I spend all of my time there, just being with him. While it's what I thought I wanted, as I sit on my own, amongst my own things, I realise that I'm completely neglecting myself, and all those who were important to me before Damien came along.

Standing up, I look in the mirror and study my reflection, paying close attention to the way my eyes seem to sink into my face due to my lack of sleep. It's not that I look ill or anything, I just look tired. And I am tired. I'm very tired.

A burst of laughter travels up the stairs, and feeling left out, I decide it's time for me to go. But not before I try to make amends by making plans to go out with everyone soon. Plans that I'm not going to break.

"Hey guys," I say as brightly as I can, as I come down the stairs. "I'm going to head back out, but do you think we could maybe make some plans for this weekend? Maybe we could go to the city or something."

"Yeah Etta," Kensi nods. "I'm always up for a party. Make sure you're here Friday, we'll all travel in together."

"Am I coming?" Jeremy nudges her, his arm resting lightly around her shoulders.

"Well, that all depends..." She leans in to him and whispers something in his ear, causing his eyebrows to shoot up high on his forehead.

"Excuse us," he says, grabbing Kensi by the hand and heading for the staircase at great speed.

She gives me a wink as they pass, and she runs up after him. "See you Friday."

"Alright," I laugh, before turning back to Aaron and Jessica.

"Do you need a lift anywhere?" he asks.

The disappointment on Jessica's face is obvious the moment he suggests leaving her on her own, while Jeremy and Kensi go at it upstairs. So I don't have the heart to drag him away from her, and I especially can't do it after what he said earlier – I don't want to give him the wrong idea.

"No thanks. I'll be fine on my own."

Turning away from them, I walk out of the townhouse and head to Damien's, checking my phone again to see if he's called, and I missed it. Although, in a way, I'm glad he's still out, I think I could do with some sleep.

***

"Henrietta," I hear whispered in my ear, startling me awake. It's grown dark and I wonder how long I've been asleep for.

"What time is it?" I mumble, inhaling sharply as I try to wake myself up.

"After nine. What are you doing here?"

"Sleeping, and waiting for you. What time did you get back?"

"Henrietta. You can't come back here when I'm working. Not after last time."

"What?" I say, sitting up in the bed. I reach over to turn the lamp on. "You weren't even here."

"Not at first, no. But I don't think it's very professional of me to have a naked girl in my bed when I bring clients around. You are naked aren't you?" he asks, sliding his hand underneath the sheets brushing his fingertips down the length of my body. "Well, you got that part right."

"Don't," I complain, flinching away from him, it's probably the first time I've ever had restraint around him. Sitting up, I keep my body covered, trying to get this all straight in my head. "Firstly, what the hell was she doing here? And secondly, why would she *ever* see me in your bed?"

"You left the bedroom door open, we could see straight in," he explains.

"And why was she here?"

"So I could walk her through the process."

"You took her into the spare room?"

"I did," he states, dipping his head to plant soft kisses on my shoulders. Knowing that he'll distract me with sex, I try to keep my wits about me. Although my resolve begins to waiver as the sheet falls away, and he takes my nipple into his mouth.

"Please show me what it is you do. I want to know Damien. I won't be ok until I know."

Sucking my nipple into a hard peak, he sits back on his knees, pulling his shirt over his head. My hands immediately reach out to touch his skin running my fingertips down over his chest and abs with my need to feel him whenever he's near.

"That wouldn't be fair. Only clients get to see the work. There are rules," he murmurs, removing his pants and sliding into the bed behind me. His hand reaching over my waist and down to my mound, a finger slipping between my folds to tease my clit.

"What if I became a client?" I whisper, closing my eyes as the delicious sensation of his touch starts to flood my body and my mind.

"I wouldn't take your money. When I create a portrait for you, it will be for my absolute pleasure." He grips my hips, tilting them so he has access, and enters my warm, wet depths.

"When will you show me?" I ask, gasping as his thrust presses firmly against my g-spot, and his fingers work my clit. I don't know how much longer I can hold a conversation for.

"Soon, my love, soon."

***

Surprisingly, the next morning when I ask Damien to come into the city with everyone on Friday, he actually agrees immediately.

"What are you doing?" I ask as he stops eating his breakfast to reach for his phone, his fingers working furiously to type out a message on the screen.

"Telling the guys. They can set something up."

"Like what? A fight?"

"Yep," he confirms, giving his phone a final tap, before setting it down beside him on the table.

"I thought you said that I could choose. Portraits or a fight?"

"Yes, but as my main money maker. If you chose fighting, it would have meant that I'd be out there every weekend looking for someone to hustle. Now I can do it for fun. Besides, we need the cash."

"But you just got a commission, didn't you?" I ask him, confused.

"Yeah, but I need money to hold us over until I'm done. She's only paid me the deposit."

"How is it that I'm feeling as though I'm the one getting hustled right now?" I comment, shaking my head at him for managing to get his own way – again.

"Take your clothes off. I'll give you your way for the rest of the day," he growls erotically, the rumble of his voice sends glorious chills racing around inside me.

I stand, and pull my dress over my head.

"You're on," I say, turning around and striding toward the bedroom, boldly naked.

***

When Friday rolls around, Damien drops me off at my place so I can get ready with Kensi and Jessica.

"Make sure they understand that I don't want any of you watching when a fight goes down. I can't make any money if they start getting hits in," he reminds me for the billionth time. He's made me promise to stay inside the nightclub when the fight happens.

"I wouldn't dream of distracting you. I don't know if I'd enjoy looking at your face anymore if it got all beaten up. I'm very superficial you know," I joke, unable to keep the grin off my face as I speak.

"That's bullshit and you know it. You'd love me with a smashed up nose – as long as my tongue still works." He winks, pulling me toward him to press his lips against mine before he heads off to meet up with the guys who are the lookouts for his fights.

Humming as we separate, he presses his forehead against mine. "I'll see you in an hour," he murmurs, kissing me once more before unlocking the car to let me out. "One hour," he repeats, calling after me as I walk up the short driveway.

"Alright, go!" I laugh, shooing him away as I head inside and call out that I'm here. Kensi, of course, is already making pre-emptive cocktails in the kitchen.

"We were wondering, since you have never slept in your room – can we turn it into a home office or a gym?" Jessica asks me when I walk through the door.

"No," I smile. "It still holds most of my clothes."

"Damn," she says with a smile, clicking her fingers dramatically. "Oh, and it's just us tonight. Kensi and Jeremy had a falling out."

"Really? What happened, you were all over each other just last weekend?"

"Bedroom malfunction. He thought he could get all up my back door without discussing it with me first, so I threw him out," she says, licking some sort of sauce off the back of her hand as she shrugs like it's no big deal.

"Couldn't you have just said 'no' and moved on?" I ask.

"She doesn't want a guy who just takes from her," Jessica explains. "Supposedly, he wasn't that great with his tongue either."

"Yeah, he was fucking hopeless. But he was plenty happy to have me lollipopping all over him whenever he got the chance. Nope. No thank you. You don't get to ride the Kensi train indefinitely based on your looks alone," she comments, heading back into the kitchen to tend to the drinks. "Are you drinking with us?" Kensi yells after me as I begin to climb up the stairs.

"Yes. I'll just take a shower first," I call back, as I grab a few things from my room and make for the bathroom.

Unlike Damien's, this bathroom is littered with beauty and bath products. It's clean, but it's cluttered, although I don't really have the right to complain. At the moment, I'm kind of spending an exorbitant amount of money for storage space. I know I could give up the room, but I just don't feel comfortable doing it. We've only been together for a couple of months, despite how I feel about him, it's way too soon to make anything permanent.

Here's the thing, while I with him, I'm in Damienland. It's this place where everything is wonderfully blissful and I rarely question anything. It's filled with sex, orgasms and clouds. Yes clouds. That's what I feel like I'm walking on. I don't know how he does it, but if we ever figure it out, we could bottle it and make a fortune – then he wouldn't feel the need to do all of this other shit to make money.

When I'm away from him, although it's not often that I am, it's as though my mind starts to clear, and all the questions that surround him and his actions start to present themselves. I promise myself I'll get to the bottom of his issues. That I'll be that one person he shares himself with completely. But ultimately, I know that's not going to happen. He's far too guarded. I just need to decide whether that's something I can live with. Although I'm not sure I'll have a choice. Because one thing I'm very sure of, is that I need him, and he needs me - we fucking *need* each other.

Taking my time, I slowly soap up my body, enjoying the warm stream of water as it flows over my body. The tattoo pen has worn away on my thigh, but I now have a new design on my stomach, this one is an intricate array of feathers and stars – it kind of looks like a peacock tail. It sweeps down from beneath my breast, curving around my belly button, until it sweeps across my abdomen.

I have to admit, I love being his canvas. I asked him if he wanted me get one of his designs, tattooed permanently on my flesh but he replied 'no', he just wants to keep drawing on me.

Omitting my bra, I have chosen to wear an emerald green, strapless dress that fits tightly around my bust, but flows freely, stopping only a couple of inches beneath my buttocks. For dignity's sake, I wear a pair of black silk panties. I've owned them for a while, but never found occasion to wear them. Tonight, I plan to dance, drink, and have fun, then go home with my man and spend the night in his arms. And hopefully, he'll make enough from the bets that he won't have to do this again for a while.

Curling my hair so it brushes gently across my bare shoulders, I apply the minimal amount of makeup, not wanting to look like I'm trying too hard. As I press my lips together, I hear the honk of Damien's horn outside.

Grabbing my purse, I shove my feet into my black peep toe heels, and make my way down the stairs.

"Tell him to come in," Kensi calls after me as I run for the door.

Nodding, I rush out into the cool night air, my eyes desperate for a glimpse of him, an hour just feels like too long.

"Holy fucking shit," Damien breathes when he sees me. "There is no way I can leave you alone looking like that."

"Well you'll have to," I grin, taking his hand and indicating that we're going inside. "You have a job to do."

"I didn't know you were going to look like this," he counters, pausing before we go inside, pressing a soulful kiss against my lips.

"There isn't a man in this world who turns my head like you do. I want you to want me – nothing more," I whisper as he grazes his mouth along my jaw, sucking on my ear lobe.

"I want you in a paper bag," he murmurs, pulling on my lobe with his teeth, sending chills through my body.

Laughing, I press against his chest, to separate us. "We are required inside. Kensi is trying to make cocktails," I inform him.

"This will be interesting," he says, taking my hand as we head inside. I lead him into the kitchen, where Kensi is preparing some sort of concoction. All I can hear is her swearing as the blender cuts in and out, rocking back and forth across the counter as she tries to steady it.

"Fucking piece of shit," she yells at it before noticing that we're in the room.

"Oh hi! Oh wow – that's a very fitted shirt you have on there Damien. Did somebody call for a stripper?"

"Oh my god! Kensi!" Jessica admonishes. "You can't talk about Etta's boyfriend like that."

"Sure I can. Come on Damo, if you're going to stay, you'll be required to remove your shirt. And since you're going to piss off on us to go play fisty cuffs with some other guys. I'm declaring this a girls' night. So we plan to do a lot of ogling."

My mouth falls open when Damien tilts his head in acceptance and moves to lift his shirt. "No!" I call out, not wanting to share one part of his body with anyone else. My stomach turns sour at the thought of anyone else drooling over his abs except for me. "Don't you dare," I warn him over my shoulder.

This only elicits a panty dropping smile from him, and I actually witness both girls turning into puddles at his feet.

Normally, I'm not a jealous person. I was fine when I was dating Aaron. Other girls would always go on about how wonderful he was. I could handle that. I actually took pride in them sighing over my boyfriend. But with Damien, I'm feeling a little irrational and have to keep a firm hold of my tongue or else I'm going to tell them to keep the fuck away from my man.

Jesus. What the hell is happening to me?

Gripping his hand tighter, I keep a very firm hold on him, not letting go for the next hour. I don't think he minds though, he seems to enjoy having me as close as possible and drops light kisses on the bare skin of my shoulders whenever he gets a chance.

When it's finally time to make our way into the city, I'm feeling a little disappointed that he won't be staying with us for the whole night. I've already had a couple of cocktails, and I'm well and truly happy for the evening when he drops us off in front of the night club.

"Aren't you coming in with us?" I ask.

"I have to meet the guys. I'll be back. No more alcohol for you. Understand?" he tells me. "I'm trusting you."

"I understand. I more than love you," I tell him, wrapping my arms around his neck as we say goodbye.

"I more than love you too. Now go. Be good," he says.

"I promise," I grin, following Jessica and Kensi as we join the line to enter.

"Bye lover boy!" they call out, giggling as we make our way inside and pay our cover charge.

Once inside, it takes a few moments for my eyes to adjust to the hazy dark of the club as Trance music vibrates through my breast bone.

"I need more drinks," Kensi calls out, dragging us all over to the bar.

"That cocktail you made was pretty strong Kens," I tell her, leaning down to speak into her ear. "I think I'll just grab some water."

She shoots me a look over her shoulder that says 'you've got to be kidding me' and proceeds to order a round of drinks for all of us. "Here, I got you lolly water instead – there's like, no alcohol in those things at all."

I hold up the bottle of poison green fluid and note that it's still

1.3 standard drinks and decide to drink slowly. I'm not interested in starting a fight with Damien over the amount I should or shouldn't drink.

Scanning the room, I watch as people mingle and dance, but really, I'm just waiting for Damien to come back.

"Drink up," Kensi instructs me. "I'm ready for another round."

"Already? Jesus Kens, you have to slow down. You're going to destroy your liver," Jessica says from beside her. She's only halfway through her drink, slowly sipping it as she people watches and dances where she stands.

Kensi waves her off dismissively and turns to push her way back to the bar, her small frame disappearing amongst the crowd.

"I'm worried about her. She drinks far too much," Jessica informs me.

"Yeah, I'm noticing. She's only tiny. Where does she put it all?"

"She can't handle the amount she drinks. Every time we go out, she ends up getting sick, and *I* have to get her home. She's my best friend, and I feel responsible for her, but it's getting a bit much. I had to stop her from having sex with some guy on the dance floor the other week," she says, shaking her head at the memory.

"What do you want to do about it?" I ask, thinking that maybe we could talk to her and try to convince her to slow down.

"What can I do? I've tried talking to her and refusing to come out with her, but she just does it anyway. At least if I'm with her, I can keep an eye on her so she doesn't do anything too crazy," she shrugs.

"I'm sorry I haven't been around more," I say, feeling bad for moving in, but never being a good housemate to them.

"Don't be silly. You've been busy with Damien. Speak of the devil," she notes, nodding toward the club entrance where Damien is entering, accompanied by the two friends we saw him with last time as well as one other.

The moment I look over at him, his eyes find me and he smiles, it's like a cord connects us and pulls us together, pushing out everything else around us. I can barely hear the music, just a static sound created by the whooshing of my blood through my ears as I stand still and wait.

"What's this?" he asks, taking the bottle of melon flavoured alcohol from my hands.

"Would you believe me if I said I was holding it for a friend?" I try, pulling at my bottom lip with my teeth.

"Henrietta," he warns, but there's still a softness in his tone, meaning that he doesn't like to be pushed, but he isn't going to make a big deal out of this.

"Damien," I return, reaching my hand out and hooking my finger into the belt loops of his jeans, pulling on them to urge him closer to me. "Dance with me," I whisper in his ear.

Handing off the bottle to one of his friends, he has eyes only for me as he wraps his arms around my waist and manages to melt us into the pulsating crowd to reach the dance floor.

We dance to a beat of our own, the music throbbing around us, at odds with our slow movement. His hands roam over my body, as his eyes drift over my face, he always seems to be studying me, like he needs my image burned into his memory.

I find that he communicates so much with me through his gaze and his touch, it's as if tendrils of emotion rise up out of him and enter me, entwining with my very being, connecting us in some kind of strange symbiosis.

When he dips his head to take my mouth in his, everything stops, all time, all sound, is gone. All that exists is the two of us in a world built only for us.

I have no idea how much time passes while Damien and I sway together on the dance floor, our bodies pressed tightly together and our mouths connected like we're drinking in each other's life force.

Eventually though, we're interrupted and catapulted back to reality when one of Damien's mates taps him on the shoulder and whispers something in his ear.

"Who was that?" I ask.

"Just a friend," he says, before adding, "I need to go. We need to find your friends." Extending to his full height, he scans the room seeking out Kensi and Jessica. "Over there," he says, pulling me through the crowd.

"Hey!" Kensi yells, her grin broad and her face shining.

"She's smashed," Jessica explains, looking fairly unimpressed.

"I'm leaving Harry with you. Stay here," Damien instructs, eyeing Kensi warily. "I think she needs some water."

"I'll get her some," I say before adding, "Wait a second, who the hell is Harry?"

Damien shifts his gaze to the space over my left shoulder, turning around I spot a well built, dark haired guy with Asian features who looks more like a Special Forces security guard than somebody's actual friend.

"Seriously – I'm being babysat?" I ask disbelievingly. "I thought we were supposed to trust each other?"

"I do trust you," he murmurs into my ear as he runs his finger along the edge of my dress, skirting the flesh of my breasts with his fingertips. "I just don't trust everyone else."

He turns his head and leaves a lingering kiss on my cheek before stepping away. "Do not leave this club," he instructs. "I'll be back as soon as I can."

"Come on Damo!" one of his friends calls from behind him.

Nodding at his friends, he turns to leave. From the look on his face, I can tell he's having second thoughts about leaving me, but with one last glance over his shoulder toward me, he disappears through the club's back door.

Kensi moves in next to me, watching after him and his friends. "We need to get out there to watch," she declares.

"No. He doesn't want me out there."

"Kensi. I think we should just stay here," Jessica puts in, looking clearly uncomfortable at the thought of witnessing a street fight.

"What's he going to do? He won't even see us there," she slurs a little, her balance a little off as she teeters on her heels.

"Yes, but he'll know we left. We have a sitter," I inform her, pointing at Harry who's standing with his arms crossed stoically behind me, witnessing our conversation.

Pulling on my arm, Kensi leans up to speak close to my ear. "He won't catch us if we make a run for it," she suggests, to which I shake my head.

"No," I state.

Biting on her lip, she looks from Harry to me, to Jessica, her mouth curling in a grin before she bolts for the door, her tiny frame making it easy for her to duck and weave through the crowd faster than the rest of us.

"Kensi!" Jessica calls out. "Shit, we have to go after her," she panics, pulling at my arm to follow.

I take one step with her before an arm shoots out to stop me. For the first time in my life, I react the way I'm trained to, using

Harry's momentum to tip him off balance and knock him to the ground.

"I'm sorry, I have to find my friends," I yell as I race after Jessica and Kensi, not even knowing if Harry could hear me, or if he's following as well.

As I burst through the back door, I catch up to Jessica as she continues to push through the outside crowd. "She's over there!" she yells back at me, pointing to the footpath where Kensi is standing and looking both ways.

"Where the hell is the fight?" Kensi wonders out loud, as soon as we catch up to her.

"I don't know. They must have gone somewhere else," I state, scanning the crowd for Damien. He's so tall that he would easily stand out, but he's nowhere to be seen. "Maybe we should just go back in. They'll come back and wonder where we are."

"They can't be too far. Let's go," Kensi says, completely ignoring me as she takes off down the street.

Jessica and I exchange exasperated glances. Shrugging, we follow after her, hoping we don't take a wrong turn and get lost.

"Kensi, I really think we should just go back. I don't like walking the city streets and I really don't want to see a fight," Jessica complains, her arms folded protectively across her chest as she follows a step or two behind.

"Live a little Jess, you're always so cautious," Kensi responds, turning around and walking backwards as she speaks.

"Holy crap!" Jessica breaths, her eyes widening as she freezes on the spot. Suddenly, a rush of people come flying out of a side street like rats escaping a sinking ship.

The air fills with panic as everyone scatters and one guy runs toward us yelling, "COPS!"

We all squeal like a bunch of five year old girls, clutching at each other as people race around either side of us.

"Fucking run!" I hear, as strong hands grab a hold of my waist and catapult me forward. I have no choice but to run or else I'll fall. Caught up in the panic, I look around for Jessica and Kensi, feeling relieved when I see they are running along with us, guided by Damien's two friends whose names I still don't know.

"Up here," one of them yells, pulling Kensi by the hand into another side street. We all follow, slowing our pace down when we realise that we're not being followed.

"What the fuck were you doing on the street?" demands Damien.

"We were..." I start, but Kensi interrupts as she hunches over and groans before spilling the contents of her stomach on the footpath.

"Oh Kens," Jessica complains. "Not again."

"Get them home," he instructs his mates, who nods and, supporting Kensi, escorts them out of the side street and into the throng of the Friday night crowd.

Grabbing my hand, Damien tugs me out into the crowd as well, heading in the opposite direction, toward where he parked his car.

Pulling his phone out, he swipes his thumb over the screen then holds it to his ear. "What the fuck happened?" he says after a moment, pausing as he listens then grunting out a response. "Well you fucked up." He taps his thumb again, before putting his phone in his back pocket.

"Who was that?" I ask, when he just continues heading for the car park without speaking to me.

"Why is it so hard for you to stay put?" he growls as he pulls me along briskly.

"I was going after Kensi. She bolted and we weren't going to leave her alone in the city!" I explain defensively.

"Is there a reason you took out Harry?"

"You're the one who made me start training again. You can't complain when I use what I know when the situation calls for it."

He shakes his head and sets his jaw, his anger rolling off his body as his grip on me stays firm. "You're a fucking child who can't do what she's told."

"Excuse me? I'm the child? You're the one who's running around fighting for money instead of getting a regular job – let's not even get into your fucking portrait business!" I bite back.

315

"Does this happen a lot? Getting chased by the cops?" I demand, attempting to pull my hand away from his. His grip just tightens.

"I'm not discussing this with you anymore," he states, as we reach his car and he roughly deposits me in. I open and close my fingers a few times, allowing the blood to run through them again. His grip wasn't painful, but it was certainly restrictive.

"Fine, don't discuss it - I don't want you fighting anymore Damien. I don't want you doing any of it. Get a fucking job stacking shelves or pouring beers for fucks sake. If you want to fight – enter a bloody tournament. If you want to make money from your art and design skills, make fucking custom book covers or advertising posters – I don't care what you do with it. Just stop what you're doing now. I can't take all of this secrecy anymore. It's driving me insane! I mean, I've been with you for over two months now, and I still don't know what's in your other room. I'm at your house every fucking day! What's the big secret Damien? Why can't you just share your life with me?"

Gripping the steering wheel tightly, he steers us toward the motorway, keeping his eyes ahead and his jaw clenched.

I know I should stop talking, but I can't, now that it's coming out of me, I need to keep going. "Is this how our lives are always going to be? You make the rules, and I follow them or else you crack it? Are you always going to keep tabs on me? Are you ever planning on introducing me to your friends?" I ask, assaulting him with just a few of the questions that have been plaguing my mind.

He doesn't answer me, he just keeps focused on the road as we speed down the freeway toward Penrith.

"Well?" I prompt.

"Which answer do you want first?"

"All of them."

"Fine. Yes Henrietta, this is how it's going to be. I am always going to keep tabs on you. I need to know where you are and that you're safe. I didn't introduce you, because they're not the kind of guys I want you associating with. You don't need to get mixed up in my shit! But what I want to know is – why? Why, when I specifically told you to wait with your friends at the club, you had to come outside? You could have told Harry to go after Kensi, and just waited for me to come back like I fucking asked. But no, in typical Henrietta style, you do the fucking opposite. Take out the very guy I left to keep an eye on you and somehow manage to be walking directly into the fight I specifically told you to stay away from! Do you understand what could have happened if I wasn't one hundred percent focused on the guys I was fighting? If you're around me, I can't fucking concentrate. You're the only person I see. I'm out there, fighting guys that are half cut from drinking all night. Sometimes it gets out of hand, and I need to be able to see it coming. I don't need to be worrying about you. So please, the next time I tell you to stay put – fucking stay put! And no, I won't be giving up fighting. It makes me too much fucking money!" he yells, flicking a wad of money over at me, the colourful notes raining down around me, landing on my lap and falling around the car. There is easily a thousand dollars here – maybe more.

317

We sit and drive in silence for a while. "You're a dick," I say finally, my arms folded over my chest as I ignore the money and stare ahead.

"Great. Now your name calling. See, this is why I've never had a girlfriend. You're so fucking stubborn. If you had just listened to me in the first place, we wouldn't be having these issues."

"I'm not the one who went looking for your fight, the other two did."

"I'm not talking about the goddamned fight. I'm talking about us. You're too young. You weren't ready. But you fucking pushed."

"Don't talk like you're stuck with me Damien. It's not like we're married and have kids. You can get out of this anytime you like."

"Is that what you want? You want out of this?"

"I don't know what the fuck I want anymore. Someone else is always there, making my decisions for me. I left home because I couldn't stand the rules. I couldn't stand the fear that losing my brother produced in my parents. For years they smothered me Damien! And now you're doing the same fucking thing!"

"You don't understand," he growls, down shifting as he takes the Northern Road exit.

"Of course I don't understand. Our relationship is all about fucking, I know very little about you."

"Do not call it fucking Henrietta. It has never been about fucking and you know it," he bites back.

318

"Fuck you." It's not very eloquent, but it's all I have right now. I've been drinking, and I guess I'm being irrational, but I'm just getting so sick and tired of all the secrecy and all the protection. "Just take me back to my place."

Tightening my arms across my chest, I stare out the window, not saying a word as we drive the darkened streets. We pull into the parking lot of his apartment building, and I get out straight away, slamming my side before I start to walk off.

"Get back here," he demands.

"If you won't take me home, I'll fucking walk there myself."

"Henrietta, you're being ridiculous," he says from behind me as he catches up.

"Am I? The more I think about this, the more sense this makes. I need to go home – to my home. I need some time away from you."

"Why? I've done nothing but care for you."

"It's too much! Tonight was supposed to be fun. I'm eighteen for fucks sake. I'm supposed to be going out with my friends. But you keep restricting everything I do. You're so fucking selfish. It's all about you – all the fucking time!"

"No Henrietta. It's always about you. Always," he entreats, as I insert my hands into my hair, tears escaping my eyes as I shake my head in frustration.

"God, I hate feeling like this! I just wanted to be free. I hate you for making me need you!" I cry, sobbing uncontrollably as he steps forward, wrapping me in his arms, holding me against his chest.

I just sob. I curl myself into his body and I sob.

"I need you too," he whispers, kissing the top of my head, his strong body cocooning me in its warmth.

"God, I'm all over the place right now," I say eventually, standing back from him and wiping at my eyes, hoping that I don't have mascara streaming down my cheeks. "I just… I feel strange. Maybe it's just hormones, I haven't had my period since…" I pause, touching my fingertips to my thumb as I try and count. When realisation dawns on me, my eyes meet his. "You said we'd be fine," I whisper.

"And we will be," he replies immediately, his voice stone-cold calm.

I thump my fits against his chest. "When I told you I wasn't using birth control, you said not to worry. You made me think you couldn't get me pregnant. I fucking believed you. I fucking trusted you!" I thump my fists over and over again on his chest as I scream murderous things at him.

He just stands there, stoically taking my onslaught, unwavering in his stance.

"Was this to trap me? Is that what you're trying to do? What the hell is wrong with you?"

Still he stands there, his jaw clenching as he watches me rant.

"I'm eighteen. I can't…I can't… not yet… oh my god," I lean forward, placing my hands on my knees as my heart pumps so fast that I'm struggling to get enough oxygen into my blood.

"You need to calm down," he says, reaching for me.

Flinching away, I hold my hand up, warning him off me. "Don't…touch me," I pant. "I can't have a baby. I'm not having a baby."

"We'll be fine Etta. Relax, just come home with me. We'll do a test in the morning. We can do this Etta."

"No."

"No what?"

"No, I'm not doing this. I'm not going with you. I want to go home – to my home. I just… I need some space. I need to think."

"Henrietta," he warns, his tone becoming demanding.

"Just stay away from me."

"No," he growls, reaching out and grabbing my arm. With a firm grip he starts dragging me back toward his apartment building.

"Let go, you fucker! You bastard! You Liar! I hate you right now!" I yell, slapping at his arm, trying to pull in the opposite direction. But he's too strong for me.

As soon as we're in the foyer of the building, I reach out and grab a hold of the door, using it to anchor myself and make it harder for him.

"I'm not letting you go," he growls, turning on me, pushing me up against the glass door I'm holding on to, breathing down into my face.

He takes a moment to look at me, his expression dark and stormy, his intent clear. He crashes his mouth against mine, forcing his tongue over my lips, his hands sliding around my waist, practically crushing me against him.

I try to fight it, I try to stay angry at him, but the power he holds over me begins to envelope me, causing me to respond. The moment the first gasp escapes my mouth, I feel his cock, hot and hard against my thigh.

His kiss deepens as he pulls me closer, curving my body into his. Sliding his hand down, he grips my buttocks, pulling me roughly against him. His hand moves underneath my dress and into the waistband of my lace panties. With a swift tug, he breaks the seam, dropping them on the floor where we stand.

Reaching down, he grips my thigh and lifts me onto his waist, continuing to kiss me the entire time. I wrap my legs and arms around him as he takes to the stairs, stopping periodically to press me against the wall and ravish my neck, my breasts. To grind against me.

By the time we make it to his apartment, I'm almost ready to explode. He sits me on the bed, pulling my dress over my head before urging me to lie back.

Discarding his clothing, he climbs of top of me, his glorious muscles rippling as he takes his weight and enters me.

"We belong together Etta. You're my everything. You're my life. You're the very reason I breathe," he whispers between kisses and thrusts.

With my senses overwhelmed, I can do nothing but respond to my carnal need for him. It's as if my body craves him so much that it shuts off my rational mind the moment he touches me, and I can't fight him.

Sliding out of me, he kisses his way down my body, leaving a trail of prickling heat in its wake. He settles himself between my thighs, moaning his pleasure as his tongue slides through my folds.

My hips jolt as he sucks on my nub. "You're magnificent Etta," he murmurs. "My own personal heaven." He slides his fingers inside me, sucking on my clit, pulsing my insides as he continues to seduce me further with his words. "I want you. I need you. Let me love you. Be mine forever."

My body bursts over his hand, in his mouth as his pulses continue and my hips jolt. Climbing back up my body, he thrusts himself back inside me, pumping quickly, continuing my orgasm as I start to call out.

My moans become increasingly louder as his hips thrust back and forth at great speed. He hoists my legs up, positioning my feet on his shoulders, increasing his depth.

"Holy shit," I call out as I explode again. He slams himself into me one last time, shuddering against me, spilling his juices inside me.

Suddenly my consciousness revisits me, reminding me that this is exactly what I'm upset about. It's exactly why I need to go. I can't trust him.

Passively, I go through the usual routine where he cleans me and gets us both ready for bed. When he curls us together, under the blankets, I pretend to fall asleep quickly as he plants his soft kisses on my skin.

Dampness pools beneath my face as tears slide silently from my eyes and I force my breathing to stay steady. Eventually, I feel his body relax, and his breathing evens out. It's then that I slide out of bed, quickly and quietly grab my bag, and I leave.

"Aaron," I whisper into my phone once I'm in the stairwell.

"Etta?" he asks, his voice groggy from sleep. "What's going on?"

"I need you. Can you please drive me home? I'm outside."

"What? Of course. Shit Etta, are you ok?" he asks, immediately sounding alert.

"Not really. Just please. Hurry up. And Aaron?"

"Yeah?"

"Please be as quiet as you can. You don't want to wake him."

When I reach the foyer, I spot my discarded underpants and pick them up off the floor, shoving them into my bag as I exit the building and wait outside on the path.

Seconds later, Aaron is slipping out to meet me.

"Did he hurt you?" he asks immediately.

"No. He just..." I burst into tears, instantly Aaron's arms are around me, strong and familiar.

"Let's get you out of here," he whispers, guiding me toward his car.

Once on the road, he asks, "Where am I taking you?"

"Take me to the 24hour Coles. I need to buy something."

When we pull into the parking lot, I ask him to stay in the car, I don't really need him with me while I buy pregnancy tests.

Rushing in, I head straight for the pharmaceutical aisle. Normally, I love how they shelve all of the condoms and lube, right next to the pregnancy kits. Tonight they taunt me. I can't believe I was so stupid.

I select one of every test they offer, I don't know which one is best, so it seems logical to just use them all.

As I climb back in the car, Aaron glances down at the grey plastic bag in my hands. You can clearly see the labels through the opaque plastic.

"Shit Etta," he says, meeting my eyes, his own filled with sympathy and worry.

"I know," I sob.

As we drive back to my place, he reaches over and takes my hand, giving it a gentle squeeze. "I'm here for you ok. Whatever you need. I'm here for you."

I nod, fighting the floods of tears that keep forcing their way out of me. I just want to get home. I just want to find out if it's true.

When we get to the townhouse, all is quiet. It's almost 5am and I'm sure that my roommates are either sleeping or still out partying – who knows with Kensi. Selecting the key for my room on my keychain, I unlock my door and let Aaron in.

"Can you wait here for me? I don't really want to go through this on my own."

"Of course," he whispers, moving over to my desk chair and taking a seat.

When I get to the bathroom, I unpack the tests, and remove two sticks from different packets, reading the instructions and following them for each one. Placing the caps on the end of each of them, I wash my hands and clean up the packages, taking everything back to my room to sit with Aaron and wait.

"What did they say?" he asks as soon as I enter the room.

"I don't know yet. It says to check in three minutes." I set them on the desk and stash my plastic bag with the remaining tests and empty packaging on the floor.

"Um, Etta?" he says looking at them where they lay. "I think you already have your answer."

"What?"

"Have a look."

My stomach turns sour with nerves and I shake my head. "I don't want to. Shit. I can't do this. Just tell me. They say yes don't they?"

"Um… yeah, one says 'Yes' and the other has a pink line in each window."

"Oh crap," I breathe, leaning forward and rocking my body. "God I'm such a fucking idiot!"

"No Etta. Sometimes things go wrong. It doesn't make you an idiot."

"No, you don't understand. I told him I wasn't on the pill and he said we'd be fine. I believed him. I thought that meant… oh shit, I should have insisted. I'm a fucking idiot."

He doesn't respond, and I'm too busy freaking out with my head in my hands to pay attention.

"I'm too young to have a baby Aaron. I can't do this. I can't be pregnant. I'm not even finished uni and my parents. Fuck!

327

They're going to kill me. They're going to make me go back home and they're going to kill me!"

As my mind reels, he sits there silently, listening to my ranting. I don't think he knows what to say.

"You know what? Maybe they're wrong. I'll go and drink some water. I'll take some more tests." I rise from the end of the bed and step past him to go back to the bathroom. But his hand reaches out and takes mine.

"Etta," he says gently. "The other tests will all say the same thing. They're accurate."

"No," I whisper. "I need them to be wrong."

He pulls me toward him, and wraps me in his arms. "I'm sorry," he says.

I lean against him, sinking down until I'm sitting on his lap, shock taking over my emotions. "I can't have a baby. I just can't."

20

"Henrietta!" I hear from outside. I'm still sitting on Aaron's lap, still in shock from the results of the test.

"Oh shit. He woke up," I say, locking eyes with Aaron.

"She's not here. She's never here," yells Kensi. "Now go home, we're trying to sleep."

"Check her room. The light's on," he calls up.

"Fine. Hang on."

I hear her leaving her room and trudging up the hallway to mine. "Etta," she calls as she knocks gently. "Your psycho boyfriend is outside yelling for you."

"Tell him I'm not here. Please," I beg through the door.

She sighs, so loud that I can tell she's not at all happy about this. "Fine. Just turn your light out," she says quietly. "She's not there," I hear her yell back down to him. "Her room is empty, I just turned the light out myself."

"That's bullshit. Henrietta, I know you're in there. I can see Aaron's fucking car. Do you really think I'm that stupid?"

Aaron and I both stand. "Stay here. I'll go and talk to him," he says.

"No Aaron, he'll hurt you."

"I'll be fine. Just stay here."

As he heads downstairs, I move over to the window and open it. "Please just go. I need some time away from you to think."

"Don't do anything stupid Henrietta," he tells me.

"It's a bit late for that – I already did! The moment I trusted you," I argue back.

"I'm coming inside to get you," he states, making a move toward the house, pausing when he sees Aaron in front of him.

"You need to leave. She said she wants some time to think."

"She can think just fine when she's safe with me."

"Go home, Damien."

"Get the fuck out of my way, Aaron."

"No."

They move toward each other and before you can even blink, Damien has Aaron on the ground and is standing above him, his fist cocked, ready to punch.

"Stop!" I screech, racing down the stairs as fast as my legs will carry me.

When I burst out the front door, both men are on their feet, circling each other like predators.

I run and place myself between them. "No!" I yell, putting my hands on both of their chests. My breath catches when, even though I'm angry and confused, my body leaps for joy to moment my fingers connect with Damien.

Every traitorous cell in my body seems to be begging me to go to him, never has my rational mind had a chance when I'm around him. I force myself to focus my attention on the hand that presses against Aaron, on the bond we have, and the trust that he has never broken or taken advantage of, before I speak.

"If you have one bit of love for me, you will do what I ask. Please Damien – go home. Give me some time. I need to figure out what I'm going to do. This is a very new development."

His hand moves up to his chest and closes over mine, his eyes pleading.

My heart swells to bursting in my chest, painfully reminding me of everything between us. "Please," I whisper, shutting my eyes so I don't have to look at him anymore. I don't know if I'm strong enough to keep saying no.

Slowly, his hand relaxes, and he takes a step away from me.

"What the fuck is your deal?" Aaron says as he moves. "Who the hell tricks an eighteen year old girl into getting pregnant? You're all kinds of fucked up mate – worse than I ever expected."

331

Shit. Not even me standing in the way could stop Damien's fist from flying out and hitting Aaron in the jaw. He stumbles backward slightly, and my mouth drops open as I watch him fall.

When I look back at Damien, he's walking away.

***

Over the next week, I don't hear from Damien once. As much as I said I needed space, I didn't think it would be this hard to be away from him. I've felt ill all week. I don't know if it's because of the pregnancy or because of the heartache, but I'm struggling to eat anything and keep it down.

By the following Friday, I've decided to go and see my parents. I really need to talk to my mum. I know she'll be able to help me decide what to do.

"What's wrong?" she asks, the moment she sees me. I've arrived early, so I can talk to her without dad there.

"Oh mum, I've really screwed up," I cry, bursting into tears and flinging myself in her arms. Even as large as I am compared to her, her embrace is still a comfort to me.

"Nothing can be that bad Etta. Come inside and sit down. Tell me everything."

Taking a seat on the couch in the living room, my mother turns toward me expectantly. I fill her in on how intense my relationship has become, as well as the colossal error I've made, having unprotected sex with him.

"I thought we were safe. He said not to worry," I moan, hating myself for being so gullible. "And now...now..."

"You're pregnant." My mother puts in for me.

"Yes," I nod, tears falling from my eyes, as I wallow in my own self-pity.

Sighing, my mother takes my hand in between hers. "Honey, I'm not going to tell you what you did wrong. You're already beating yourself up about it as it is. You're young, you're trusting – you always have been. And I'm also not going to tell you what to do about the baby.

"My concern, however, is what Damien's agenda is. Why would a twenty-two year old man lead an eighteen year old girl to believe everything would be fine if they didn't use protection? I mean, he's not a stupid man. He's clearly very intelligent, so he must have known.

"The only conclusion I can come to, is that he was purposely trying to trap you. To force you to stay with him. And that really worries me Etta, a man who would do that, isn't someone I want dating my daughter, let alone fathering her child." She lifts the sleeve of my t-shirt and nods toward the circular bruises in my bicep. "Are these marks from him?"

"Yes and no. I was fighting him, and he was trying to stop me from walking home in the dark. He would never hurt me on purpose mum. I know that much – he does love me."

"Do you love him?"

"Yes. Very much. I truly feel like he is the divine part of me. My body literally calls out to him when he's near. It's like every fibre of my being wants him around, and I have a really hard time saying no to him. But when I'm away, after a while, the cloud lifts and I can see what's going on. I can see how he bosses me around and tries to run my life, and I can see what a lifetime together would do to us."

"What do you think it would do?" she asks.

"It's just... the way we fight... the jealousy, and his secrets...I think we'd end up hating, or worse...killing each other."

"Do you know what you want to do about the baby?"

"I don't know mum. I'm not ready."

"You're not ready for what?" my father asks as he enters the room. My mother and I just exchange glances. I don't think either one of us actually wants to answer that question. "Not ready for what?" he repeats more insistently, looking between us both, knowing from our own reaction that something huge has happened.

"You might want to sit down for this one, dear. And you have to promise to stay calm."

"Just. Tell. Me."

My mother looks at me again, her mouth moving to make the words, but struggling to actually find them. Taking a deep breath, I close my eyes. "I'm pregnant," I blurt out.

"Mother fucker," he growls. "That little bastard. I'll fucking kill him!" The veins in his forehead seem ready to burst out of his skin. "Where is he?"

"No. Please. This is my fault. I'm the one who was stupid. Don't hurt him dad!" I plead, crying and panicked, wishing I had never come here to tell them.

"I told you!" he yells at my mother. "I told you not to let her go. And now look what's happened. Our daughter is goddamned pregnant." He lets out a roar of aggression as he twists his body and slams his fist into the wall, popping through the plaster with a loud crack.

"Stop!" my mother yells. "This isn't helping anyone. If we're going to start pointing fingers then they should all be pointed at you. You're the one who kept her locked up for all those years. I'm surprised she didn't rebel at sixteen like Craig did and end up pregnant then! You are too suffocating Barry, and if you don't calm the hell down and support our daughter instead of fighting against her, we will end up losing her for good. Is that what you want? Well? Is it?!"

Never in my life have I seen my mother yelling at my father, and by the look on his face, he hasn't witnessed it either.

He stands in the doorway, my great big hulk of a father, and looks between the two women in his life, his eyes wide with rage as he looks for something he can do to fix this. But there's nothing he can do. This is one situation that is completely out of his control.

"Fine. I'll back off. But she's moving back home. Understood?" he says, before disappearing from the door.

"Where is he going?" I ask my mother.

"I'd say he's going to pack your room up and bring you back home."

"Oh no," I say, grabbing for my phone to warn Jessica and Kensi, the last thing they need is to be freaked out by a visit from my father.

"Well, what do you want us to do?" Jessica asks.

"Just let him do it. Don't get in his way," I say quietly, knowing that being back home with my parents is the only way I'm going to make the break from Damien. If I stay out on my own, I'll just end up back with him. "I'm sorry Jess. I really am so, so sorry."

"Me too Etta. Me too. Just let us know if you need us."

21

After another week has passed, I know what I have to do. Damien still hasn't made contact with me, and even though I haven't contacted him either, I take it as a sign that he's letting me go. He used to talk of never letting me go, of always needing me by his side. So the fact that he hasn't even attempted contact speaks volumes to me.

As much as I know that our relationship isn't healthy, I can't help but be completely heart broken. I still haven't returned to university. I'm not ready and I've missed too many classes. I'm going to defer my studies for a semester. Just until I get my life together.

I enlist Aaron to go with me to pick up my things from Damien's apartment. Jeremy has reported seeing him at uni, so it seems as though he's just moving on with his life without me – how nice for him... With this knowledge in mind, I choose a day when I know he has class, and ask Aaron to wait for me downstairs in the car, so I can make a quick getaway.

"I can come in if you like," he suggests.

"No, I don't think it's right to take you in there. It's still his space."

Using my key to get inside, I push the door open, peaking around the edge of it. Shockingly, the usually pristine apartment is littered with beer bottles and pizza boxes. My stomach heaves a little at the smell, so I cover my nose with my hand and make my way toward the bedroom.

Everything in there is exactly as it was when I left it. It's as if it's some sort of a shrine to our time together and reminds me of what my parents did with my brother's room. The dress I wore to the night club is still sitting on the floor at the foot of the unmade bed, covers pushed into the middle, showing that two people had been in there.

Reaching down, I pick up his shirt, and hold it to my face, inhaling deeply, breathing him in. Tears spring to my eyes as my heart aches for everything that I love about him.

I find myself wondering if we should try and work this out. Try and start over – with different ground rules. Would he accept that? Would he share his life with me properly and let me freely live my own, or would he always be trying to control me?

Knowing that the latter is most likely true, fresh tears begin to fall as I move around the room and pack up my things. Pulling the handle up on my suitcase when I'm finished, I stand it up and take one last look around the room before I make my way to the door.

Half way there, I hear a muffled noise – it sounds like music playing. I pause, listening for the direction of the sound. My eyes shift immediately toward the door of the spare room.

With my heart hammering in my chest, I leave my bag by the front door and make my way to the other room. The padlock is hanging open, so I know it's unlocked. Nervously, I take a deep breath to steel myself for whatever it is I'm about to see then turn the handle and push the door open.

If I thought my heart was broken before, it just shattered into a million, irrecoverable pieces.

Inside, it looks very much like the set of a television show, or a photographic studio. On one side is a desk with a laptop set up on it, as well as some photographic gear. Behind that are images. All over the walls, there are images. Admittedly, they're very artful, but erotic looking, featuring women, men and couples. On the other side, the walls are all black, and there's even a black four poster bed, covered with crimson material and bedding. It would all be rather impressive, and I could even see past the nakedness of the subjects in the portraits, if it wasn't for what was going on in front of me right now.

In the middle of the bed is Damien, with a good week's worth of beard growth. He's passed out. He's stark naked, his cock hard in his sleep and glistening from recent use. And if that wasn't bad enough, he's not alone. Curled up next to him is Bec, her long dark hair, flowing out on the pillow in chocolate waves as her naked limbs drape over Damien's body.

As an extra kick in the guts, she has a hand drawn tattoo on her thigh. It's not flowers and butterflies like the ones he's drawn on me, it's skulls and thorns. But it's unmistakably his hand.

My breath catches in my throat, as a fresh bout of tears pours out of my eyes, I shake my head, not quite believing that what we had was that easy for him to get over. That easy to move on from.

Choking back my sobs, I back out of the room, planning on making a very speedy and very quiet get away. But I'm not so lucky. My phone starts ringing the tune I have programmed for Aaron. I've obviously taken too long and he's calling to check on me.

Fumbling with my bag, I grab it and silence it as fast as I can, but I'm too late. He's already sitting up.

"Fuck," he croaks, his voice sounding like sand paper. He tries to stand, and clutches his head as he stumbles toward the door. "Etta?" he says, as if he thinks I might be an apparition.

"I just came to get my things," I state, forcing my words out through my tears as I grab the handle of my bag and place my hand on the door. "I would have woken you to say goodbye. But, you have company."

"What?" he asks, looking confused, before glancing over his shoulder to the sleeping Bec. "Oh no. Shit." He mumbles to himself, his eyes wide with disbelief.

"I'm glad you didn't have trouble moving on from our...our everything. I obviously meant a lot to you."

"Etta, you have to believe me, I don't even remember her coming over. Please. You mean everything to me. You are everything. Please don't go."

"Go and fuck your new girlfriend Damien," I say, dropping my key on the floor and exiting the apartment, knowing that I have the time it takes Damien to get clothes and shoes on to make it to the car.

"Etta!" he calls from behind me as I reach the foyer. He appears with only a pair of pants on, obviously in too much of a rush to worry about shoes and a shirt.

I pause at the door but keep my back toward him.

"Please, just talk to me. We can work anything out. We belong together. You're carrying my baby."

"I'm too young to have a baby with you Damien," I say in response.

"What's that supposed to mean? Tell me you didn't... please tell me you didn't." his voice grows panicked. "No Etta."

"It means I took care of it," I tell him. "You're free."

"No," he groans, the emotion and pain thick in his voice as I hurt him with my words.

"I'm sorry," I tell him, refusing to look at him. I can't bear to see the heartbreak on his face, I don't trust myself not to give into him. I just push through the door and walk quickly for Aaron's car where it's waiting on the curb.

"NO!" Damien roars, slamming his fist into the row of letterboxes hanging on the wall.

"Shit. Get in," Aaron says, taking a hold of my bag and dropping it in the boot, racing back to the driver's seat and jumping inside.

"Are you ok?"

"No. Just drive," I say, as I do up my seatbelt.

Aaron starts the engine, the radio bursting to life with Gemma Hayes' version of *Wicked Game*.

As a tear rolls down my cheeks, I hear Damien screaming after us. Banging on the window. Trying to open the door.

"Go!" I cry, squeezing my eyes shut tight. I can't look at him. I'm scared that if I do, I'll go back. As the engine roars, catapulting me away, I can't help but think how fitting this song is. I never dreamed that the man I fell in love with, so completely would be so wrong for me. I close my eyes and keep my head forward, knowing that if I catch a glimpse of him right now, I won't be able to go on.

"You're doing the right thing, Etta."

"I know. It doesn't stop it from hurting though." Openly I sob, huge wracking sobs that shake my body and turn into anguished howls.

Aaron keeps talking to me, trying to calm me down. But I can't. My heart feels so destroyed that I can't imagine it ever being repaired.

Closing my eyes, all I can see is Damien's face. He truly was my everything, my life, my breath, my heart. But loving him was like a sickness, one I don't think I'll ever recover from.

My love for Damien is a teardrop that will hang inside my soul for all eternity.

Epilogue

A hint of book two

Damien

It's been three years since Henrietta walked out of my life. She took my heart, my love, and my light with her that day. And I hated her for it. I hated her for giving up on us, for getting rid of the baby.

I went out that night, and I got into a massive bar fight. I hurt a lot of people and did a lot of damage. As a result, I spent the last two and a half years in prison. The judge was pretty hard on me because of my martial arts background and the fact that my street fighting had made me a 'person of interest'. He said that I was a walking weapon and knew exactly what I was doing.

I guess he was right. I wanted blood that night, and I didn't care where I got it.

But now I'm out, and I'm determined to find her and make things right. Time can heal a lot of things, but it can't make love go away. Not the kind of love I have for her anyway.

What I feel for her is soul consuming. I need her. I don't think I can live much longer without seeing her again. I know I can win her back. I just need to take things slower this time.

The GPS navigator on my phone tells me that her house isn't much further. It took me a while to find her. She's moved to Phillip Island in Victoria and is unlisted, so I had to coax her location out of friends.

But now I've found her, and I can't wait to see her.

Henrietta

Walking around the house with a basket in my hands, I lean down and pick up random items that have been strewn around the house, shaking my head, but smiling to myself all the while.

Pulling out the vacuum from the hall cupboard, I plug it into the wall and switch it on, gathering all of the dust bunnies that have accumulated under our couch.

My brow pulls together as I think I hear the doorbell over the drone of the motor. Hitting the off button, I move to the front door and look through the screen.

"Yes?" I ask the man who has his back to me. But I don't need to see his face, as soon as I get close enough, my body lets me know who it is. "Damien?" I whisper, not quite believing it's him.

Turning around, he gives me his most charming smile, and I feel my mouth go dry with a need for him I've never managed to get rid of. "Henrietta," he says softly.

Henrietta

I forbade anyone to call me Henrietta after we broke up, the sound of my full name just seemed to hurt too much – my heart couldn't take it.

"What are... what are you doing here?" I ask, my voice breathless just looking at him.

"I came to see you Henrietta. I haven't stopping thinking about you. All this time, you're the only one I've cared about," he explains.

"You need to forget about me."

"I can't."

***

Aaron

"What's this?" Evie asks.

"It's a shell," I explain, taking it from her tiny fingers and turning it over in her palm, smiling as her little mouth tries to pronounce the words. It comes out more like 'Wha dis'. But I understand nonetheless.

"What's this?" she asks again, this time showing me a piece of seaweed.

"It's seaweed. Let's go and see if mummy is finished with the cleaning. Do you have your bucket?"

"Yes," she says, rushing over on her chubby little legs to grab the plastic yellow pail out of the sand.

"What about your spade?"

"Here!" she squeals, waving it over her head as she rushes toward me, flicking sand everywhere as she runs. "Shoulder ride!" she yells, a big grin on her face as I hoist her onto my shoulders and start the short walk home.

"My love you daddy," she says suddenly, hugging the top of my head and planting a sloppy kiss in my hair. My heart fills up and bursts a little. Who would have thought such little hands could hold so firmly onto my big heart.

"I think we have a visitor," I muse as I round the corner and the cul-de-sac, where we live, comes into view. There's a black Commodore VE parked on the curb out the front of our house.

"A visitor," Evie parrots, always happy to repeat the last two words of most sentences.

"Holy shit," I breathe, suddenly coming to a stop at the base of our driveway.

"Holy shit," she parrots again, although I barely hear her. I'm too shocked to find Damien standing at the door, talking to Etta.

The moment she sees me, she shakes her head then touches her hair to try and cover up her slip. I take the hint and start to move away. But Evie has seen her mother.

"I want mummy!" she yells, wriggling on my shoulders, wanting to get down.

It's enough to alert Damien to our presence. He turns around with a smile on his face, but it vanishes almost instantly when he sets eyes on Evie.

"Is that... is she...?" he stammers, pointing at the little girl I call my own, as she rushes toward her mother, her jet black hair streaming behind her as she runs, brandishing her bucket for her mother to see her new treasures.

Damien's hand covers his mouth as he watches her. He knows. Of course he knows. Holy shit. I think my whole world just exploded.

The End…for now.

ABOUT THE AUTHOR

Lilliana Anderson

New Adult Author

Bestselling Author of the A Beautiful Series, Alter and the Confidante Trilogy, Lilliana has always loved to read and write, considering it the best form of escapism that the world has to offer.

Australian born and bred, she writes New Adult Romance revolving around her authentically Aussie characters as well as a biographical trilogy based on an ex-Sydney sex worker, named Angelien.

Lilliana feels that the world should see Australia for more than just it's outback and tries to show characters in more of a city setting.

When she isn't writing, she wears the hat of 'wife and mother' to her husband and four children.

Before Lilliana turned to writing, she worked in a variety of industries and studied humanities and communications before transferring to commerce/law at university.

Originally from Sydney's Western suburbs, she currently lives a fairly quiet life in suburban Melbourne.

Visit my website at www.lillianaanderson.com

Connect with me:

For updates or to ask questions/ send comments,

*you can contact me at **lillianaanderson@live.com.au***

*follow me on twitter **@Confidante_Lili***

*visit my website **www.lillianaanderson.com***

or facebook where I am most active-

http://www.facebook.com/pages/Lilliana-Anderson-Author/444649528938470

http://www.facebook.com/lilliana.anderson.12

Thank you so much for taking the time to read my work. I hope to have a very long writing career, producing books and characters you'll come to love.

If you enjoyed reading, please take a moment to let someone know. Use the social media options on your device to share this book on Facebook or Twitter, and if you have time, leave a rating and review – I love to read your comments.